THE PRICE OF SILENCE

Print ISBN 978-1-945419-97-3

Ebook ISBN 978-1-945419-98-0

LCCN 2021942860

THE PRICE OF SILENCE

A BARTHOLOMEW BECK NOVEL

RICK TREON

FAWKES PRESS

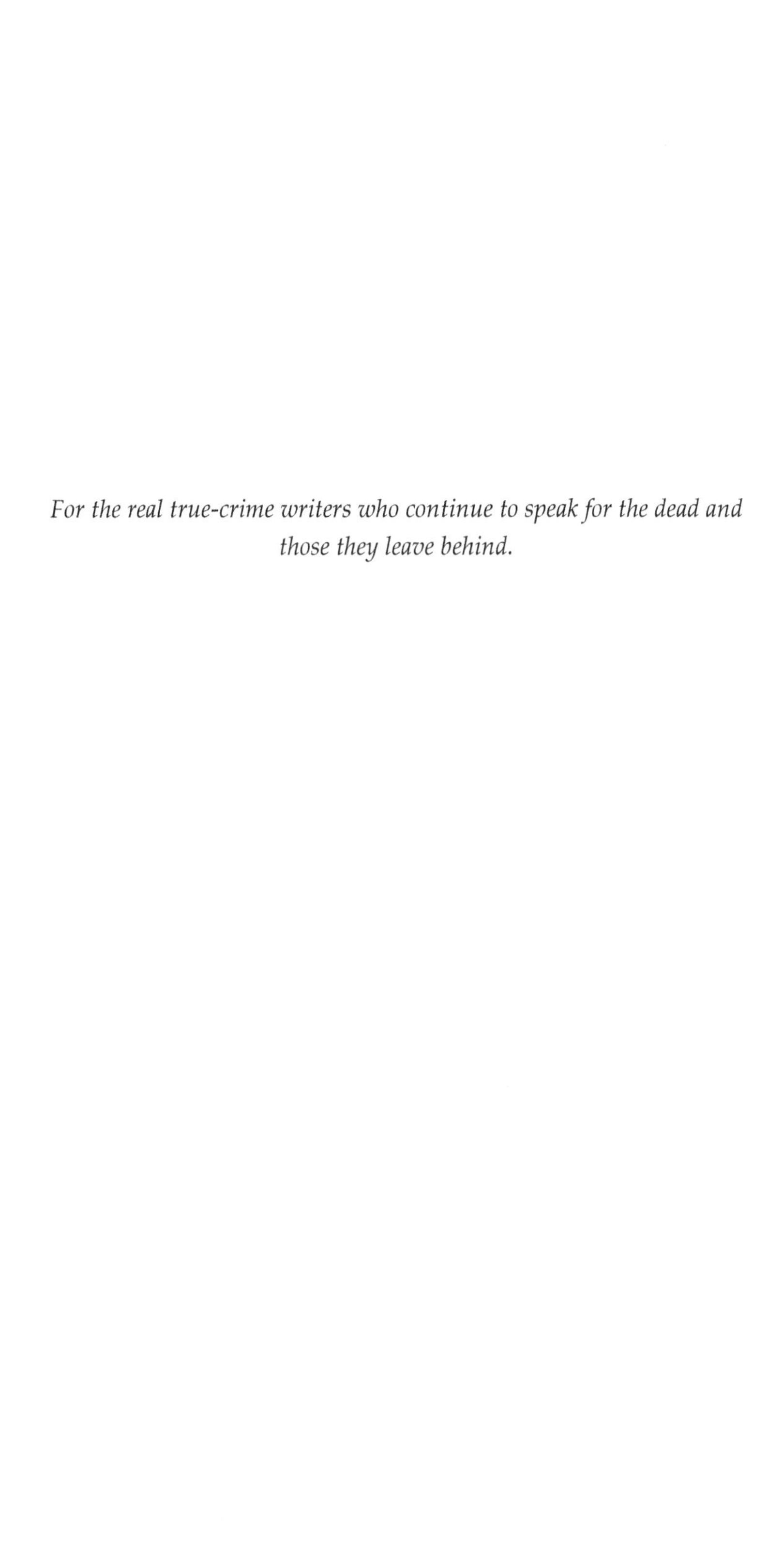

For the real true-crime writers who continue to speak for the dead and those they leave behind.

State authorities, congressman hid son's connection to infamous Texas murder

By Veronica Stein vstein@lonestarledger.org

In 2004, the DNA of Paul Henry Schuhmacher was entered into the Combined DNA Index System—commonly known as CODIS— following his conviction of second-degree sexual assault. Five years later, his genetic code matched a sample from the rape kit performed on Summer Foster, who was killed in their hometown of Hinterbach on July 4, 1999.

But according to a high-ranking official in the Texas Department of Public Safety, the match was buried for more than 15 years because Paul is the son of U.S. Rep. Grant Schuhmacher.

BECK
PRESENT DAY

As he called my name for the third time, I wanted to punch him square in the nose—even with a hangover that warranted dark sunglasses while dragging luggage across a bright lobby. But the downtown Dallas hotel was crawling with other writers, which meant even a mildly antagonistic encounter could turn into a news story.

Especially if it involved Parker Mallory.

So instead, I pulled up short of the glass doors and turned to face the wisp of a man strolling toward me, a reporter's notebook in hand.

"Finally." Parker ran his fingers through blond hair before pulling a pen from behind his ear. "You really thought you could sneak out of here without commenting on the story?"

I had no idea what Parker was talking about, and my head pulsed as the words passed across his thin lips like machine-gun fire.

Rather than trying to figure it out, I pulled down my burnt orange ballcap. "Look, it's early, and I have no idea what—"

"It's nearly eleven." Parker never let me get a word in, always bloviating over my drawl. "And my editors know you're here, so I have to either quote you or write that *literary darling* Bartholomew Beck is dodging the media."

Though still foggy from the night before, I was coherent enough to realize engaging with a journalist on the record was a terrible idea, even if all I did was ask what *it* was. Nothing I said in this state would look good in the pages of *Manhattanist Magazine* or one of its prominent national websites, so I grabbed the handle of my larger suitcase.

"Like I said, I don't know what you're talking about."

"Quit playing dumb, Bart."

Walking away from Parker was the smart move, but he'd poked me by intentionally using the nickname I loathed.

I smiled despite my worsening headache. "Oh, I get it. You're referring to last night's big win for Beck and Stein?"

That hit Parker harder than any haymaker I could've mustered.

Though he'd risen to fame in his late twenties by writing a series of Pulitzer-winning exposés for the *Post* and producing long-form investigative pieces for *Manhattanist*, the towhead journalist had also written several highly praised true-crime books.

His latest had been at the top of the *Times* bestseller lists.

Then came *The Ultimate Alibi*—a true-crime thriller about how journalist Veronica Stein and I narrowly escaped death at the hands of a madman while working undercover on an oil pipeline in the Texas Panhandle. While that was an exciting premise, what made it an instant Number One was the villain: Paul Schuhmacher, disgraced son of US House Representative Grant Schuhmacher.

And Parker's book, a page-turner in its own right, about the apprehension of a serial killer thanks to consumer DNA testing firms, would've won all the nonfiction crime writing awards were it not for *The Ultimate Alibi*.

Instead, Veronica and I had just completed our sweep at the final convention of the year.

It was the worst losing streak of Parker Mallory's privileged life. He'd even skipped the boozy afterparty at the hotel bar, which had made for a helluva Saturday night for the rest of us.

Parker was still formulating his response as I wrangled my bags, but he leaned in while brushing past. "I'll tell Veronica you said hi. I'm sure you won't want to speak to her for a while."

I tried ignoring him again. Parker and Veronica, who met at the year's first major event in New York, had been nearly inseparable the last few days. They were both single, high-profile journalists, so the connection made sense—though I had a feeling it was hate sex for Parker as much as anything else.

And no matter how much they hooked up, their relationship would never be as strong as the one Veronica and I shared. Though we weren't romantically involved, tragic events would keep our lives and livelihoods forever entangled. In fact, we were meeting later to discuss our next project.

I didn't know what the hell Parker had meant and lacked the mental capacity to decipher it, so I grabbed my other suitcase and headed toward the exit, the leather computer bag barely balancing on its extended handle.

I'd packed far too much for such a short trip. Dallas was only four hours north of home, and that included the crawl through downtown Austin, but I couldn't be caught re-wearing anything throughout the four-day writers' conference. And since all my ensembles were distinct, I'd taken three pairs of dress shoes in addition to new sneakers, which were screeching to high heaven as I shuffled along the floor. Even my crossing-the-lobby shirt was collared, though I'd left it untucked over my jeans.

My muscles were also lagging, which made my rolling wardrobe that much heavier as I pulled them. The problem wasn't a lack of strength, though I was much weaker than two years ago, when I'd spent my days lugging around equipment on the pipeline with my best friend, Jorge Hernandez.

No, the struggle stemmed from drinking too much the night

before and taking my usual dose of prescription sleep medication.

Right number of pills.

Wrong amount of Scotch.

My residual impairment was too much, and the entire mess came crashing down in the middle of the lobby, forcing me to Tetris everything back together and escape with half a dozen cellphones pointed at me.

Between news coverage of the deadly encounter with Paul, the buzz around the book, and the recent profile of Veronica and me in the *Wall Street Journal*, I was more recognizable now than at any point in the twenty-plus years I'd been in publishing. And while visibility was important, Gavel Press wouldn't like a viral video of me avoiding a prominent reporter, even if it was taken out of context.

But all I could do was take my time and avoid showing my frustration as I left. The cameras were still trained on me as I crossed through the sliding doors, and a few people followed me out into the surprisingly warm October morning.

I pulled out my own phone to look like I was distracted, keeping my eyes on the screen as the valet brought around my matte black Dodge Challenger. There had been thirteen unread texts and three missed calls when I'd woken up an hour ago, which seemed unusually high for the weekend. I hadn't checked them since none had been from Veronica, who enjoyed working in the early mornings. She'd left long before I came out of my coma and may have already been in Austin.

The device buzzed in my hand. It was another text from the *Journal* reporter who'd published the rosy profile, *Beck and Stein: A 21st Century Capote and Lee.*

Tapping the green banner revealed a string of messages asking me if I'd *seen it yet?* and if I could *comment on the story.*

I panic-scrolled through the rest of my unread texts.

One included a link to the *Lone Star Ledger*'s latest headline.

2

BECK

PRESENT DAY

The new car was one of several expenses I'd come to regret. It was unnecessary, like most of the clothing in its trunk.

But it was great for road trips.

I liked listening to audiobooks or podcasts and thinking for hours, usually about the plot for my next novel or visualizing another bestseller—which I needed.

That wasn't a big concern until a few hours ago. But the possibility of exposure was high now, and few things could derail a true-crime career like the revelation that an author had lied.

And that's what I'd done.

Twice.

So had Veronica. But instead of enjoying our success and moving on, she'd put our reputations and livelihoods at risk to take a meaningless swipe at one of the most powerful men in the country.

What hurt worse, though, was that she'd lied to my face.

The sleeping pills had just hit my stomach when Veronica started banging on my hotel room door. She hadn't gone to the afterparty, so I assumed she wanted to celebrate our win.

Instead, she sat on the couch and told me Caroline Walker, one of the Texas Rangers at the heart of our book, had called earlier that evening.

Paul Schuhmacher's DNA had been linked to another case—the murder of Summer Foster, my childhood neighbor in Hinterbach, Texas.

I'd stayed awake long enough to hear Veronica explain that his DNA had been found in Summer's rape kit along with that of Butch Heller, the man who was executed for her murder after I testified against him.

The test results had leaked long ago, but the second DNA sample had never produced a match.

I had no idea the mystery sample had come from Paul, a classmate of mine at Hinterbach High School. But he'd been convicted of raping a college classmate, and Walker wondered if the attractive high school librarian had been one of his earliest victims.

The conviction also explained why Paul was in the CODIS system.

But Walker didn't have to request a comparison. She just had to dig up test results that had been buried to avoid scandalizing Paul's father, US Congressman Grant Schuhmacher.

And that's a hell of a story, Veronica had said. She was right, but that's not the only reason she wanted to write it.

Veronica had been on a mission to take down Grant Schuhmacher since we finished edits on *The Ultimate Alibi.* Congressman Schuhmacher rose from mayor of Hinterbach to chairman of the House Energy and Commerce Committee, and it was an open secret that he'd used less-than-legal means to fund those campaigns.

She'd leveraged the buzz around our book to write pieces in national magazines like *The Atlantic* and *Vanity Fair*, in addition to smaller, more frequent pieces for her regular employer, the *Lone Star Ledger.*

A few of the rumors made their way onto the *Ledger's*

website, but the journalism nonprofit couldn't justify posting most of what she wanted to write, even if her stories generated more hits than the rest of the newsroom combined.

But Veronica's goal was to expose him in the glossy pages of one of the mags, particularly *Manhattanist*. That and the book would keep her in demand for years—a long-term strategy I might have to adopt, too.

A story like this one could get Veronica one step closer to her dream and further tarnish the Schuhmacher name.

It would also give Grant a reason to expose our lie.

Veronica was one of three other people alive who knew what really happened to Summer. But Veronica joined me in the coverup after I saved her from Paul—who'd already killed one woman while working on the pipeline before threatening to chop up Veronica and spread the pieces across the Southwest.

Grant Schuhmacher also knew, along with Summer's psychotic ex-boyfriend, Franklin Jones.

Jones was a hermit with his own reasons for staying out of the public eye. He even provided a benign comment for our book, which was necessary prior to publication.

Grant Schuhmacher had done the same, then stayed quiet on the matter for years.

But that was about to change.

THE CALL WENT to Veronica's voicemail again, but I knew where to find her. The *Ledger* had a weekend editor, and I'd been there often enough over the last few years that Amber referred to me as Veronica's "work husband."

I was only two hours away, and she'd let me in—even on a Sunday.

I nearly jumped when I received an incoming call a moment later. But it wasn't Veronica returning my many messages.

It was Shayla Hickman, an old source with secrets of her own.

I hit the green receiver on my steering wheel. "Shayla?"

"Yeah."

I was both ashamed and excited to hear her voice again. We'd stopped communicating after it became clear my manuscript about her father's murder wouldn't get published. Part of me had wanted to get to know her much better, but she'd been too vulnerable. Instead, I dove into an ill-advised relationship with another woman involved in the case.

"It's been a long time. How—"

"This isn't a social call. Jorge Hernandez was seriously injured in a pipeline explosion."

I tried to string together several pieces of seemingly disconnected information. Shayla had never met Jorge, and I didn't remember mentioning him in our conversations. And last time we spoke, she was a sheriff's deputy in North Texas, not the Permian Basin where Jorge was working.

I was so lost, a trucker honked at me for drifting into his lane.

"Beck?" Shayla asked through my speakers.

"I don't understand."

"Your friend's at the hospital here in Big Lake, down by San Angelo. He's in bad shape, but I don't know the details."

I gripped the wheel with both hands to steady myself. But the more Shayla spoke, the more questions I had. "Jorge is hurt? In Big Lake? How do you know?"

"I've been a deputy in Reagan County a few years now. I was called to the scene to assist the paramedics. I recognized Jorge's name from your book and checked his ID against news photos."

Shayla was all business. I, on the other hand, was freaking the hell out.

"So, he's at the hospital in Big Lake, and that's all you know?"

"Yeah, that's what I've been saying. Do we have a bad connection or someth—"

I'd apologize later but continuing our conversation would've been pointless. I was too busy looking up the hospital's address and burying the gas pedal.

3

BECK

PRESENT DAY

I sucked in a breath before answering another call from Jorge's wife, Grace, who was driving to the hospital from the Panhandle. A nurse had been calling Grace with updates, but I couldn't convince the take-no-shit woman on the other end that I was his brother.

"What'd they say?" I asked.

"Surgery. Long one. Seven, eight hours."

I heard her take a drag from the latest of what was surely an unending chain of cigarettes, but not the noise of an open car window.

"You there already?" I asked.

Another hurried puff. "Just parked."

She'd been driving on more four-lane highways coming from Borger and probably hadn't been pulled over in her minivan. But my car was a cop-magnet, and I'd been stopped for speeding twice already. The first time, a young, unsympathetic highway patrolman gave me a ticket. An older sheriff's deputy caught me the second time. He just shooed me along with his condolences.

The stops didn't keep me from pushing my car, though, so I knew I was close. I tapped my phone and brought up the GPS.

"I'm only ten minutes out. Want me to pick up food since we'll be there waiting all night?"

"Oh my god, yes. First thing you see."

As I spotted a Taco Bell coming into town, Grace relayed everything she knew. Jorge was thrown from the blast and fell hard enough to tweak his back and pinch a nerve. He was screaming so badly they had to sedate him, and surgery was the best option for avoiding long-term damage.

While I waited for a party pack of crunchy tacos and two drinks, Jorge was probably on his stomach. I imagined something like a rotary saw sticking out of his flayed back, the whine giving way to the sickening sound of metal against bone—the one Paul's leg made when I cut him with Jorge's grinder.

I shook off the nightmare and picked up my cell. I couldn't do anything about Jorge, but I could call Veronica again. She wouldn't pick up—and I didn't know what I'd say if she did—but Veronica was his friend, too, and deserved to know.

"Listen, I'm still pissed about that story, but I'm not calling about that," I told her voicemail. "Jorge has been in an accident at work. He's in surgery. He'll be there all night, but I'll call when I know something."

The welding rig behind me honked as I ended the call. I waved an apology then grudgingly pulled up, not yet ready to put another meal on my credit card and sit all night worrying.

I WAS STILL groggy as the doctor began talking, but her face relayed the most important information.

Jorge had survived.

"He'll be able to walk in a day or so, and you'll be able to take him home in three," she told us. "It may be a year before he gets full mobility back, but everything went very well, so it could be much sooner."

I turned to Grace, who thanked the doctor while gripping the gold cross hanging from her necklace. She didn't ask for details, but I couldn't help myself.

"What did you have to do in there?"

The doctor slipped her hands into the pockets of her lab coat, annoyed. "Like I told Mrs. Hernandez over the phone before you arrived, Jorge landed hard and likely has a concussion. He was disoriented but said his back and legs were in excruciating pain. We scanned him and saw he had a herniated disc, which was pinching his sciatic nerve. Ordinarily we'd prescribe a muscle relaxer, ibuprofen, and rest. But given the circumstances, we felt surgery was more prudent."

She paused for a moment and turned back to Grace, who was staring past the surgeon. "He's lucky we went in. Your husband's lower back was already severely damaged, and some of the scar tissue was very old."

Grace nodded. "He'd been complaining about his back. But he was able to work."

The doctor didn't look sympathetic. "He should've seen a doctor a long time ago."

Grace's expression hardened. "Who are you to judge us?"

I rested a hand on Grace's shoulder but turned my attention to the surgeon. "When can we see him?"

"A few more hours. He'll be out of it, but I'll have someone find you when he starts coming around."

The doctor was only a few steps away when Grace started cursing under her breath in Spanish.

"I know you're mad," I said. "But she's just trying to help."

Grace began rubbing the cross with her thumb. "I was cursing at Jorge. Why wouldn't he tell me if he was in so much pain?"

I had no answer, other than they couldn't afford any short checks. Not long after I stopped working with him—after Veronica and I were almost killed at a remote jobsite not far from his house—Jorge suffered the same fate as the rest of the country's oilfield workers. He found short stints at plants near Borger, but the glut of unemployed welders meant he settled for lower wages and frequent layoffs. By the time the economy stabilized, the Hernandez family had no savings.

"Maybe you should call everyone and tell them how the surgery went," I said.

She stood and nodded. "Sorry for losing my shit."

Grace dug into her bag and was only halfway to the exit when she lit a cigarette.

Nobody said a word.

4
———

BECK
PRESENT DAY

I t was nice to hear Jorge's laugh, even if it hurt him a little. He'd been groggy when we first entered the room, repeating the phrase *we've got to finish tie-ins* and asking me—his former helper—to hand him something.

But by mid-morning, Jorge seemed thankful for the company. He was giving me shit about being a big shot and ignoring old friends when Grace kissed him on the forehead.

"I'm going to get food," she said. "What do you want?"

Jorge shook his head. "I'm not hungry. I think it's the medicine."

She sighed. "Well, I'm starving. Want anything, Beck?"

"No thanks. I'll go find some lunch and a motel after you get back."

Grace shook her head. "I'll bring you both a burger, just in case."

She squeezed Jorge's bare foot as she passed the edge of the hospital bed. After she disappeared into the hall, Jorge turned to me.

"It was crazy, bro." He was whispering so Grace wouldn't hear. "You'd've been freaking out."

I shook my head. "The old me, maybe."

Jorge waved away my comment, then winced in pain.

Though he always bought a copy, Jorge never read my books. I'd told him an abridged version, though, including how I saved Veronica by nearly chopping off Paul's head with a machete.

"Whatever, dude. You remember the last fire? You were pissing down both legs."

"Shut up." I smiled. We'd been telling each other to *shut up* for decades, a shit-talking ritual I missed.

As usual, Jorge was exaggerating my fear, though I had discovered that firefighting was not in my future.

We'd been on a main line in Oklahoma, walking along an endless string of teal-colored pipe and stopping to weld every forty feet. Rather than welding with the welding machine in Jorge's rig, we were working beside a tack rig—a gray tank fitted with four machines, their leads strung out to the side as it rolled down a dirt highway through the pastureland. In front of the tack rig, a six-man team worked with a side boom, a yellow machine of war with an arm to hoist and position the next piece of pipe.

On our third day, a rogue spark lit the dry grass behind the tack rig. There was supposed to be a portable water tank there to douse any fires, but we later heard the pump had broken weeks before and the company declined to repair it, citing the already high cost of the project.

So instead of fighting the fire with water, everyone but me ran toward the flame and began stomping and smothering it with piles of loose dirt. They were all wearing fire resistant shirts and jeans, but I'd doubted the effectiveness of second-hand FR shirts and pants purchased out of some dude's garage.

Everyone else on the job either trusted the gear or didn't care.

"How's Ronnie?" Jorge asked, using the nickname the pipeliners had given Veronica when she was working under-cover with us.

I thought about telling him the truth. That she'd written a

dangerous story and I was pissed at her. That she'd been ignoring my calls and I was getting hounded by reporters.

"She's good," I said instead. "We won another award. I was on my way to meet her in Austin to talk about our next book when I heard about the accident."

"Good deal, man. You two still *not* hooking up?"

I was trying to think of a way to steer the conversation away from Veronica when someone knocked on the open door to the room. I turned and saw a tall, skinny guy in jeans and a white T-shirt. His beige ballcap featured a bass and sat on a thick mane of dull blond hair that hung past his shoulders.

Jorge smiled and lifted his arm a few inches before wincing and returning it to his side. "Chuck D, c'mon in. Beck, this is my buddy, Chuck Davis. Chuck, this is the author friend I've been telling you about."

As he got closer, I saw that Chuck D was a bit older than Jorge and me, probably in his early forties. I stood and shook his hand. "Great to meet you. You work with Jorge?"

"Yessir. I'm in charge of the tie-in crew."

"He was out there when it happened," Jorge said. "How close were you?"

"Not very. I went to the shitter during break, so I was driving back and taking a snap when it happened."

Jorge perked up. "No shit? Get out your phone so we can watch it. Mine's busted, and Beck's too cool for Snapchat."

Chuck took off his hat, revealing a mullet whose party half was bleached by the sun. "Are you sure? I mean, you're laid up and a couple of other guys got burned."

As Jorge considered this, I couldn't help myself. "How badly?"

"Not too bad. Cody's at the burn unit in Lubbock, but he called and said it was just a second-degree on his forearm and a little on his side. His helper was released from here last night."

Jorge smiled. "See, man? Everyone's okay. Get out your phone."

Chuck shook his head. "You're stupid."

"No, *you're* stupid."

They shared a laugh. My smiling mouth belied a tinge of jealousy. Jorge had a comedy routine with his new friend, and I wasn't part of it. But what should I expect? For my charismatic friend to stop making new friends while I was off writing and congratulating myself?

Chuck pulled out his phone and tapped on the screen a few times before holding the device low so Jorge could see it.

The video, shot through a dusty windshield, showed a trench running along the right side of the dirt path. Maybe half a mile in front, a yellow-and-black track hoe stood still, its arm reaching into the six-foot-deep ditch. I knew it was holding a forty-foot-long piece of pipe, which had been held out when the bulk of the line was welded together.

Chuck told his audience that they were *finally starting their first weld of the day after Cody's piece of shit machine wouldn't start up this morning.* Had the explosion not happened, Jorge and Cody would've welded both ends of the piece that had been held out, connecting two long stretches of pipeline that had been lowered into the trench on both sides of a caliche road.

I recognized Jorge's hunter green truck, and assumed the white truck was Cody's.

"You're right about his machine," Jorge said as he watched. "That's why you always buy a Lincoln and not—"

Jorge was interrupted by the explosion, accompanied by a short-lived flame rising above the trench. We winced as Chuck yelled *What the fuck?* over the sound of Jorge shrieking. It worse than I'd anticipated. Much worse.

I was thankful the video didn't shown Jorge, who, despite being ten months younger than me, had taken the role of older brother. I pictured his spinal cord being snipped in half with bolt cutters. What else could cause that much pain?

The torture only lasted a couple of seconds before its merciful end.

"Jesus," I said. "How did that happen?"

Chuck again adjusted his hat, and I found myself wanting to chop off the straw showing underneath. "The company is saying it was a burp."

I looked over at Jorge, who had told me about another burp —when a buildup of fumes finds its way to any outlet it can find —when he first broke out as a pipeline welder. That story and the video did not jibe.

"Man, we both know that wasn't a burp," Jorge said. "Someone had to have opened a valve upstream. We're lucky they closed it so quick."

Chuck shrugged. "Hey, that's just what the corporate honchos said at our meeting this morning. Only time they've been out here since the project started."

Jorge shook his head. I trusted him more than this Chuck D character, even if the former was in charge. The older I got, the more I believed what my father told me the morning before I started my first job at fourteen: *You'll be smarter than most of the people you work for.*

The only exception had been when I'd worked for Jorge. Which reminded me of something missing from the video.

"Where was your helper?" I asked. "I didn't see him in the video."

"He called in Saturday night and said he needed the day off. I told him it was fine. Shit, I'm tired of working seven-tens, too. But I need the money."

Working ten hours a day, seven days a week could be brutal. I'd done that once when we were coming up on a project deadline.

"How many weeks you been doing that?" I asked.

"I was about to start my third." Jorge pointed his chin at Chuck. "Ol' Chuck D's a real hardass, aren't you?"

Chuck was busy typing on his phone. "Hey, I gotta get back. The sheriff's involved because we had to call for the ambulance, so now there's a shit ton of paperwork and stuff I have to do."

Jorge seemed disappointed that Chuck was leaving so soon.

I wasn't.

Grace walked in a few minutes later, two Dairy Queen bags in one hand and a large to-go cup in the other. As the smell hit, I realized she'd been right about the extra burgers. After offering one to Jorge, who still passed, I unwrapped mine and pigged out.

"Told you," Grace said. "So, there's some asshole reporter out there who wanted to know if I was… well, me. He also said he knew you, Beck."

I forced down a large bite. "What did he look like?"

"Short white dude in a suit. Blond hair. I told him to fuck off, but he didn't look like he was leaving."

Parker Mallory.

I set down the burger and told Grace I'd handle it.

Parker palmed his note pad and jumped out of the chair when he saw me push open the double doors.

I didn't wait for him to come my way. "What are you doing here?"

He powerwalked across the tile floor, clicking that damn pen of his. "I can't believe you're surprised. First there's the news that Grant Schuhmacher's son was sexually involved with Summer Foster. The same son who, twenty years later, tried to kill you, the man who saw Summer's murder and wrote a book about it."

"Yeah, and we talked about that yesterday morning—"

I stopped. I'd left the hotel right after the conversation, then got the call that Jorge was hurt and drove straight to Big Lake. "How the hell did you even know I was here?"

He smirked. "Then I hear your best friend, whose truck and tools you used to kill Paul Schuhmacher, is hospitalized in a workplace accident. And now I have confirmation of that."

I repeated my question, but my fair-haired nemesis started writing in his notebook like he couldn't hear me. "Mostly I just needed to get some sensory details. Your mood, angry. Your appearance, disheveled." He leaned in. "Hasn't showered in at least a day and a half."

I had at least four inches on Parker, and even if he were deceptively strong, I could still muscle up for long enough to knock him on his ass or send him to one of the rooms with a broken nose.

But that would only make things worse, so I turned and started walking back to Jorge's room.

"I have a story, Beck, and I'm going to write it," he said. "Do you want to comment or not?"

I did, but instead I slogged forward and let my impotent rage simmer.

5

BECK
PRESENT DAY

I listened to the voicemail one more time before getting out of my car. The missed calls, voicemails, texts, email, and direct messages all numbered in the double digits.

Veronica's message was the only one that mattered.

Hey, I am so sorry to hear about Jorge. I'm praying he's okay. Also, I know you're pissed at me, but I need to talk to you about something.

I shut off the ignition and cursed under my breath. I wasn't in any hurry to see Veronica after the shitstorm she'd caused, but I had no choice. Between that and the knowledge that I was the subject of an angry investigative journalist, I knew I needed to get back to Austin.

I'd left with the understanding that I'd help Jorge retrieve his pull-behind camper in a few days when he could travel on his own. Then, rather than call and set a meeting with Veronica, I decided to ambush her. It seemed only fair after what she did to me.

I was still rehearsing my speech as I hit the elevator button, calling it down to the ground floor of her building. *You're damn right I'm pissed. You were leaked information about the subject of our book, then you withheld it from me for long enough to write a story you knew would bring undue attention to me and my past.*

I was resolute in my argument as the elevator dinged, but it all disappeared as the door slid open, revealing a fidgeting Veronica. She was surprised to see me but didn't seem as off balance as I'd hoped.

"Did you get my voicemail?" she asked.

I nodded, then let the silence eat at her.

"Look," she said, "about the story—"

"Which story? The one you wrote, or the one your boyfriend is working on that's going to ruin us?"

Veronica's eyes widened as her face turned red, though I didn't know if it was anger or embarrassment.

I went with embarrassment and kept needling her.

"Oh, out of the loop, are we? Feels pretty shitty, doesn't it?" I said. "I am happy you had the decency to call back when you found out about Jorge, though."

My mouth was still open when her palm connected with my cheek. Veronica was already tall and handled herself well, but she'd spent much of her money on eating better food and exercising. And, as evidenced by the left side of my face, she'd gained some upper body strength.

I'd guessed wrong, and her slap brought me back to my senses.

"You done being a prick?" Veronica asked.

I nodded and rubbed my face, which already felt like sandpaper after more than two days without shaving.

"Now," she continued, "by *my boyfriend*, do you mean Parker?"

"Yeah. He was waiting for me in the hospital. Said he'd heard about the accident and is going to add it to his story."

She looked around, then started walking toward the Congress Avenue exit, grabbing my arm as she passed. "Let's grab a late lunch."

THE HOSTESS RECOGNIZED US IMMEDIATELY. She'd been working there in the same black shirt, pants, and shoes for at least a year and a half.

"So good to see you again. I think we have your usual booth available. Follow me."

Veronica and I had been there nearly every day last year. Most of our book had been written at our respective condos and the *Ledger*'s offices, so when we could finally come up for air, we were eager to eat and drink anywhere else.

Veronica hadn't spoken since we left for the restaurant. I'd given her space to think, but that patience was almost up as we sat.

"So, are you going to tell me what's going on?"

Veronica nodded, as though giving herself the go-ahead to tell her own story, but she kept her eyes focused on the cream-colored tablecloth.

"Parker and I were sleeping together," she said. "We hooked up back in New York and made plans to spend last week together."

I tried to put on my best poker face at the mention of his name. "I figured as much."

"And you're right about the story. Walker called me Thursday night and told me about the DNA match."

I leaned back into the booth's leather cushion. "You kept it from me for three days?"

Veronica finally looked up. But her eyes weren't filled with fight. Or anger. Or fear. She was guilty, an emotion that, this far into our relationship, had been reserved exclusively for me. And after what we went through three years ago, then working together to relive it nearly every day since, I could read her well enough to know the story was about to get much worse.

"What aren't you telling me?"

Veronica was taking a deep breath when the waiter approached from behind her. "Can I start y'all off with a drink?

It's not quite happy hour yet, but I can make an exception for the famous Beck and Stein."

I had a feeling I'd need one, so I asked for the oldest Scotch they had and the cedar-planked salmon. Veronica ordered an unsweet tea and a Caesar salad.

"Grilled chicken on that salad? I'll throw it on for free?"

"No. But I'll tell you what—you bring us the food and drinks quietly and don't bother us again until we ask for the check, and I'll tip you fifty percent on the card and leave a hundred-dollar bill on the table."

The waiter smiled and left without another word.

"So, Walker calls you on Thursday and tells you that Paul's DNA was found in Summer's rape kit. Then what?"

"That's not all she told me. The DPS got those results back more than a year ago. After that, Walker got resources to re-investigate her murder with Paul as a suspect."

I knew it would be bad, but this was turning into my worst nightmare. "Does she know?"

"I'm sure you'd already be in jail if she did."

I felt a tinge of relief, but it passed quickly as Veronica's frown deepened. "But you wouldn't have brought it up if she didn't find something."

The waiter silently placed a glass of tea in front of Veronica, who lifted it and drank slowly. "She found your fingerprints. On one of the tablecloths in Summer's yard."

"So what? I testified that I tried to resuscitate her."

Veronica downed the rest of her tea and shook her head. "That's what I told her. But she said they weren't where they should've been. Walker and her team also examined the crime scene photos more closely and pulled other items out of storage and tested them. Apparently, they found major inconsistencies with your version of how Summer was killed."

I noticed the waiter approaching with my drink and subtly shook my head at Veronica. I grabbed the glass before he could set it down and coughed after a long drink. "What inconsistencies?"

"She was cagey. The only concrete details she gave me were Paul's DNA and your prints being out of place."

I tried to calm myself. Teams of lawyers had tried for decades to get Butch Heller's conviction overturned. They'd pored over all the same evidence and come up short, so what could be different now?

"If my story wasn't airtight, it would've come out during Heller's appeals process."

Veronica laughed. "You're kidding, right? After a conviction, the court system is biased against the defendant. Sure, his first appeal was based on ineffective counsel, and if the standard wasn't so goddamned high, that would've worked. I've read those transcripts. Butch's lawyer hardly even cross-examined you—"

I gestured for Veronica to lower her voice, something I had to do frequently when she got going on a subject. She was getting animated, and not just because a man had been wrongly convicted.

Butch had been like her father, and I'd helped put him on Death Row. She said she'd forgiven me after I saved her life, and that Butch had made his peace with dying before his execution.

But there was still something there, an animus that may never completely fade.

Veronica drained the last of her tea and crunched an ice cube.

"What about all the testing they did after his stay of execution?"

"The scope of the court's ruling was limited to DNA testing. Plus, as you pointed out, your testimony put you at the crime scene as a witness and Good Samaritan."

But apparently, I'd left something behind. That night was still fresh in my mind. The anger. The blood. The panic after I realized she was dead.

"Are you sure there isn't an arrest warrant with my name on it?"

"No. But why would they wait? Everyone knew exactly where you were all weekend."

I mentally crossed Walker off my list of allies and penciled Veronica back onto it. "Thank you for leaving me out of your story. Was Walker pissed that you didn't report everything she wanted to leak?"

Veronica shook her head. "She wasn't leaking anything. She was trying to quietly warn me that you were hiding something."

Of all the things I'd just learned, that surprised me most. "You weren't on the"—Veronica put a finger to her lips and flashed her *what the fuck?* scowl, so I leaned in and lowered my voice—"on the record?"

She checked to make sure the waiter wasn't coming. "No. Not at first."

I chewed the inside of my bottom lip before responding. "You mean you called her back and chased a story you knew could hurt me? Hurt us?"

"That's where Parker comes in."

I closed my eyes and bit my lip again. I thought back to Thursday night, when he and Veronica had become reacquainted at the opening-night cocktail hour. I got bored watching them flirt, so I set out to mingle and didn't see them again until the next afternoon, when we were all on a narrative nonfiction panel.

"Beck, I need you to stay calm for a few minutes and just listen, okay?"

I looked around. The happy hour crowd was filing in, and the hostess smiled when she caught my eye. Veronica had chosen this restaurant—a nice place where the waitstaff knew us —so I wouldn't make a scene.

"What did you do?"

6

BECK

PRESENT DAY

As we turned the corner for the *Lone Star Ledger* offices, a college intern greeted us below a television showcasing its homepage. And there, plastered across nearly all sixty inches, was Veronica's headline above a mugshot of Paul Schuhmacher, Grant Schuhmacher's congressional portrait, and the first few sentences of her story.

There wasn't much to it, but the smallest piece of new information gave reporters from *The Kerrville Daily Times* to *The New York Times* a reason to post versions of the story on their websites and social media, whose users never tired of articles about murder and politics.

I distracted myself by deleting dozens of texts, voicemails, emails, and direct messages every hour from reporters seeking comment.

I kept checking my phone because I needed to monitor two situations.

Jorge, who was still in the hospital but was scheduled to leave Big Lake in less than twenty-four hours.

And Parker Mallory.

"Your friend had better know something," I said. "Otherwise,

I'm just going to call that reporter at the *Journal* and get out in front of this."

I followed Veronica through the bullpen almost involuntarily. It was my second office in the evenings and on weekends, when her top editors weren't in. The evening editor, Amber, didn't care and usually greeted me when I passed her desk, but my face must've matched my mood and she swiveled back to a pair of oversized computer monitors.

Veronica picked up a yellow legal pad from her desk, which was far less cluttered than I remembered, and we went into the empty conference room. She sat and flopped the pad on the thick wooden desk before digging into her purse, presumably for a pen and her phone.

I closed the door and stood beside her.

"Will you sit down," Veronica said rather than asked. "You know I hate it when you hover."

"Just call her."

Veronica had scheduled an after-hours call with an editor at *Manhattanist Magazine*. Emily Dreyer had worked with Veronica on a piece about undercover investigative journalism the week our book released.

She also worked closely with Parker.

Veronica tapped the screen and put her cell on speakerphone.

"Veronica?" Emily's voice sounded hushed, though I might've been imagining the cloak-and-dagger tone since we were trying to get an editor to betray one of her reporters.

"Thanks for doing this."

"Don't thank me yet. I don't have anything for you."

Veronica acted like she was going to slam her fist on the table but stopped. "Dammit, you said you were going to help me on this. You said we were friends."

I'd witnessed their relationship. As far as I could tell, Emily genuinely liked Veronica. Their story had detailed how I'd talked Veronica into coming to work on the jobsite with me and Jorge. She had joined me in being a welder's helper to investigate the murder of another pipeliner, a woman whom Paul had left inside a piece of large-diameter pipe.

It was an emotional piece for Veronica to write, but she said Emily had been supportive. When we were in New York receiving our first award for the book, all three of us had spent a night in the hotel bar getting drunk and having a helluva time.

"We *are* friends," Emily said. "You know that."

"Then tell me what Parker is writing for you. I told you he manipulated me. That slimy piece of shit slept with me, then got me to do his work for him. I don't care if all you have is a budget line or whatever y'all call it. I need to know right now."

Veronica looked up at me with soft eyes. Less than an hour ago, she'd explained to me that she was in Parker's room—in his bed—when Walker had called to *warn* her about me. Veronica had taken the call in the bathroom.

But when Parker asked, she told him she'd gotten a lot of off-the-record information about Paul and the murder of Summer Foster. Parker told Veronica she should call back her source and get something on the record. When she said it could damage me, Parker said, "It doesn't always have to be the Beck and Stein show. You're allowed to do what's best for you."

I flexed my jaw and shook my head. Veronica was looking for a sign I was ready to forgive her, and I was far from doing that.

"That's the thing," Emily said. "He hasn't pitched me a story in more than a month. He's ducking me, actually."

Veronica crossed her arms and leaned back. "I don't understand how that can be true. I heard him talking to someone about the story he's chasing. Hell, they had to keep him from working on it that night."

That night was Saturday. While I was down at the hotel bar drinking and gladhanding, she was on the phone with Amber in Austin, confirming details and workshopping the headline and web presentation. Then, before seeing me, she went to Parker's room. This time, he got a call and went to the bathroom. But

Veronica put her ear to the door and heard his side of the conversation:

"Yes, it'll run tomorrow. Come on, we have enough to ruin his life. What more do you need? If you want me to sit on this, I'm going to need more money. Okay, I'll wait for your call in the morning."

"I hate letting you down like this," Emily said. "And I'm sorry about Parker. If he ever answers, I'll let him know he's done writing for us."

Veronica ended the call and rubbed her forehead.

"Well, that was a waste of time," I said. "I can't believe you let the situation get this bad. I'm sure he's going to shit all over you in his story, too."

Veronica stood, violently, her chair rolling back and hitting the wall of the conference room. "Quit acting like I'm the bad guy here."

"But you *are*." I spoke softly, unable to mask my hurt. "You lied to my face after learning Parker was getting paid to write a hit piece about me."

She took a step toward me. "I wasn't sure you were the subject. That's why I didn't say anything and didn't answer your calls. I wanted to confirm it before coming to you."

The door to the conference room opened and Amber rushed in. "Did you two know this was coming? Is that why you're here?"

Veronica and I whipped around. She asked the question, though we already knew the answer.

"Did we know *what* was coming?"

7

BECK
PRESENT DAY

The headline and first two paragraphs were enough to make my stomach turn.

Congressman, law enforcement claim bestselling author covered up his own murders

By Parker Mallory @PMalloryWriter

WASHINGTON — New evidence in a decades-old homicide has raised questions about whether a key witness lied, and one prominent congressman connected to the infamous case alleges the witness—now a bestselling author—covered up his own role in the brutal slaying.

And the murder of Summer Foster may be the first of four committed by Bartholomew John Beck.

Four? I tried doing the math but couldn't. Summer and Paul made two, though the second was justified beyond doubt. I could even make the leap to calling Butch's execution a murder. My brain already did that at night.

But that's it.

I clicked to continue the story, but the *Post* wanted me to pay, so I asked Veronica for the *Ledger*'s login.

"You sure?"

"How much worse can it get?"

She took the phone and pecked in the information, then handed it back like it was a cyanide pill.

I started reading at my own risk.

Parker began by quoting Schuhmacher, who said I'd lied about killing Summer and killed Paul twenty years later.

No surprises there.

The next section began with the subhead, "He used a machete," so I knew it would detail how I fended off Paul in the temporary grave he'd carved out of the High Plains.

But Parker surprised me with a few new details. Despite his deficit of character, he was one of the best journalists out there.

For instance, he'd detailed the final hours of Paul's victim, Sylvia Davenport, who he killed and left for me to find on the pipeline jobsite near Fritch.

Paul's alibi for the time of death was a Labor Day party attended by many of his coworkers, including Davenport.

Davenport was seen leaving with another man, Jameson Cooke. Security footage showed them pulling into the motel in Fritch where Cooke was staying, but it never caught her leaving in anyone's vehicle.

But after investigators reviewed the footage again, they became suspicious of a pickup with a welder in the bed that entered the parking lot at 4 AM and only stayed for 10 minutes. The driver was wearing a ballcap and, as they later learned, a wig of long blond hair. It exited the parking lot with the same driver but no visible passenger.

The truck was registered to Jorge Hernandez.

"At that point, we were back to suspecting Bart Beck, who said he was at the Hernandez residence all night, with only them to confirm it," said an investigator who worked on the case, who spoke on the condition of anonymity.

"So, we looked back over the notes and we saw that Hernandez had

mentioned being awakened by the sound of what he thought was his truck early Saturday morning. He admitted to a habit of leaving his keys in the truck, so he went out to check but found it safe and sound. He and his wife separately gave the time as 5:35 AM because they debated before starting their day with a strong pot of coffee."

That timeline was consistent with when someone would have returned the truck after stealing it, kidnapping Davenport, then taking her to the jobsite to kill and pose her body. During separate interviews, the Hernandezes said they saw Beck sleeping on their couch, and they didn't hear the front door open or close.

"We expanded our video search using that timeline and discovered that Hernandez's truck was seen stopping at a gas station about a mile from his house," the investigator said. "The driver put in a small amount of diesel, likely making sure the tank was back at the level from before he took it. That video was clearer than the motel's. The driver was too tall and wasn't fat enough to be Bart, but he was about right for Paul Schuhmacher and had similar-looking tattoos on his arms."

The agents believed Paul stole Hernandez's truck to leave physical evidence in a vehicle to which Beck had easy access.

"He wanted to make it look like Bart had done the deed," the investigator said. "That also fit with his staging of the body to look like that other woman Burt found dead twenty years ago. One of us working the case told the other writer of that damn book it would've been the ultimate alibi if not for that stop at the filling station."

A warrant was issued for Paul Henry Schuhmacher's arrest a week into the investigation.

However, the Texas Rangers didn't find Paul until after Bartholomew Beck had killed him.

"He used a machete and nearly cut Schuhmacher's head clean off," the investigator said.

Based on the contempt in the quotes, the anonymous source was Lieutenant Owen "OJ" Johnson, Ranger Walker's partner on the Davenport case. And for a moment, I was distracted by learning new information.

But then the story got back to me and my second victim. Parker used *The Ultimate Alibi* as the source, which was close enough to the truth.

Until Agent Fucking Orange and Schuhmacher started chiming in again.

"We never got to arrest and interrogate Paul Schuhmacher," the investigator said. "We closed the Davenport case, but only because we didn't have enough to arrest Bart Beck or anyone else."

Stein claims Paul confessed to Davenport's murder while he drove her from the Texas Panhandle town of Borger to the location of his death. Beck wrote that she later relayed that information to him after he nearly decapitated Paul.

Grant Schuhmacher still mourns the loss of his son and knows there is a possibility Paul killed Sylvia Davenport.

"Like I said, I know my son was capable of hurting other people, especially women," he said. "I just wish we'd been given the chance to hear what he had to say and, if warranted, have his day in court.

"If you look strictly at the facts, a significant amount of Ms. Davenport's blood was found on tools in Jorge Hernandez's truck, which Mr. Beck had easy access to. He was also seen arguing with the woman hours before her death. And the authorities could not positively identify my son in that all-important video footage.

"There's actually more evidence that points to Mr. Beck than there is my son. But because he killed Paul, we'll never get to know what really happened to Ms. Davenport. Or to Paul, for that matter.

"Can I see Paul killing her? Yes. Can I see Mr. Beck killing her? Absolutely."

Davenport was my fourth victim.

No.

My stomach was sour and roiling as I spoke to Veronica, not taking my eyes off the phone's screen. "I can't believe they're trying to put Sylvia's death on me. I haven't been innocent in a long time, but they can't do this."

When I didn't get a response, I looked up.

She looked as ill as I felt.

"Keep reading."

I swallowed, trying to tamp down the geyser in my gut.

In the next section—"Trying to hide"—Parker described how Walker uncovered the fact that Paul had slept with Summer the day she died.

Both Schuhmacher and the Rangers took issue with Veronica's slanted story, which was predictable.

Then the story shifted to "A deadly love triangle," which is where I learned just what Walker had been up to while re-investigating Summer's case.

Among the items unboxed during the last year was a white tablecloth. It was of particular interest to the Texas Rangers because there were a set of fingerprints that had no match.

It began with a review of crime scene photos by a department with much more experience investigating heinous crimes than the local law enforcement in charge of the original crime, Schuhmacher said.

One photo captured a swath of blood on that tablecloth, concentrated at the corner nearest the tool shed where Foster had stored the screwdriver and a small sledgehammer, which, for more than 20 years, has been considered the murder weapon.

At one end of that streak were three fingerprints.

When that tablecloth was taken to the DPS lab in Austin, techs ran the fingerprints again and examined the cheap cotton more thoroughly. They confirmed the fingerprints belonged to Bartholomew John Beck and the blood as Foster's.

Lab techs also performed a blood spatter analysis, which hadn't been done during the initial investigation. The tablecloth was not listed as one of the items to be tested after the Supreme Court granted Heller a stay of execution in 2009.

The examination showed a wider pattern of blood emanating from the corner, and an expert eye revealed a long-hidden truth: The side of

Summer Foster's head was caved in by the corner of that table, not the sledgehammer that was later used to fool investigators.

Another fact was also apparent. The hand that smeared that blood —Beck's hand—had wiped through that blood after the fact in a manner that indicated he was trying to wipe away evidence.

Now I understood why Walker—who'd been an ally during the Davenport investigation—had told Veronica to be wary of me.

She knew I'd killed Summer.

I was close to the end of Parker's story, so I had to keep reading, convinced I'd read the worst and could predict the end.

But after he asked why I'd killed Summer, Parker began shredding what had been left of his journalistic integrity.

According to Schuhmacher, authorities now believe Beck killed Foster in a jealous rage.

Everyone interviewed at the time said Beck was not at the Independence Day celebration in Foster's yard. They also said Paul was seen coming and going along with his friends.

When the festivities moved to the park so people could watch the fireworks show, Paul's whereabouts are even less certain, and Beck was nowhere to be found. But everyone knew Foster had stayed behind to begin cleaning up after the party.

"I was the last person to leave her yard for the fireworks show, and she was alone at that moment," congressman Schuhmacher said. "But I never did see my son in the park."

According to the new theory, Paul sneaked over and had "a quickie" with Foster. Beck had the same idea and caught them as they exited through her back door.

"They're telling me Mr. Beck must've chased my son away," Schuhmacher said. "And as athletic as my son was, Mr. Beck was freakishly strong. I bet he still holds all the high school lifting records."

After disposing of his romantic rival, Beck turned to Foster, an attractive, fit woman he'd watched from across the street as his teenage hormones raged. She had gotten even closer to the family the year before while acting as a voluntary personal track and field coach for Beck's older sister, who died in a car crash in January of 1999.

Authorities believe Beck coveted Foster and was under the impression he was the only student to whom she was paying special attention.

When that belief was shattered, the new evidence suggests Beck slammed the side of Foster's head into the corner of her own picnic table, then dragged her to the tool shed and went to work on her with the hammer and screwdriver. He then wiped his prints from the screwdriver and tried to make it seem like he left the blood on the tablecloth after attempting to help her, which would also explain his prints on her body, clothes, and the hammer.

When he heard Heller approaching in his car, Beck ran and hid nearby while watching Heller find Foster's body. It was then that Beck realized he could frame Heller by lying to the police and, three years later, publishing a book with Heller as the villain.

Along with Stein, Beck revisited his fictional version of the events in The Ultimate Alibi, *a title Schuhmacher said is a "big middle finger" to law enforcement.*

"I mean, it's right there on the cover," the congressman said. "I know it's supposed to be about how my son almost had the ultimate alibi for Ms. Davenport's murder, but it's really about Beck's alibis for the murders of Foster and Davenport. Finding the body was his ultimate alibi for Summer's murder. Then the book he wrote was Beck's alibi for the Davenport woman. I mean, who'd be stupid enough to leave a body the same way that you wrote about, right?"

Authorities point to the romantic relationship with Davenport twenty years later as establishing a pattern. Beck was violent toward her, and she ended up dead after rebuffing him.

There is also the possibility Beck killed Paul Schuhmacher to finish getting his revenge for his relationship with Foster.

None of the sources in this story would comment on whether the Sylvia Davenport or Paul Schuhmacher cases have been re-opened.

"But I think it's certainly a possibility," Grant Schuhmacher said.

"And I hope they nail him for the murder of one of those women, because he may not be done killing."

I dropped my phone onto the conference table, unable to read the final section. It asked "Who's next?" and I didn't want to know what future deaths they wanted to add.

But before I could stand and leave, Veronica answered the question.

"I can't believe Schuhmacher said you tried to kill Jorge, and that he'd be your fifth victim if he dies," she said as I turned to her. "And that kicker? Batshit crazy."

When she realized I didn't know what she meant, Veronica walked over and handed me my phone, where I read the end of Schuhmacher's quote.

"And if I were Ms. Stein, and I knew what really happened to my son and Sylvia Davenport, I'd be worried about becoming the sixth."

8

BECK

PRESENT DAY

I ignored Veronica's voice from outside the bathroom. She opened the door and called my name, but I continued sitting beside the toilet, the back of my head hurting after repeatedly slamming it against the cold title.

My eyes were closed when she opened the stall door.

"I am so, so sorry," she said. "This is all my fault and—"

"Save your apologies." I kept my eyes shut. I wanted just a few more minutes of pretending I wouldn't have to deal with the fallout. "I'm not in here trying to kill myself. Give me a few more minutes and we can talk about it."

Veronica didn't say anything, and, for a moment, didn't move. She eventually took the hint and let the stall door squeak shut. As she walked across the bathroom, she whisper-yelled "What the fuck?" and I wondered who was getting the earful.

Not that it mattered. The damage was done.

A sick part of me respected Parker's work. He was a talented fabulist. The key, as those of us who've done it in such spectacular fashion know, is making sure there is plenty of verifiable truth woven through the narrative.

While reading Parker's story, I remembered throwing Summer into the picnic table, then realizing she was dead. Then the panic. Cursing as I mutilated the area around the wound to cover it up. Crying as I stabbed her lifeless eye with the screwdriver, then cursing again as I realized I shouldn't leave my fingerprints on the handle.

It was dark that night after the fireworks ended, and I had no idea how much blood Summer had left on the tablecloth. No matter the quantity, I had to explain it, so I swiped my hand across the corner. I used the table to stand up, I'd say, but my hand was so slick from tossing the hammer and trying to help poor Miss Foster that I slipped and fell back down. It seemed as foolproof as the rest of my story.

I didn't know about bloodstain pattern analysis until 2006 when *Dexter* debuted on TV. I worried when the US Supreme Court allowed for re-testing a few years later, but the twenty-four-year-old technique had just suffered a major blow from the National Academy of Sciences, which gave many lawyers fuel to consider it "junk science."

That defense wouldn't work after Parker's story, though. Texas courts started holding pattern experts to higher standards in 2019, and no jury would question the state crime lab.

My first instinct—after emptying my stomach—had been to turn myself in. That had been my plan three years ago when I was sure Veronica would expose me as Parker and Grant Schuhmacher had just done. But she didn't, choosing instead to keep my secret as a reward for saving her life.

And if Parker's story had stopped at the deaths for which I was responsible, I might've walked a half mile to the Austin Police Department's downtown station and thrown up my hands in surrender. I could even have lived with the mischaracterization of why I was so angry at Summer that night. Either way, I would be found guilty of murder. During sentencing, I could try to convince a jury my rage wasn't about a love triangle, but rather grief and anger over the death of my sister. That might get it dropped to a second-degree felony, which would mean only twenty years rather than life.

But Schuhmacher and his attack dog got greedy.

I couldn't let them add Sylvia to my body count. If I were found guilty of murdering her, there would be no reduced sentence.

And without this story, prosecutors may have only considered charging me for Summer's death. But Parker's case was convincing. Add the fact he was backed by a sitting congressman, who would no doubt put pressure on the district attorneys in Hutchinson and Nimitz counties to file charges, and I had to assume an arrest on one charge would mean three indictments. Hell, they might pile on a charge for Butch's execution.

I opened my eyes. I didn't know how, but I wasn't going to let an arrogant ass like Parker or a corrupt shitbag like Schuhmacher do this. My guess was Veronica felt the same way and was already working on a plan.

I made it halfway out of the bathroom before throwing up again.

I WAS RIGHT ABOUT VERONICA. She'd been on the phone with Walker, and I caught the end of the conversation as I opened the conference room door.

"Well fuck you very much," she said, then slammed her phone on the desk.

"Better hope you have a good case."

Veronica didn't look amused. "For someone trying to, quote, help me, Walker's a real bitch."

Veronica's phone buzzed. She turned it over, revealing a fresh spiderweb above the green banner indicating a new voicemail. "Dammit."

"What'd Walker say?"

"Not a damn thing. I asked if she was one of Parker's sources, if the parts about the blood spatter and new theory were true. You know what she said?" Veronica didn't give me more than a beat, and I wasn't quick enough to guess. "*I tried to warn you about him.*"

I'd figured as much, but that hint of confirmation still felt like a knee to the gut. Hadn't I just been in this situation a few years ago?

Not quite.

I hadn't killed Sylvia Davenport.

Veronica's phone buzzed again, a second reminder about the voicemail. She picked it up and cursed again before tapping the damaged screen.

I turned around. I needed to go home for a shower and time to think.

I'd nearly reached the door when Veronica elbowed me out of the way, threw open the door, and jogged toward Amber's desk, cubicle decorations falling as she brushed past them.

She'd left her phone on the table. It hadn't gone dark yet, so I hit play.

Veronica, it's Dave. We read the story and, well, Christ, your story said Schuhmacher declined comment, then he turns around the next day and denies it in the goddamn Post. *I know he's as crooked as a three-dollar bill, but yours was a one-source story and that source was anonymous. Plus, he says the Texas Rangers are questioning what you wrote in your book. The bottom line is you ran out of leash and our donors are already calling me. We're suspending you. I've emailed Amber and told her to take down everything you've written and put out the press release the lawyers and I worked up. Call me back when you get this.*

By the time I got to Amber's desk, Veronica was hunched over the monitors, reading the email. The *Ledger*'s statement was short and bland, but it said they were *looking into these serious allegations* and would *review all of Stein's past reporting.*

"This is such bullshit," Veronica said. "If you were a real journalist, you'd tell Dave to go fuck himself."

"Look, Miss Moneybags, I need this job."

I tapped Veronica on the shoulder before she could lay into Amber again. "You left this," I said, holding up her phone.

"You need to go," Amber said. "Dave's already on my ass about getting this posted."

I waited by Amber's desk while Veronica went back into the conference room to get her things. "Will they fire her?"

"Who knows," Amber said. "I believe Veronica, but we can't look like we're spreading fake news. We hear that enough as it is. And nobody's going to believe us over the *Post*."

"Your editor's definitely no Ben Bradlee."

"He's a spineless piece of shit," Veronica said as she hustled past us.

I rushed to catch up and joined her. I didn't say anything, but as soon as the elevator doors closed, she answered the question I wasn't asking.

"No, I didn't reach out to Schuhmacher. I knew he wouldn't say anything on the record, so I wrote that he declined to comment and filed the story. Of all the lies I've told and secrets I've kept, I can't believe a throwaway no-comment line is what's going to ruin everything."

I nodded but stayed quiet until we were both standing on Congress Avenue again.

"Parker had that story ready to go," I said. "He had it written before he got to Dallas and was waiting for yours. Schuhmacher paid him to write that story."

"I know."

9
____

BECK
PRESENT DAY

I stood naked. Wet. At peace, if only for a few minutes. A long shower can wash away the thin, outer film of worry. I continued the good vibe by shaving, the smell of sandalwood more welcome than usual, given how ripe I'd been twenty minutes earlier.

Not yet ready to leave, I slopped over to the long marble counter where I'd set up stations, an assembly line for making myself presentable to the public.

I brushed on the deodorant that had come in a kit with the rest of the smell-good crap. I flossed. Brushed. Stepped on the scale—a bad idea after four days of eating hotel food and drinking, followed immediately by unhealthy levels of cortisol, fast food, and hospital vending machine snacks—and even tried styling my hair with whatever the hell *pomade* is.

I turned around to the stone-lined shower, the one I'd told the realtor was bigger than the living room in my last apartment in Fort Worth.

And then there was the six months I'd been homeless, traveling with Jorge in his camper or sleeping on his couch in Borger, usually sharing it with one or more of the family pets—though never their pig.

Perhaps that's why my first advance check from *The Ultimate Alibi* went toward the condo. I'd never need a quarter of the space it provided, but boy did I want it. And for the first time, I could afford something nice for myself. Well, I could afford the down payment, which was larger than I'd have needed for one of the fantastic houses nearby. And the mortgage rate was higher. But no house could give me the view or proximity to Austin's nightlife. Totally worth it at the time.

After using every health and beauty product I owned, I walked to the other end of the room, slipped on the white robe I'd bought from a New York hotel earlier that year, and opened the door that led to my crumbling life.

If I was going to face it, I might as well be comfortable.

Bathroom tile gave way to polished concrete until I reached the rug in my walk-in closet, where I'd stowed the luggage. On the other side of the closet was my room with a bed that matched those in the luxury hotel suites.

Furnishing the place had nearly cleaned me out, but when the next check came, I decided to buy the Challenger. Though I'd needed a new car, the model that could get to sixty in less than four seconds was a little much for Austin's constant congestion. The electronic dash that could do everything but launch a missile was also unnecessary.

But I was smart and paid cash, which meant when I sold my novel just as *The Ultimate Alibi* was launching, I only owed my mortgage payment and utilities. I'd even saved myself money by not hiring a business manager to handle my money, which felt like a fifteen percent bonus.

That's how I justified doing the one thing every rich son should—putting a down payment on a plot of Montana land and working with my parents to design a custom home. My dad's carpentry shop was bigger than our house in Hinterbach had been.

They hadn't been to my Austin digs, which was how I got away with furnishing the living room with the most modern glass and brushed metal furniture I could find. My father, the master carpenter who'd been selling custom furniture for years, didn't know most of my pieces were on the fourth floor of a storage facility north of the UT campus.

The two exceptions were an executive writing desk and bookshelf, which would've been gathering dust in my office were it not for my housekeeper. I hadn't written anything substantial in six months. Maybe eight.

Turns out, I was not a prolific storyteller, and cranking out a novel a year in addition to my true-crime partnership with Veronica would never happen. After recalculating my situation, I'd finally realized my debt would wipe out my guaranteed income in five years.

That figure dropped to one after my father suffered a near-fatal stroke. After he was released from the hospital, I hired a full-time health care provider to help my mother while he recovered. Mom didn't ask for the help, but she didn't need to. Her son had two *New York Times* best sellers. Why should she worry about money during a time like this?

That's when I hastily cashed in the easiest asset I could find. Against my agent's advice, I practically gave away my rights to *Cold Summer* so Gavel Press could reprint it in the afterglow of my newfound success.

That would pay dividends over time. But until then, I was back to putting my groceries on credit.

AFTER RUNNING out of ways to procrastinate, I sat on my leather couch, studied my phone like it was a bomb, then deleted everything but one voicemail and one text.

To avoid the bad news for just a bit longer, I listened to Grace's message first.

Hey Beck, just wanted to let you know they're letting me take Jorge home tonight. He's already walking. He's wearing a back brace and he'll be on good pain pills for a day or two, but that pendeja doctor made it seem way worse than it is. Anyway, we're about to get him in the van. Talk to you later.

I leaned back with the phone and tapped the green dialogue bubble, ignoring the unread message from Shayla Hickman for a bit longer.

Glad you're doing so well! Don't forget to call when you're ready to get the camper.

I saw the three dots almost immediately.

Thx bro will do call u ltr

Jorge's text would've been the same jumble of letters whether he was high or not. It usually grated my writerly nerves, but after seeing that video on Chuck's phone, I'd have been happy with a string of emojis.

I hit the back arrow and stared down the unread text.

Call me ASAP. It's about your friend.

I'm not sure if my reticence came from the subject matter or the messenger.

Shayla was in law enforcement—now in Reagan County, apparently—so whatever she had to say would sour my mood. I had a feeling, though, that I'd have been nervous to call her if she'd been offering a lifetime supply of Blue Bell ice cream.

"All right," I said, talking myself into calling. "Let's get this over with."

The phone rang four times before she answered.

"Hold on," Shayla said before sucking in a breath. "At the gym. Let me step outside."

Shayla had been working out the night I went to her old house, the one in Weatherford that had belonged to her dead father and estranged mother. I'd been waiting for her to give me information then, too, though I'd asked for that conversation.

"Okay," she said.

"Your text said you needed to talk about Jorge's accident?"

"That's the thing. It wasn't an accident."

Jorge and I were right. It wasn't a burp. "How do you know?"

"The gas company initiated a standard investigation, which included looking at the valves that were supposed to be shut off and locked in place. Sure enough, they'd been tampered with."

I sat forward. "Tampered with how?"

"I didn't follow all of it, but one of the project managers took me to some kind of station and said two of the valves had been opened. A chain should've been wrapped around the wagon wheels so they couldn't be turned. But when we walked up to them, the padlocks were cut and the chains were on the ground."

"Someone opened up the bypass valves at the block station."

"Yeah, that's it," Shayla said. "The guy said it had to be someone who knew what they were doing. They had to open the right valves in the right order and be quick to close them, otherwise it would've been a lot worse."

I stared at the black television hanging from the sea green wall. Someone had tried to kill Jorge and the rest of those pipeliners.

"Holy fucking shit," I said.

"Yeah. Our theory is it was someone who worked on that pipeline."

I'd met pipeliners with criminal pasts—some of them violent, maybe assault with a deadly weapon, though most were drug or theft related—but everyone's goal was putting in ten and leaving to spend their paychecks. The basement was 15 dollars an hour.

Skilled labor like welders could pull in 60-plus, and everyone got a hundred or more per diem.

Money was the only reason they were out there, so who the hell would want to intentionally hurt one of their own?

And why?

"You have any suspects?" I asked.

"We just found all this out earlier today. I'm good, but I'm not that good."

I could hear the smile in her voice, a welcome relief after how we'd left things.

I tried to stop picturing her in the old high school shirt and sweats she used to work out in, slowly shifting my focus back to the fact someone may have tried to kill my best friend and his coworkers.

But not all his coworkers.

I stood and began pacing. "Did Jorge tell you his helper wasn't there yesterday?"

"No."

"He called Saturday night and said he needed the day off."

"What's the helper's name?"

"Hey, you're the cop, not me."

"Sheriff's deputy, thank you very much," Shayla said. "But seriously, call Jorge and get the guy's name and phone number."

I told her I'd do it, then thought about ending the conversation. But I didn't want to, and she hadn't said goodbye, either. "So, why is a sheriff's deputy discussing her case with a lowly civilian?"

"I know you spent a day with him, and he probably told you things he wouldn't tell us. I know Jorge is a permanent resident, but immigrants never say much to anyone with a badge. Looks like I was right."

She paused, and I prepared for a goodbye.

Then she surprised me. "Plus, it gave me a good excuse to call you again."

I could hear her smiling through the phone. Was she flirting with me?

I decided to find out. "How'd you end up in Big Lake?"

"After everything came out that night, I realized I could finally let go of what happened. But first, I needed to get out of that goddamn house, so I started looking for a new job the next day."

If she had been flirting, I'd blown it by giving Shayla a reason to remember her awful childhood. She put our conversation out of its misery with an awkward goodbye and a reminder to get information about Jorge's helper.

I took my sour mood back to the bathroom and poured two pills out of a prescription bottle. The psychiatrist I saw after killing Paul said it would be a temporary fix but sleep never came without the medicine. And every night before they kicked in, the souls of each life I'd taken spoke to me.

Summer. Paul.

Butch Heller.

Though I hadn't put the needle in his arm, I condemned him to death and thought it would bring me satisfaction. Butch was the drunk who killed my sister in that accident and left her to be found hours later. Hadn't he deserved to die?

The answer was irrelevant. He haunted me all the same.

But as I waited to drift off, my mind was consumed with more pressing thoughts. Parker's story and Jorge's non-accident were connected, and even in my drowsy haze, the answer was clear.

Grant Schuhmacher was engineering my demise.

10

BECK

PRESENT DAY

Veronica was waiting for me on the small sidewalk patio. The Italian *caffé* was one of five shops on the ground level of her building, the second-tallest residential tower west of the Mississippi.

Veronica chose hers because it was a straight shot down South Congress to her offices.

I chose mine because it was the tallest.

She pointed to the plastic to-go cup opposite her mug, which was holding down the corner of a dossier labeled *Special Agent Casey Kelley*.

"Thanks." I sat and greedily sucked down a third of the iced chai. "I know we owe everyone another book proposal, but is now the best time to get back into the Kelley file?"

Veronica had been pitching me the murder of Casey Kelley for months. He'd been the special agent in charge of the FBI's field office in San Antonio before his throat was sliced open more than twenty years ago. The case had been ruled a mugging-gone-wrong since it happened behind a dive bar and his pockets had been picked. Authorities assumed the items stolen included his FBI badge and credentials, and his service weapon, since both were missing from his home.

One newspaper, citing an unnamed law enforcement source, said the killing may have happened during a sexual encounter that turned into an armed robbery. The source said Kelley was found with his junk hanging out. Additionally, half the bar's patrons said a man followed Kelley into the hallway leading to the bathroom and back exit, but the other half swore they saw a woman. The one thing they agreed on was the leather jacket he or she was wearing.

The article quoted the bartender, who said he went to check on him after a few minutes because he hadn't paid his tab. He was worried Kelley had skipped out on the check. He claimed to have discovered the body and called 911 at 6:08 PM.

The story ended with the police source saying law enforcement had no leads.

That much was true, and after a swift investigation, the FBI said the murder was unrelated to his status as a high-ranking special agent.

But there were several red flags. The fact that his throat was cut, as opposed to a more traditional stabbing, seemed odd—if you were looking for oddities. He was also fifty-seven and about to retire, so why even bother to kill the man? Kelley wasn't known to carry around cash, according to one of the newspaper profiles she'd compiled, and his dress was always understated, especially off the clock.

And wouldn't he have told the mugger he was a fed? That would scare off your run-of-the-mill dirtbag.

The theory favored by his widow and one coworker, Special Agent Terry Jackson, was that Kelley had been killed to stop a high-profile investigation, though that lead had never panned out. So, with no physical evidence in the grimy alley, it was called a tragic case of wrong place, wrong time. Everyone at the Bureau was satisfied with the hero's sendoff Kelley received.

Everyone but Jackson, who was now the FBI's public affairs officer in San Antonio, which is how he'd met Veronica and put the bug in her ear about his old friend's death.

The file in front of her now was little more than a collection of clips from the Washington and San Antonio newspapers. She'd procured a printout of the FBI file's topsheet, which made the folder feel a bit heavier, though the document didn't include any revelatory information. All we had was Jackson's vague promise to provide something soon.

"So, this is kind of wild," Veronica said, "but Agent Jackson called me last night. He thinks Congressman Schuhmacher had Kelley killed. And after reading the *Post* story, Jackson thinks we can work together to prove it. I know you think he's half crazy, but—"

"Actually, I believe him."

Veronica leaned back in her chair. "Just like that? What happened to your speech about sources having an ax to grind and needing physical evidence?"

Now it was my turn to discuss a wild phone conversation. Veronica went from confused to chasing a story faster than I could take another drink of my tea. By the time I conveyed Shayla's information, Veronica had filled a page in her reporter's notebook and was peppering me with questions.

"And you don't have the name of Jorge's new helper?"

"Not yet. He hasn't returned my call."

"Dammit. Can you call again right now?"

"I guess."

Veronica stared at me. She always won these contests, and this time was no different.

I reached into the front pocket of my jeans, but before I pulled out the phone, a young man approached our table and took off his expensive-looking aviators.

He locked eyes with Veronica. "I'm so sorry to interrupt, but are you Veronica Stein?"

She nodded but didn't seem pleased. "Can I help you with something?"

The kid flashed a fluorescent smile and rested the glasses on a thick head of chestnut hair. "I normally don't do things like this, but I'm a huge fan. Both of your journalism and your book."

He turned to me. "And you must be Mr. Beck."

I nodded and extended my hand. He removed his from the strap of a leather messenger bag and shook it enthusiastically.

"It is such a pleasure to meet you both. I absolutely loved *The Ultimate Alibi*."

"Do you have a copy for us to sign?" I asked.

"I don't, and I can't tell you how disappointed I am."

Veronica reached for her purse. "I think I have some book plates in here with our signatures on them."

"Oh that's okay," he said. "I have something in here that'll work."

He opened the bag and emerged with two sets of tri-folded papers, which he placed in the middle of our table.

Veronica and I locked eyes.

Before we could reach for the documents and start reading, the man cleared his throat. We looked over to find him standing farther away with his phone pointed at us.

"You've been served."

Veronica hastened his exit with some choice profanity as I unfolded one of the packets.

"Schuhmacher is suing us," I said.

I'd been sued once before, over one of my lesser works in which I'd failed to say someone was an *alleged* child molester. The publisher's lawyers said I could file the document in my circular bin, which I'd done without reading it. The case was thrown out because the woman suing me had been tried and convicted of the crime.

But this is America, where a reader could sue me for a shitty sub-plot if it upset them enough.

Veronica picked up her copy and began speed reading. "This is bullshit."

"I know. First, he pays Parker to write that hit piece, now this—"

"No," Veronica said, still reading. "I mean, yes, that's also bullshit. But I'm talking about the suit itself. He's coming after us for libel on behalf of his son, but you can't libel the dead. That's one of the first things you learn in J-school."

I could decipher criminal complaints, affidavits, and a detective's murder book with the best. But as a journalist, she'd read more civil lawsuits and would have to interpret some of the legalese for me.

I flipped another page and acted like I was trying to make sense of it.

"Oh hell," Veronica continued. "He's saying he can sue on Paul's behalf because, quote, Texas civil law clearly states that libel is a defamation expressed in written or other graphic form that tends to blacken the memory of the dead." She finally looked up from the document. "Even if it literally reads that way, I know there's too much precedent that says otherwise. This'll never make it past a judge."

I found that paragraph. But I was maybe halfway through my paperwork, and Veronica was near the end of hers.

I turned a few more pages. The first document was over quickly, but another suit had been folded in.

I handed her the second packet. "I think I'm being sued individually for something else."

She started speed-reading again but stopped after only a few seconds. "Jesus. He's suing for wrongful death on Paul's behalf."

Now it was my turn to flex some legal knowledge. "He can't. The statute of limitations is two years in Texas."

She looked at me, likely trying to decide if I knew that for professional or personal reasons.

"It comes up during murder cases when you talk to family members." That was true, but book research wasn't why I initially read Chapter 16 of the state's civil practice and remedies code.

Veronica kept reading.

"He's claiming the new evidence that's surfaced in Summer's

case should re-set the clock. Parker's bullshit story is his main argument."

Two lawsuits, neither of which had a chance of going Schuhmacher's way. "What lawyer would file this kind of garbage?"

I flipped to the last page and found the attorney of record.

Samuel Clemens Foster.

We used to call him Sammy.

I stared at the name, frozen, until Veronica leaned over and read the name.

"Wait. Is that—"

"Summer Foster's son," I said. "And now he knows I killed his mother."

Veronica didn't seem convinced. "We don't know that. There must be hundreds of Fosters out there with a first name that can be shortened to Sammy."

"Not with that middle name. Summer named him after her favorite author, Mark Twain."

Veronica leaned back and stared past me. "Let's say you're right. What does he gain from filing Schuhmacher's frivolous lawsuits?"

"You mean the man who has a high-profile reporter on his payroll."

Veronica's eyes went wild. Less than a minute later, she cursed so loud a barista walked out and asked if she was okay.

Congressman sues infamous author for wrongful death, libel

By Parker Mallory
Special to the Post

WASHINGTON — U.S. Rep. Grant Schuhmacher has filed a wrongful death lawsuit against Bartholomew John Beck, the bestselling author who killed the congressman's son in 2019.

Schuhmacher, R-Texas, is also suing Beck, his publisher, and another author for libel on behalf of his late son, Paul. Beck and his co-

author, Veronica Stein, accused Paul of murdering a woman in the pages of their book, The Ultimate Alibi.

Schuhmacher, said he's bringing the wrongful death suit "because new evidence has been brought to my attention that clearly shows Mr. Beck has murdered at least one person, and my son threatened to expose the truth.

"Mr. Beck was simply tying up loose ends when he killed Paul under the guise of self-defense."

The libel lawsuit accuses Beck and Stein of lying about the events surrounding Paul Schuhmacher's death three years ago. The book was published by Gavel Press—an imprint of PHC Publishing Group—which is also named as a defendant.

Beck and Stein have not yet been reached for comment.

PHC declined to comment because its lawyers "have not yet had a chance to thoroughly review the lawsuit," according to a written statement.

The Lone Star Ledger, which employs Stein, pulled all her stories from its website and released a statement saying they were reviewing all of her past reporting.

The lawsuits come as law enforcement investigates whether Beck is responsible for the murder of his former neighbor, Summer Foster, the subject of his first book.

"I don't know what's going to come of any criminal investigations, but I know without a doubt that Mr. Beck is a liar," Schuhmacher said. "I can't abide him disparaging my son's name for his own profits."

The suits were filed in Nimitz County—where Paul Schuhmacher's permanent address was listed before his death—by Samuel Clemens Foster of the Dallas-based law firm Duggan, Chatsworth & Howell.

Samuel Foster is Summer's son.

"When congressman Schuhmacher called and said he had reason to believe someone other than Butch Heller killed my mother, I immediately wanted to help," Foster said. "We'll see what the Texas Rangers say about my mother's murder. In the meantime, I can make sure Bartholomew Beck is held accountable for one of the other people he's killed."

The story continued with background from Parker's first article. The editors at the *Post* made sure a few paragraphs were dedicated to discussing the legitimacy of the suits. A Georgetown Law School professor agreed with Veronica. Summer's orphaned son said he was willing to *let a judge decide*.

"What do we do now?" I asked.

She picked up the phone and started texting. "I'll get recommendations for libel lawyers. I can ask about ones who specialize in defending wrongful death lawsuits, but I wouldn't rely on a bunch of reporters to know much about that."

I almost told her not to bother with any of it. We'd never out-lawyer Schuhmacher. He might not get to pursue his lawsuits, unless he had a lot of leverage over the Nimitz County district attorney, or the DA was willing to put their reputation on the line for cash. Both were possible.

But the fate of Schuhmacher's suits were irrelevant. If he kept repeating his story to the media, it would become the truth, no matter how much he manipulated the facts.

He was running a fake news campaign against us.

We'd have to run one against him.

"Get hold of your FBI source, too," I said. "Let's find out what he knows."

11

BECK

PRESENT DAY

I felt less optimistic about Special Agent Terry Jackson as we walked into a *saloon* on the northeast edge of San Antonio. That's what the sign said on the faux-rustic swinging doors, anyway.

A phone call should've gotten the job done. But when Veronica brought up Schuhmacher and the conspiracy surrounding Agent Kelley's death, her FBI source said he'd only talk in person.

"What does Jackson look like?" I asked.

She scanned the bar. "I don't know. This is the first time he's demanded to meet in person. His photos on Facebook and LinkedIn look like a generic bald dude."

Nobody seemed to fit that description. There was a bearded hipster in a trucker hat at the bar, and an older brunette with graying roots in a corner booth, and a family of four on a road trip, judging by the annoyed look on their faces and SeaWorld T-shirts.

"Wonder why he's so paranoid now?" I asked.

Veronica was about to speak when a black suit and matching sunglasses appeared in my periphery.

"Not paranoid. I just don't feel like being fired and brought up on charges for unauthorized leaks to the press."

Agent Jackson took off his shades and nodded hello to Veronica. He started walking to a booth in the corner and didn't bother to make sure we were following him.

I picked up the lunch menu while Veronica got to work schmoozing her source. "Thanks for agreeing to meet on such short notice."

"Skip the flattery. I'm already going to be late getting back."

Veronica pulled a pen and steno pad from her purse.

"We need everything you have on Grant Schuhmacher."

"You don't have enough paper or ink. For today's purposes, let's start with the day Casey Kelley was executed."

When the place's lone waitress approached, Jackson told her to bring us three waters before shooing her away.

"In February of 2000," he said, "Case had been working a lead on Schuhmacher for a little over six months."

Veronica started writing. "So people called him Case, not Casey?"

Jackson smiled for the first time since walking in. "Yeah. Some of us called him Hard Case Kelley behind his back. He wasn't the warm and cuddly type, but if he trusted you, you were family."

Veronica nodded and kept writing. It's a detail she might've used in a book, but for our purposes she was trying to get Jackson to let down his guard. And she was good.

The waitress came back with the waters. I drank half of mine in one pull.

"Sorry I interrupted," Veronica said. "You said Agent Kelley had been investigating Schuhmacher for six months?"

"Actually, it was more like eight months. Schuhmacher was using laundered money to fund his election to the state senate."

I decided to play bad cop. "The Texas Rangers investigate local political corruption. Why was the FBI involved?"

Veronica shot me a look, then softened her expression and turned expectantly to Jackson.

"To start, the bank he used was backed by the FDIC. But you're right, we probably wouldn't've given two shits if Schuhmacher hadn't been involved with Jim Flynn."

I recognized the name but wanted to make sure. "The lobbyist who got all those politicians in hot water twenty years ago?"

Jackson nodded. "Got your attention now?"

I leaned in. Veronica was also engrossed, writing notes for the half-dozen magazine and book ideas that were no doubt flashing through her mind.

"How did I not already know this?" Veronica asked. "I've been researching Schuhmacher for years and never heard that rumor."

"Since it involved such high-level suspects, Case and I were the only ones working that angle, and it was mostly Case." Jackson spun his sweaty glass as he spoke. "He wanted it to be his last bust before retiring. He even talked about slapping the cuffs on himself. It's how we'd all like to go out, you know? Big, splashy arrest, then ride off. Not like me."

Jackson was deep in thought. I wanted to move the conversation along. Veronica picked up on my impatience and tapped my foot under the table. She wanted to keep him reliving the past. That's when a source gives up the good stuff, so I didn't interrupt Jackson as he continued.

"At the time, I was wrapped up in a joint task force with the DEA. This was the early days of the opioid crisis, and we were investigating how dealers were getting the drugs. In the end, we found out nurses had been sneaking fentanyl out of local hospitals. I got to arrest Lenny *Pretty Boy* Floyd as part of a massive bust, but the judge ruled some of the evidence was inadmissible. Some procedural screw up that let the assholes go free. Between that and what happened to Case, I asked for a transfer to the Public Affairs desk and never left."

Jackson paused and looked at his glass like it was showing him the future he'd lost when Case died. He kept staring until someone burst into laughter at a nearby table, jerking him back to the present.

"So, February twenty-first," he said. "Presidents' Day. Case hadn't proven any connection to Flynn, but he was meeting someone with physical evidence that would be too much for Washington to ignore. Then he was supposed to go visit his mother in her nursing home."

Something about his story didn't add up. "If the evidence was so damning, he should've known the meeting would be dangerous. Why didn't he bring back-up?"

Jackson closed his eyes and rubbed his forehead. "Because the source said he would only meet with Case, and I didn't have the balls to stand up to him." He shifted his gaze to a spot on the far wall. "He could've taken them all down and retired a hero, and it's my fault he never got the chance. I know that."

"I don't buy it," I said. "There's no way you'd've let him go on his own."

Jackson pointed at me. "Look, we had the day off. I didn't know he was missing until I called his mom's nursing home four hours later. By then Case's wife was already calling every hospital in South Texas. I checked security video at the nursing home that evening and confirmed he never walked in."

Veronica tapped her pen on the notebook. "Why was Case meeting his source on a federal holiday? Why was he working in the field at all?"

Jackson turned to Veronica. "Stop writing."

She looked like she wanted to protest, so I put my hand on her forearm. If Jackson didn't want a record of what he was about to say, it might finally be information we could use.

She carefully laid her pen on the table.

"Our investigation was off the books."

Veronica and I looked at each other.

Kelley and Jackson had gone rogue. That's why Kelley was dead, and Jackson was using us to get the justice he never could.

Veronica spoke first. "When and where were they supposed to meet?"

"Three in the afternoon, somewhere near Hinterbach. He didn't give me a specific location, though."

She turned to the last page of her notepad. "According to the report you sent me, the medical examiner put Kelley's time of death between five and seven in the evening. Definitely enough time to have met with the source and driven back."

Jackson took a drink. "We used beepers back then. At about 3:40, he let me know the meet had gone as planned. Three hours later, an SAPD officer called in a 10-60. DOA."

I felt for Jackson and could tell Veronica did, too, so we let him have a moment. But no matter how guilty Jackson felt, I knew he was wrong. Kelley had stopped to have a drink before visiting his mother and was a victim of a mugging gone wrong. It was the simplest explanation.

"I still don't understand why you think Kelley's Schuhmacher-Flynn investigation has anything to do with his murder," I said.

"Follow me."

Jackson led us to a silver sedan and popped the trunk. Veronica leaned in and I stood over her shoulder. It was empty save for a manuscript-sized box.

"I got this in the mail last year. Its original contents included a ledger, a handwritten note, and a sandwich bag with a piece of bloodstained tissue inside. It was shipped from a small town southwest of Killeen. Security cameras only caught someone in a hoodie. We think it was a woman, but there's no way to be sure."

Veronica stepped closer and stared as though trying to see through the cardboard. When that didn't work, Jackson opened it and revealed a stack of copy paper.

"The originals are in a safe at home, but you are free to look at these." He pulled out the first sheet and handed it to Veronica. "Here's the note."

I leaned over her shoulder.

Special Agent Jackson,

I know who sliced Special Agent Kelley's throat. Enclosed is the ledger he had on him, which I retrieved after watching him die, along with a recent sample of the killer's DNA.

I can't live knowing nobody was punished for his murder.

Can you?

He lifted the photocopies and revealed a small manila envelope.

"I kept the baggie in my freezer just in case. Should make a great DNA sample."

He handed the box to Veronica, who looked around like she was making a coke deal before dropping it back into the trunk.

"What the hell are we supposed to do with this?"

He picked up the hot potato and handed it to me. "I can't use Bureau resources to run the blood. But if you two can find someone to do it for you, we'll have a lead."

Veronica laughed. "Looks like we're shit out of luck. You're the only one I'd trust enough to do this, though I'm not sure about that anymore."

I was about to agree. But then I remembered my conversation with Shayla the night before.

Shayla, who is working on a fresh case.

Shayla, who's already in contact with me about that case.

Shayla, whose secret I'd kept all these years.

"I know someone who might help."

Veronica looked confused but didn't question me. She'd save that for the ride back to Austin.

"And I'll do it," I said, "*if* you help us."

I couldn't gauge Jackson's reaction through his sunglasses, but he didn't immediately object, so I continued.

"I need you to find out if the DPS is seriously looking at me for murder."

He nodded. "I already know they're not coming after you for Sylvia Davenport. She wasn't an informant for our office, but I heard more than one person was fired over her death. If there was evidence you killed her, you'd already be in prison, but I'll ask some friends in the DPS about the others."

Veronica and I started walking to my car but stopped when Jackson called my name.

"If you're worried about getting arrested, I'd toss your cellphone out of the car window on the drive back. Find a landline and have someone buy you a burner, but make sure they aren't directly connected to you or whoever you call. And don't go back to your place."

He pointed to Veronica. "Or hers."

12

CASE KELLEY

FEBRUARY 21, 2000, 1:18 PM

One hundred sixty days. He'd been mentally checking them off for more than six months.

Case normally didn't see the need to celebrate his birthday. Judy always baked him a cake, and she used to try and make it fun for the kids when they still lived there. But Ray and David hadn't been around for years, and since then, Case had been content with his piece of cake and small gift on his birthday.

That all changed in one hundred sixty days.

By the end of that day, he'd no longer be Special Agent in Charge Casey Kelley. He'd be citizen Case Kelley, former member of the Federal Bureau of Investigation who got to the San Antonio field office by way of the SAPD. A local boy done good.

Now Judy was planning a retirement barbecue. Lord knows what Jackson would plan at the last minute.

Case would receive the plaque showcasing his badge above a gold ribbon with FIDELITY BRAVERY INTEGRITY written in black. Below would be three gold service keys—coin-sized medallions with the same three words written on them—and to the left would be his credentials, the word RETIRED drilled in the top and bottom sleeves, all behind Lucite.

But for now, the badge and credentials sat on his dresser.

Case was still deciding whether he should shove them into the back pocket of his jeans when he heard Judy's footsteps in the hall.

He made a snap decision to take them. In one motion, he grabbed the black bifold, then slipped it into his pocket while walking to meet Judy at the door jamb.

"Better hurry if you're going to deliver the pie to Terry and make it to your mom's on time," she said. "Plus, Darcie is expecting me soon."

Case tucked a lock of Judy's dark brown hair—still damp from their shared shower—behind her ear. How had he kept this beautiful, younger woman happy all this time?

"I was just on my way out," he said. "Pie on the kitchen table?"

"Yep. And don't forget to grab a pint of vanilla from the freezer. He said he wanted to give his date dessert à la mode."

He pecked her lips. "Yes, dear."

"I CAN'T BELIEVE you talked Judy into baking for you," Case said. "By the way, what's this date's name supposed to be?"

Jackson stabbed the crust with his fork and smiled. "Stacy. And us single guys need home-baked pie every once in a while. You can get it whenever you want now that you're retired."

"Not for another five months."

Case's partner sucked in a piece of wayward apple. "Counting the days yet?"

"Way too early for that."

Case didn't know why he lied. Jackson was relatively young and cocky as hell, but that's part of what Case liked about him. Though Jackson was only a few years in, Case was trying to set him up for a long career, maybe finish as an ASAC running the McAllen office.

Something about being nearly retired had Case on defense. But he had no time to think about that.

"I need to get going if I'm going to make it before my source," Case said.

Jackson dropped his fork into the pie dish. "Always show up first. That's the first thing you taught me about meeting CIs. Your second was to never go without backup. Just take me and I'll hide out nearby. Better yet, how about I go and get this evidence, and you get a head start on spending time with your mom and her new nurse boyfriend."

Case laughed despite himself. His mother was expecting him, and she'd likely be in the company of the nursing home's newest hire. And Case might've considered it—if he weren't working off the books. In retrospect, Case shouldn't have told Jackson anything about the meeting. But he wanted Jackson prepared to move quickly when the time came, so keeping him in the loop had seemed like a good idea.

"Like I said, this is my mess," Case said. "If things go sideways, I can't have you involved, not officially. You have a hell of a career ahead of you, and I won't let this ruin it."

A solo meet was risky, but Franklin Jones was a conniving bastard, not a violent one. Plus, he hadn't left his estate in at least eight months.

But that didn't keep him from contacting Case.

A week earlier, another one of Jones's pompous letters arrived at his desk, always addressed to the attention of *Agent K, a.k.a. Casey Kelley*.

Case wished he'd have taken down Jones the year before. But Jones promised he could provide evidence that would lead to the arrest of Hinterbach Mayor Grant Schuhmacher, who was running for state senate. That bust was too tempting.

Jones's letters had produced no solid leads, but now he was finally ready to provide the books he'd kept—a history of dirty money coming in and clean money coming out, with Schuhmacher's real estate firm providing the laundry service. Jones

gave Case a time and place to meet his Guy Friday, Darren, who
would give him the ledger.

This should conclude our business, Jones had written. *Good luck,
Agent K.*

"I know you want to feel like this thing is finished," Jackson
said, "but why don't you just sit back and ride the desk for five
months, then retire with that pretty wife of yours?"

That had been the plan. Eight months ago, Case, Jackson, and
a few others made a major bust that should've been the exclama-
tion mark on the end of his storied history at the Bureau.

But the bust came with a catch. Jones was willing to give up
his corrupt uncle, the bank's chairman, but he wanted to keep
the cash that had been embezzled and stashed under his name.

At first, Case told him to take a flying leap, but Jones came
back with a proposition. Jones claimed he could prove Schuhmacher was laundering money through Jones's bank, and that
some of the money had come from Washington lobbyist Jim
Flynn. Case asked his bosses about Flynn and realized what a
major investigation he may have found.

Jones knew that, too, and said he couldn't have his name
associated with that mess, not even as a confidential informant.
But Jones agreed to give Case proof of Schuhmacher's involvement—in exchange for confidentiality, the cash, and an alibi for
July 4, 1999. He'd met with Case and Jackson earlier that
evening, so what harm could come from shifting the time a few
hours?

Case made the deal, then spent more than half a year trying
to make it worthwhile. Jackson and his bosses in Washington
thought the Jones matter was settled, though they thought Case
was too soft on Jones. Under normal circumstances, they'd have
been right. But Case had a chance to reel in Jim Flynn.

Then he didn't.

Flynn was a slimy K Street lobbyist, to be sure. He dealt with
the left and the right, a truly bipartisan charlatan. But could Case
prove Flynn was involved with anyone in South Texas? When he

told them he was working a promising lead, Case's superiors asked him to forward whatever he discovered to Washington.

Then relax. Retire. Know that you put a lot of bad guys in prison, which is more than most men do with their lives.

It all sounded fine. But he'd never rest easy unless he took this Schuhmacher thing all the way.

He'd have to come to his superiors with something big.

Case stood. "You should be happy I'm meeting with this guy. If I can't get it sewn up in time, you'll be the lead agent on one hell of a bust."

"Yet another reason I should come with you."

Case walked outside and got in his pickup. "This Darren guy is looking for me, and only me. I'm not going to risk spooking him. Plus, you need to focus on that drug task force investigation."

"I know," Jackson said. "I take it you still haven't heard anything from your old informants here?"

Case shook his head. "I've spent the last six months asking around about your *Pretty Boy* and gotten nowhere. Time for you to focus on that again. The pricks in Houston are breathing down my neck."

Jackson shut the truck door. "Fine, I'll dive into the files while you're gone. Just promise me you'll bail out of there if anything looks wrong."

"Ten-four."

13

BECK

PRESENT DAY

The phone felt heavy in my front pocket. I'd driven about twenty miles up I-35 before stopping for gas.

"Thanks for paying," I told Veronica as she flopped into my passenger seat.

"Thanks for driving. So, are you going to lay low like Jackson said?"

I still didn't have an answer as we sat beside a pump at the New Braunfels Buc-ee's. "Not sure yet. I have to drive to Big Lake to deliver the DNA to Deputy Hickman either way. I'm much more interested in what you found out about Sammy."

Veronica pressed the button to lower her window, letting in a refreshing blast of cool autumn air. "Not much. According to the bio on his law firm's website, associate Samuel Foster joined them nine years ago, just after getting his law degree from Northwestern."

"I can't believe that's the same guy I grew up with. He used to love Hinterbach. But after it happened, nobody knew who his father was, and he didn't have any other living relatives."

"Where'd he go?"

"Lived with neighbors his senior year, the Schmidts. I think he went into the Army after that."

Veronica shook her head. "Marines. Background check says he did a few tours and left with an honorable discharge. Then San Diego State for undergrad before law school. He's hot shit."

The background checks Veronica did were good for biographical information, but never included the important stuff. Why law school? Why not stay in California?

Had he read *Cold Summer*?

"I want to get back to this friend of yours," Veronica said. "You really trust her enough to do this?"

Veronica knew the basics. I'd met Shayla while researching an unpublished manuscript. She'd been a deputy for the Parker County Sheriff's Office, and I used her to get information about a murder there. We'd lost touch until Shayla contacted me when Jorge was hurt.

Veronica didn't know—would never know—what kind of childhood Shayla had suffered. Or that her father was the victim I was researching. Or the circumstances surrounding her father's death.

A car pulled up behind us and honked, so I started the car and headed for a parking space. "I trust her as much as you trust Jackson."

Veronica gave me a *fair enough* face. "Call her."

I ignored the mountain of messages and found Shayla's number in my contacts. I debated dialing her from my phone but decided to give Shayla plausible deniability if the plan went south. Then there was Jackson's warning.

"Let me use your phone," I told Veronica after stopping near the edge of the parking lot.

Veronica looked at me blankly.

"Just in case."

No change in expression.

"If anyone asks later, you can say you were working on a story about the investigation into Jorge's explosion. She's a source. Nothing wrong with that."

Veronica pulled out her cell. "I can't believe you're letting Jackson get to you."

I pecked Shayla's number into her phone, put it on speaker, then turned off my device.

"Deputy Hickman."

"Shayla, it's Beck."

"Oh, hi. Did you get a new phone since Sunday?"

"I'm calling from a friend's phone. Mine's busted."

I hadn't planned on lying to her, but that sounded a hell of a lot better than *I'm worried about being found and arrested, which is why I need you to help me fight a powerful congressman hellbent on destroying my life.*

"Oh, gotcha," Shayla said. "Well, I don't have much in the way of an update. We haven't found Jorge's assistant, Alfredo Juarez. His address is in Borger, so we have the local PD and sheriff's office looking for him."

"Anything weird with his finances? Large cash deposits?"

Shalya laughed. "Look who's playing amateur detective. No, nothing like that."

Veronica covered her mouth to muffle the laughter.

"I appreciate you letting me know what's happening with the case," I said, "but I had something else I wanted to talk with you about."

"What's that?"

"If I drove to Big Lake tonight, would you meet me somewhere? It's important, and I'd rather talk in person."

The silence only lasted a few moments, but it was enough to make me nervous.

"Is it about that story?"

I could lie again. But what would I say? And if she agreed to meet based on that lie, how would she react when I told her the truth?

"It is. But you should know that I didn't—"

"I know," Shayla said. "And yes. Meet me at the beer house tonight. Will seven o'clock work?"

I looked at Veronica. She nodded.

"Sounds perfect," I said. "What's the name of this beer house?"

Shayla laughed again. "That *is* the name. The Beer House. It's just off Highway 67 as you come into town. You can't miss it."

I looked at Veronica after I ended the call. She had the biggest shit-eating grin I'd ever seen.

"That woman likes you," she said. "And you clearly lied to me about your, quote, research for that book."

I avoided taking the bait. "So, are you coming with?"

Veronica pointed at the phone. "Oh, I definitely want to see all of that in person. But you have to drive me back to my car. I'm not getting stuck in the middle of nowhere with you. Especially if you decide to stick around for an extra night or two."

I was running from the Texas Rangers and planning to ask a sheriff's deputy to break the law for me, with no guarantee she'd help.

And yet, I was smiling.

"Shut up."

14

BECK

PRESENT DAY

I cringed every time a rock bounced off the undercarriage of my car. Getting to the Pumpjack Hotel meant driving through a massive RV park on a multiacre patch of caliche.

Veronica slammed the door next to me in a violent cloud of cursing and dust. "Thanks for the crack in my goddamn windshield. Next time, I'm picking where we stay."

"Like I said before we left, this was the only vacancy in town. Unless you want to drive by the billboards again and make some calls?"

As we'd caravanned west through Big Lake, several advertisements had offered workforce housing, some with accommodations for five occupants per unit. I pictured trailer houses with hazardous additions.

"Well, we're about to check into a hotel made of shipping containers," she said, "so maybe I should."

The Vegas-style sign, complete with an animated pumpjack, had been visible above the RVs and small pre-fabbed cabins. The structure below claimed to be a hotel. But up close, the Pumpjack was a collection of conexes stacked like brown LEGO blocks.

The containers were often retrofitted to serve as jobsite storage sheds. But it had never crossed my mind to pile them three stories high, paint them beige, and charge people fifty bucks a night to stay inside.

"It'll be okay for one night," I said, trying to convince myself, too.

We walked to a door with OFFICE painted in red.

What I saw inside made me stop in the doorway.

It may have been used to ship all manner of goods once, but the conex now looked and smelled better than most of the places I'd lived. The laminate floor looked better than real hardwood, the sheetrock walls were painted a light cobalt, and off-white baseboards and crown molding made the place indistinguishable from any other office.

Veronica seemed less impressed and pushed past me to the front desk, where a pleasant-looking older woman sat reading a Larry McMurtry paperback. She greeted us with a hearty, "How y'all doing?"

Veronica plastered on her widest smile. "We're great. We have a reservation under Beck, but I was really hoping you had two rooms available instead of one."

The fan of western literature looked past Veronica. "You must be the nice young man who called earlier today. Like I said, you're lucky someone moved out today. I expected us to be all booked up until the holidays."

The woman, who'd introduced herself as Greta when I'd called from my condo, turned her attention back to Veronica. "I'm sorry hon. But why would a lovely couple like you want two rooms?"

I knew the answer. Veronica and I would be staying in the *penthouse*, meaning it only had one full bed. The other had been removed and replaced with a desk and dining table.

People had been assuming we were a couple for years, but it never failed to irritate Veronica. "We're not together. We're colleagues and would prefer not to sleep in the same bed."

Greta's eyes went wide, and she leaned back in her chair. "I see. Well, there's not a whole lot I can do about that. You might try the dollar store and see if they have a blow-up mattress. If they don't, you'll probably have to drive to the Walmart in San Angelo. It's only fifty minutes if you speed a little."

Veronica turned and handed me her credit card, trying to hide how upset she was at Greta's answer. "I'm going to get my suitcase."

I approached the desk to pay. "We appreciate the tip, Greta. The room will be just fine."

Her smile returned and she began narrating. "Excellent. Let me just pull it up. Room 208. Change the name from Alfredo Juarez to—"

"What was that name?" I asked.

"Well, he called himself Fredo, like in those *Godfather* movies. But his license and credit card said Alfredo."

My adrenaline spiked as she continued. "That's the sweet young man who moved out in such a rush. In fact, it wasn't even him who came and packed the suitcase. Mr. Juarez called and said a friend would be by to gather his things and settle the bill. He didn't even ask me to pro-rate it. Just let me keep the balance. He paid cash, so it made for a very generous tip."

Damn, no credit card information. "What did Fredo's friend look like?"

Greta narrowed her eyes. "I really don't think I should tell you that. Now, may I get back to checking you in?"

I nodded and apologized for being nosey. As she took Veronica's AmEx, I turned to study the room.

It didn't take long for me to find a discreet camera attached to the molding.

15

BECK

PRESENT DAY

The Beer House wasn't as fancy as the Pumpjack Hotel.

The building, which was about a half-mile east of town, didn't promise top-shelf booze, but it was a clean warehouse constructed of white corrugated tin with a high ceiling and large concrete dance floor. The parking lot was also large, and the nearest space was at least fifty yards from the door.

But unlike the hotel, the Beer House's interior hadn't been fitted with walls, ceiling, or a floor. The tables and chairs were foldable and from a big box store, and the bar itself was made of raw two-by-fours and plywood.

The jukebox was modern, though, and there were two industrial ceiling fans pulling up a thin layer of cigarette smoke hovering under the steel I-beams.

Veronica sidled up to me. "So, which one is your girlfriend?"

"You're going to have to cut that out when I find her. Don't forget, you're carrying someone's blood in your purse."

She nodded and began scanning the room. "What does she look like?"

"About your age, but not as tall. Works out a lot. She had really long, dark hair the last time I saw her."

We scanned the bar. Only two couples were dancing to the

Johnny Cash song, and both women were far too old to be Shayla, who was barely thirty.

Nobody at the tables seemed right, though a few of the women wore cowboy hats, obstructing their face.

Veronica tapped me on the shoulder. "There, at the bar. It's got to be her."

She pointed to a woman sitting on a metal stool. Though her ponytail was pulled through a sky-blue snapback, the nearly black hair stood out against the matching T-shirt.

I nodded and led us through the tables, trying to avoid ribbons of smoke and drunken gesticulations. The seats on either side of her were still empty, which surprised me. If memory served, Shayla Hickman would easily be the most attractive woman in the place.

We were still a few steps away when she turned. My untucked button-down felt tight across my gut and I hated my naked head. I should've been wearing a hat like everyone else in the place. At least I was smart enough to avoid the designer jeans, though the old Wranglers cut into my waist when I sat down.

"You didn't tell me we'd have company," Shayla said. "You must be Harper Lee."

"Actually, they compared me to Capote." Veronica nodded to me. "He's Miss Lee."

Shayla laughed. "I didn't read the story, just heard about the headline from a friend. Pleasure to meet you."

I relaxed a bit knowing Shayla was comfortable. "Thanks for agreeing to see me."

Shayla turned to find the bartender, a young woman with a baby bump, and held up her empty longneck. "And whatever my friends are having."

The bartender opened a refrigerator filled with loose bottles and energy drinks. There were four taps behind the bar, two each for light domestic beers and their heavy counterparts.

Rather than making the woman deliver bottles all night, I ordered us a pitcher.

"So," Shayla said, "what's this big secret you couldn't tell me over the phone?"

It was time to get Shayla on our side before asking for my favor. "I actually have something even better to tell you first. Alfredo was staying at the Pumpjack."

"Wow," she said as the bartender sat down our pitcher and three red cups. "You've really underestimated my skills. We already knew that. The manager let us in yesterday. Everything was still there, plus he still had to pay for the next week. He'll be back."

I filled my cup, debating on whether to act like a smart ass or not. I decided to play it straight. "No, he's not. When Veronica and I checked in earlier today, Greta told us a friend had packed up his stuff and paid for the week in cash."

"I asked her to call me when he showed back up. Guess she took me literally. Did you get a description of this friend?"

I shook my head. "Greta stopped short of telling me that. But there's a security camera in the office."

"Good," Shayla said. "I'll talk to her tomorrow."

I took another drink and prepared to make my case for Shayla to run DNA. But before I could start, a guy in a camo shirt approached us. He wore a matching cap, which sat atop his signature haircut.

"Hey partner, I thought Jorge was resting up at home?" Chuck D asked.

Veronica turned. Shayla didn't.

"He is," I said. "I'm here about something else."

He looked confused. We both knew I had no other reason to be in Big Lake, so I tried changing the subject by pointing at Shayla. "Chuck Davis, this is Shayla Hickman. Shayla, this is—"

"We've met." She was terse. Whatever their last interaction was, it hadn't ended well.

Chuck, on the other hand, was all smiles. He turned his

yellow teeth to Veronica. "But you're new here. I'd never forget a face that pretty."

Veronica smiled, the fake one she usually reserved for chatty Karens at book events.

Chuck took it as a sign to keep going and sat next to her. "Are you friends with the famous writer or Mrs. Officer?"

"My name's Veronica. I write with Beck. How do you know Jorge?"

They talked for a minute about his job out on the pipeline and her experience as a helper—minus the near-death experience—so he invited her to meet other members of his crew. They were sitting at a table in the near corner.

"Is Jorge's helper over there?" she asked.

"Hell no," Chuck said. "That sonofabitch drug up on us. Haven't seen him since before the accident."

Veronica stood and turned to me. "Watch my purse."

Since she asked me and not Shayla, I knew she wanted me to convince Shayla to run the DNA. Alone.

I glared at Veronica.

She widened her eyes.

I widened mine.

Chuck interrupted our staring contest. "C'mon, the guys'll love meeting someone who knew Jorge."

When they were out of earshot, Shayla turned to me. "So, are you two a thing, or what?"

"No," I said. "We just work together."

Shayla smirked. "None of my business either way."

"There's no 'either way.' There's just the one way."

She took another drink. "Sure thing."

"What about you and Joe Dirt over there? He seemed to know you pretty well."

When she didn't come back with a quick one-liner, I realized the girl who'd been abused by her father was still in there. Whatever happened between Shayla and Chuck must've been worse than I'd imagined.

A burst of laughter interrupted our awkward silence, and we turned to see Veronica holding court, Chuck's arm across the back of her chair.

Shayla finished her beer and poured a refill. "I'm glad you found out about Alfredo, but I still don't know why you wanted to meet in person."

I did a quick mental run-through of what I wanted to say, then reached into Veronica's purse. "I have something for you."

The envelope looked innocuous enough, but Shayla still flipped a switch from *woman at the bar* to *sheriff's deputy with more than ten years on the job*. "Stop."

I slid it to her anyway. "Let me explain."

"I don't want to know what's in there or how you got it. Your friend's alive and recovering, and we have good leads to go on now."

I nudged the envelope closer. "Thanks to me."

"Yes, thanks to you."

I'd been dreading the next part of my argument all day. "You owe me."

Shayla's father, a fundamentalist preacher, was a prick who liked to mentally and physically abuse Shayla and her mother. He had religion on his side— his interpretation of it, anyway— and was in the middle of doling out more punishment when Shayla pulled the trigger.

Though publishing the truth would've exposed a wrongful conviction and resurrected my writing career, I never regretted keeping the secret.

I'd given Shayla my word, and I'd do it all again.

I touched her forearm. "Look, I'm not trying to guilt you into anything. I just need a favor. And it's not very risky."

Shayla picked up the envelope and placed it in her lap. "That had better be the last lie you tell, or I'm out."

Veronica plopped onto her stool and put an arm around Shayla. "Oh man, do I feel sorry for you, hon."

Chuck and the guys had obviously bought her a few rounds while I was talking about stab wounds and government conspiracies.

"I see you got his side of the story," Shayla said.

"Oh, I know he's full of shit. He's just jealous that a woman kicked his ass."

I was in the middle of taking a drink and nearly spit it out. The women turned to me.

"You don't think she could kick his ass? I know she could kick yours."

I held up my hands in surrender. "I absolutely know that. I was just picturing Shayla dragging Chuck around by his mullet."

They joined me in laughter, and for a moment I forgot why we were there. "What's the real story?"

Shayla turned and gestured to the crowd. "There aren't many choices here for a young, single woman, and Chuck lives here and has a steady job that pays well."

Veronica shook her head. "Still."

"I know. But he wore me down after a few months, so I let him take me out. He was gentlemanly enough. Brought me flowers, even. Then dinner at the Sugar Creek Grill before driving me home."

"Then he went in for a kiss, right?" Veronica said. "As if you owed it to him."

"Exactly. I turned my cheek. He wasn't happy, but he turned around, so I unlocked my door and—"

"Wait," Veronica interrupted. "He didn't say anything like that. He said you kneed him in the nuts, punched him in the face, then used your pepper spray."

"I know the story he tells everyone."

I had a bad feeling about how it really went down. "What happened after you unlocked the door?"

"He must've been listening for it. He rushed me just as I was opening the door."

Veronica and I looked over at the table, where Chuck was still yukking it up with four other dudes.

"Chuck pushed me to the floor, then called me a bitch and said he was getting laid, one way or another. I let him get close enough to kick and got him square in the nuts, but he didn't fall."

I swallowed the lump in my throat. "Tell me he didn't—"

"No. He stumbled after I kicked him in the balls. I found my purse and got him with the pepper spray." Shayla smiled. "While he was crying and grabbing at his face, I went to work on his body. I know he was pissing blood the next day."

Veronica finished her beer. "What a piece of shit."

"He tells his version of the story to everyone he can. Between that and being a sheriff's deputy, I might be the most hated woman in this town."

My face got hot, but confronting Chuck would only lead to trouble, so I signaled the bartender and pulled out my wallet. "Thanks again for agreeing to help."

Veronica squealed and kissed Shayla on the cheek. "You won't regret it, I promise."

Shayla shook her head. "I already do."

Her comment stung, but I did my best to hide it. "How long is all of this going to take?"

"A couple of days, and that's if I can sweet-talk the lab tech. I'll ask to see the motel video tomorrow, but if Greta won't let me, getting a court order could also take a day or two."

I gave the bartender a fifty and told her to keep the change. Veronica excused herself to the restroom, so Shayla and I made our way to the door.

"What will you say if someone catches you?" I asked.

"That the blood is from a suspected child molester. My contact in Austin has a soft spot for abused kids. But if that DNA matches to someone high-profile, like this congressman, I won't be able to keep it quiet."

"I know. And I'm sorry for asking you to risk your job, but I'm desperate."

"I know. But so is that FBI agent. You know he's using you, right?"

Before I could respond, I heard a table flip behind us. We turned to find Veronica hustling our way, laughing and swaying as she pointed to the door. Behind her, Chuck D was wiping beer out of his eyes and hurling curses in her direction.

Shayla gestured to Veronica. "Good luck with that tonight."

We said our goodbyes and I helped Veronica into my car. When we were on the highway heading back into town, I began to think about what Shayla had said about Jackson.

I turned to Veronica, who looked ready to pass out.

"How well do you know Agent Jackson?"

16

TERRY JACKSON

FEBRUARY 21, 2000, 1:33 PM

Terry was still working on a speech when Judy opened the door. He was only halfway from his car to the porch, the cleaned dish in his hand.

She was in jeans and a loose T-shirt, probably one of Case's. "I thought we agreed you shouldn't come back here."

He held up the dish. "I just came to return this."

"Don't lie to me."

Terry hadn't seen her since Halloween, when they'd all gotten drunk and Case insisted he crash on their couch.

He ascended the steps and stopped a few feet from her.

"I can leave it here on the porch if you want."

"That might be best."

Terry didn't want to do that, so he gave Judy the opportunity to change her mind. He searched her eyes, bluer in the natural light, the dark ring around the iris more pronounced. It took a few moments, but he watched them soften and accept what they both knew.

She turned around and walked into the house.

But she didn't close the door.

"How've you been?" he asked.

"Put the dish on the counter."

He did as she asked and watched her walk past the brown microfiber couch. Though it had a pullout bed, Terry hadn't used it that night. He passed out in his pearl-snap shirt and comically oversized belt buckle, drooling on one of the flowery throw pillows.

Judy sat across from the couch on a matching loveseat. "Why did you really come over?"

The answer was awful. Terry had tried to forget the morning after, when he woke up to the sound of Case shutting the front door and saw Judy in one of her husband's Texas A&M sweatshirts and nothing else. But the images wouldn't leave him be.

Terry was back in that living room because he knew Case would be gone for several hours. He'd put on a good show for his mentor—his friend—and insisted on being part of Case's unsanctioned operation in Hinterbach. But if he'd really wanted to be there, Terry would've just gotten in the passenger seat of the truck and refused to move.

Instead, Terry waited until Case was on the road, then drove as fast as he could to Judy, who stood and crossed her arms as he tried to articulate his feelings.

"You know what," she said. "It doesn't matter. I have plans. You need to leave."

He thought about doing it, turning around and working on the task force stuff like he'd promised Case. But Terry was finally sitting across the room from Judy after four months of wondering what it would be like to see her again. Terry had to find out how she felt.

She'd baked him the pie, after all. "Why are you so upset with me? We were both there. We both wanted it."

She turned her back to him. "I love Casey. We were happily married for more than twenty years. Twenty amazing years, and never once did I want to be with anyone else."

Terry stood and took a step toward her.

Judy continued. "And you know what? I didn't ask for this. I tried so hard—so fucking hard—to ignore it. To ignore you."

He took another step. He was inches from her now, breathing in the fruity smell of her shampoo.

"And you know what else?" Judy said. "I shouldn't have to suffer the rest of my life over one mistake." She whipped around, tears pooling. "And that's exactly what you are. A mistake."

Terry understood it now. They'd spent the last four months in different worlds. He was the one pining, thinking about how full his life would be with her in it, hoping she and Case were secretly unhappy and she would come running to him.

He didn't regret what happened.

She did.

She'd been punishing herself, praying that he'd leave her alone to shove aside the memory of that night.

The sex had only lasted ten minutes. Neither of them spoke afterward, unless you counted her instructions to get dressed, leave, and stay the hell away from her. Case only walked for twenty minutes in the morning, and she needed to be out of the shower by the time he got home.

But now that he'd returned, Terry had to get even closer to her. "I know it was wrong and could hurt Case, and I hate that. But what happened was special. *We were special.* Together."

He grabbed Judy's hand. She didn't pull away.

"I'm sorry," he said. "I never meant to make you hurt like this."

Terry started to turn toward the door.

Judy tightened her grip.

17

BECK

PRESENT DAY

The world was shaking. No. Just the blow-up mattress we'd found at the local hardware store. Dollar General didn't have any in stock, but the clerk was asked so often he knew the correct aisle and shelf at the other retailer.

The source of my violent awakening: Veronica's foot. "I brought a muffin. You're welcome."

I rolled over to see a pair of lime-green running shorts and a blue tank-top walk into the bathroom. My head once again found the cheap pillow when she turned on the shower, which was loud, given my proximity to both the water and the floor.

My brain chugged to life. Shayla would be over soon, hoping to get a look at the Pumpjack's surveillance video. If she could, we might know who aided Jorge's helper in his disappearing act.

Veronica, meanwhile, was about to leave in search of a lawyer to help defend us against Schuhmacher's ridiculous lawsuit.

After scrambling to my feet, I perused the papers we'd fanned out across the desk. All we'd figured out was that the names Schuhmacher Enterprises and Flynn Consulting were included among the entities who were, presumably, sending and receiving cash from whatever criminal enterprises they were working with. The dates went back to the mid-nineties.

Was it enough to prove malfeasance on the part of now-Congressman Schuhmacher? We had no idea. But it was enough to make him appear guilty. Even if the blood—and possible link to the murder of Case Kelley—went nowhere, we had enough to convict him in the court of public opinion.

As I walked back to secure my breakfast, Veronica passed the desk and started gathering the paper.

"What time is your girlfriend coming?"

"Will you stop saying that?"

She didn't look up. "Probably not."

I sat on the edge of the of the bed. "I don't know when Shayla's coming. She has to get the DNA sent off first."

Veronica shooed me off the bed so she could finish packing. "What else are you doing today?"

I didn't have a good answer. Other than aiding Shayla in any way I could, all I wanted to do was hide. I no longer had the urge to toss my phone like Jackson had recommended, but until I got word there wasn't a warrant out for me, I had no choice but to assume it could happen at any time.

Then it hit me. "Maybe I'll write something."

"That would be a nice change of pace."

"Shut up."

I TRIED USING MY COMPUTER, but the wireless internet was strong inside the room, so instead of pounding out sentences, I read thinkpieces on websites like *Culturist* and *Slate* about me and my *complete lack of respect for readers and other authors.*

Both articles had quotes from Parker Mallory.

I looked out the window to make sure a Reagan County Sheriff's Office vehicle hadn't pulled up. No luck. Just the laundry building—two more conjoined shipping containers—Greta's beater, and my Challenger. Then I checked my phone to make sure none of the missed calls or texts were from Shayla.

It was nearly eleven and still no word.

Since the laptop was just a distraction, it was time to revisit the journal I was supposed to write in every day, a recommendation from the therapist I'd been seeing on-and-off for more than a year.

My regular doctor had stopped prescribing me sleeping medication, saying it wasn't physical. She recommended the therapist, who said she'd write the script if I at least tried to do the work. My thoughts would remain private, but I brought it to my weekly sessions until she was satisfied.

The journal itself wasn't anything special. The black faux leather cover felt more like rubber, and the pages were too thin to use anything but a ballpoint pen without ink leaking through.

The words inside were even less impressive, and not at all what I was supposed to have written.

A written account of how I felt about killing two people and condemning another to death was a sure ticket to prison. So, I used the pages to write notes for future works of fiction. I'd tried everything but starting a scene with *Once upon a time, on a dark and stormy night,* and so far, the freewriting hadn't produced anything worth typing up.

But the Pumpjack might make an interesting setting, so I put pen to paper.

Nothing came out. I shook the cheap thing and drew circles until the paper tore, then tossed the pen aside. I was about to give up when I remembered the scratch pad and flat, rectangular carpenter's pencil that was supposed to be on the desk.

Veronica must've knocked them off when gathering the ledger, so I looked underneath.

Below the hotel logo were the indents of a previous occupant's scribblings.

There was no guarantee the writing was Alfredo's. It could be from weeks or months ago. But if it was from the person who skipped town the day of my best friend's accident, I had to find out what he thought was so noteworthy.

I'd only seen it done on TV and in movies, but I used a light touch—which was no easy feat for me—and swiped back and forth across the paper, grateful that Greta was committed to her working-man theme.

PBFCU / 83954

A credit union. The number was likely an account number, one with a substantially higher balance than a week ago.

Shayla ignored my call until it went to voicemail. I pocketed the note and programmed the GPS on my phone for the sheriff's office.

A crisp fall wind greeted me as I walked onto the wooden landing outside the room, which was built like a wraparound porch that connected the stacks of conexes.

My door was a few feet from the staircase that led to a common-use area—a courtyard of sorts—complete with a circular fire pit about five feet in diameter, a small, black charcoal grill, and a homemade picnic table. It reminded me of the one in Summer's backyard, so I sped up on my way to the parking area.

I rounded the corner just as a sheriff's SUV rolled to a stop next to my Challenger. My phone buzzed, and I was surprised to see Shayla's name. Couldn't she see me?

I declined the call and waved.

But when she stepped down from her SUV, Shayla shook her head slightly and walked straight to the office. Her eyes were hidden behind amber aviators and the rest of her face was shaded by the brim of her khaki cowboy hat, so I couldn't gauge her mood.

Just before stepping inside, Shayla swung her arm behind her back and motioned for me to back off.

Something was wrong.

18

BECK

PRESENT DAY

I stared out of the penthouse window, waiting for Shayla to cross the courtyard. I'd thought about texting her my room number, but she knew I was in the one previously occupied by her lead suspect. She'd be climbing those steel steps any minute.

The phone was still in my hand when it rang.

Veronica.

I answered, hoping for good news. "You find us a lawyer?"

"Ditch your phone and your car." Her voice was frantic. "Don't use your credit cards."

Shit.

"Jackson called you."

"Yes. Now leave. I'm turning around to come get you. I'll be at the Dollar General in an hour and a half."

She hung up the phone before I could ask for details. I opened my computer and was Googling whether I could just remove my SIM card when Shayla crossed the window and pounded her fist on the door.

"You have to get out of here," she said. "We just got an APB. You're wanted on suspicion of murder."

"Veronica just told me. But before I leave, I have something to give you."

I pulled the note from my back pocket and handed it to her.

"That's not Alfredo's bank. I told you, we've already looked at his finances. No strange activity."

"Maybe it belongs to whoever you just saw on the security video."

Shayla shook her head. "Greta won't talk. I'm going to have to come back with a court order."

"So run the bank info. Maybe you can find out who it is that way."

"That takes a court order too, genius. And I'll never get one by saying I was slipped the information by a man wanted for murder."

"So don't tell them where you got it."

She crumpled up the paper and tossed it at my feet. "It has your fingerprints on it. You're a really bad criminal."

She was right. For all the research I'd done and cases I'd read, I wasn't looking far enough ahead. Leaving evidence in Summer's backyard was how my name ended up on a murder warrant.

But this bank account wasn't just about me. It was about getting the people who opened that valve and put Jorge in the hospital, too.

And to get them all—from Schuhmacher down to a welder's helper—I'd have to start acting like the criminal I was.

"Do you have gloves and an evidence bag?"

Shayla narrowed her eyes. "In my center console. Why?"

I picked up the wad of paper and flattened it on the desk. "I'm going to copy the note again and tear off the top sheet of paper. You go down, tell Greta you need to look in the room because the new occupant is a murder suspect. If she pushes back, say you think the woman I was with may be up here in danger."

Shayla nodded slowly. "Greta will have to come up with me to open the door. She'll be a witness that I found the pad, did the pencil trick myself and bagged it."

"Right. I'll leave my stuff, go downstairs and hide, then run behind the laundromat while you're in here. After you've collected your evidence and she's back in the office, pull around and get me. I'm meeting Veronica at the dollar store in about an hour."

I wasn't sure if she'd do everything I wanted. Sending DNA to be tested under suspicious terms was one thing. Collecting fabricated evidence wasn't so bad, especially if it couldn't be proven. But using her sheriff's SUV to help me escape? No way.

"Okay," she said. "But you two should stay split up. If they're monitoring your movements, they're keeping tabs on her, too. You can stay at my place until we get everything sorted out."

I stood frozen. Stunned. "That's a huge risk. You don't have to do that."

"I've already sent in the DNA. If you get caught, I took that risk for nothing." She nodded to the note pad. "Write down Veronica's number so we can call her. Then tear off four or five sheets and copy the bank info."

I did as she said, then watched a sworn officer of the law leave my room so she could put her career on the line for me.

SHAYLA'S new house was nice enough for a single person, the kind of house she should've had in North Texas when she was barely starting out as a deputy. But as I stood in her living room, dingy and smelling like the previous occupant was a heavy smoker, I wondered if she regretted giving up her family's two-story home in Weatherford.

It had three bedrooms and an old-fashioned reading room.

It also held memories of her father.

Shayla walked into the kitchen and began writing on a small yellow notepad on the edge of the counter. I followed her in and saw that the pad and pen were below a dull beige handset mounted on the wall.

She'd written *This phone* and the number she'd given to Veronica as we drove from the Pumpjack to her house. If asked, Shayla would say she'd been calling my close friends in an attempt to locate me. We'd tried to call Jorge, but he didn't pick up, so she left a message with her home phone number. Nothing suspicious there.

"Make yourself comfortable. There's also tea and beer in here. Food's in the pantry. I'll be home after my shift." She shut the refrigerator door and brushed past me on her way out. "Since you're a wanted man now, I may get access to that bank account and video before then. I'll just make sure we get footage from all day yesterday so I can see our mystery accomplice."

As soon as she shut the door, gravity pulled me into her faux suede sofa. How had it come to this? I'd abandoned nearly everything at the Pumpjack. My car, phone, computer, clothes, journal full of awful prose—all left to be confiscated and logged as evidence. It could all be replaced, though the notebook's contents would provide endless fodder for the internet if leaked. I'd end up a goddamn meme.

Perhaps taking stock of what I still had would keep me calm. I still had a pair of too-tight jeans, a faded blue T-shirt, boxer-briefs, boots, socks, keys, and a checkbook-style wallet.

I pulled out the leather billfold. A handful of wrinkled cash totaled seventy-three dollars, which represented all of the hard currency to my name. I also had a platinum card and two other useless pieces of plastic. Even if they weren't approaching their max, using them would lead the authorities straight to me. A driver's license and small stack of business cards rounded out the collection.

Then I remembered my bottle of sleeping pills, which I'd left beside the sink. I'd need something later if I wanted to rest, so I stood and walked down the wallpapered hall to Shayla's bathroom.

Like the rest of the house, it was as clean as it could be. The tub looked stained, but not moldy. The toilet looked much newer. Beside it stood a white waferboard vanity and plastic sink, likely from the same Ace where Veronica had bought the blowup mattress.

But the most important feature was hanging above the sink.

I opened the medicine cabinet and found little to work with. Ibuprofen and acetaminophen. An expired antibiotic prescription. A generic antihistamine. The closest thing to a sleep aid was the box of off-brand Nyquil. I ripped off two squares, which gave me four pills. I'd probably need three to get to sleep and one more when I woke up in the middle of the night.

At that point, I should've walked out of the bathroom and returned to the sofa. Maybe turned on the TV and mocked the idiots on a daytime small-claims court show. Found some popcorn to help set the mood.

Instead I found myself at the threshold of Shayla's bedroom. What was I looking for? Nothing, really. A glimpse into the life of my hostess. Perhaps something to help spark a conversation later.

The room was obviously her sanctuary. The shag carpeting had been stripped to the hardwood, its polished sheen now only covered by the rug below her bed, the frame a lighter grain that complemented the floor.

Mountains and evergreens hung over her bed. Surrounding the frame was textured sheet rock painted the color of Hill Country bluebonnets in the spring.

Opposite the bed was a familiar dresser. I snuck across the room despite the fact I was alone. Above four ornate drawers were a bowl with loose jewelry, a collection of makeup products, and a birthday card. I picked it up. A voluptuous cartoon woman was puckering her bright red lips on the front. The dialogue bubble wished the card's recipient *a happy 29th birthday, sexy lady!* The inside featured a lipstick kiss on the right half above *Enjoy the last year of your 20s!*

A personalized note filled up the left.

Shayla,

Hope you have a good one. You deserve it. Now go celebrate the next 365 days. They're your last until the Dirty Thirty!

Love always,

— Caitlin xoxo

As I replaced the card, I remembered the last time I'd seen the dresser. It had once belonged to Caitlin Parks, daughter of the infamous Mistress Samantha.

I'd seen it during a tour of the Parks house six years earlier while investigating the murder of a Weatherford pastor at the hands of Samantha Parks. Caitlin, then an SMU law student, hoped a book about the case could help convince the governor to commute her mother's death sentence to life without parole.

That's when I met the pastor's daughter, Shayla, who confessed to shooting her abusive father and covering it up with the help of Caitlin and Samantha.

The gun had come from the bottom drawer of the dresser.

I was reaching for that drawer when Shayla's phone rang. I jumped, feeling the adrenaline of being caught snooping through her life. It took a moment to realize the call might be for me, so I was almost at a dead sprint when I reached the kitchen.

"Hello?"

"Oh, I must've called the wrong number."

I'd never felt so happy to hear Jorge's voice. "No, you got it right."

"Beck?"

I explained Shayla's voicemail and my situation. When I got to the part about staying at her house, Jorge took the opportunity to give me shit.

"So, this lady cop. Is she hot?"

I laughed. It felt good. Normal. I leaned against the kitchen wall like a man who wasn't on the lam.

"You know," Jorge said, "this actually works out great for me. What are you doing at seven tonight?"

"Probably getting an update from Shayla. Why?"

"Nope. You'll be helping me with the camper. I'm on my way down there now."

I stopped leaning against the wall. "Should you be driving? Please tell me someone's with you."

"Dude, quit worrying. My back's a little sore, but the brace is keeping everything where it needs to be. I just need you and your girl to come help with the camper."

"At seven?"

"You know I like to drive at night. Besides, I have something to tell Missus Officer about that motherfucker Alfredo."

I reached for the notepad. "You know where he is?"

"Yep. He's in Vegas. A buddy we met at a job in Minnesota saw him playing blackjack. He left the table, but my friend sent me a snap. I'll show you when I get there."

I finished taking the info, then returned to worrying. "You should just turn back and let someone take it up to you. Maybe Chuck can do it when he gets a day off."

Jorge sighed, the crackle loud in my ear. "Look, I'm coming tonight. The lady who runs the RV park has called me twice for this month's payment. I can't pay her, so whoever takes the camper has to do it after she's gone home for the night, and I'm not going to ask anyone to lose sleep when I can just do it myself. And now I have help, so it'll be even easier."

I opened my mouth to tell him I would cover the month's rent, but then remembered I couldn't.

"Fine. Tell me where this place is, and we'll be there."

19

PATTY BUTLER
FEBRUARY 21, 2000, 2:42 PM

Patty wished she had her book of crossword puzzles. She'd already solved ones in the *Daily Times* and the *San Antonio Express News*, and she was bored stiff.

She'd been waiting with Darren in his single-cab pickup for nearly fifty minutes, parked between a rusted-out Beetle and a Pinto in the overgrown backyard of a similarly run-down house. They were also bumper-to-bumper with a classic Ford truck. Probably from the fifties or sixties. Patty didn't know for sure, but Darren did. He'd been staring at it with nearly as much lust as he did her.

She popped the folded newsprint on his leg. "Honey, he's right there." She pointed through the branches of a dying tree to a makeshift parking lot, where a truck with faded paint was parked next to a chain-link fence. Behind the wheel was a man whose sunglasses, focus, and posture—even while sitting— screamed *I'm the cop you're looking for*. "Just walk out there and get this over with. Plus, I know how your leg gets to hurting when you sit like this for too long."

Darren squeezed her hand. "You know the first one to blink loses. We need him to leave his truck, then I'll go. And Mr. Jones said the exchange was supposed to happen at three. So, we're going to wait until three."

Patty shook her head. *Mister* Jones. Darren always respected a chain of command, which was weird considering he operated outside of the law. Patty didn't like how Darren cowed to Frank, nor did she care for how much of her husband's time was spent running Frank's errands.

Then again, earning extra money from Frank had been Patty's idea.

"I know babe," she said. "But you already beat him here by twenty minutes, so you know he doesn't have backup. And the sooner you give this FBI guy Frank's books, the sooner we can start tailing him to his house and get back."

Darren smiled. Though his teeth weren't straight, and he couldn't quite pull off the movie-star stubble, her heart melted a bit every time she saw it.

"You're the one who says discipline is how we avoid getting caught. It's only fifteen more minutes." Darren handed her the A section of the *Express-News*. "This'll take up a few of them."

Patty usually skipped the news sections. There's a chance she'd read about one of her old friends, the ones she ran with in her teens and early twenties before she met Darren.

She avoided the obituaries for the same reason.

Back then, she was what her second-to-last foster mom had called a *petty criminal*. Kiting checks and lifting wallets. Light B and E when the newspapers piled up outside a house.

That's how she got into crosswords. Patty would steal the papers and do them when she got back to wherever she was crashing. One day she robbed a house with a six-inch-thick dictionary and collection of encyclopedias. She got more use out of the volumes than whatever brat had let them collect dust.

Now Patty had enough money to buy those crossword books at the grocery store and always kept one around the beauty parlor and in her car.

But not in Darren's pickup.

Patty took the paper and scanned the front-page headlines. Nothing piqued her interest, so she found the crime briefs. No familiar names. The regional news section began with a story about the murder of that poor woman in Hinterbach, less than four miles from where she sat.

Darren said he'd been there that night. He'd watched Frank walk to the yard, then come back a few minutes later. It was enough time to have killed her, Darren was sure of that. But Frank didn't have any blood on him, and he wasn't out of breath or high from adrenaline. In fact, Darren—who was no stranger to causing pain with his bare hands—said Frank was calm. Not in a good way, but creepy, like a man who'd wanted to do bad things but had been interrupted.

Now the trial was about to start for the man they say did it.

About three-quarters of the way down the story, she saw Frank's name.

Heller's attorney claims authorities didn't thoroughly investigate Franklin Jones III, Foster's former boyfriend who, according to county records, was the subject of a restraining order taken out by Foster nearly two years ago.

"There were red flags that the police and district attorney ignored," the public defender said.

District Attorney Martin Gamble said Jones was considered a suspect until he provided an incontrovertible alibi.

He declined to provide further information about Jones, the recently retired president of Hill Country Bank and Trust of Kerrville.

Darren wasn't Frank's alibi, but he could've bought one from just about anybody.

Patty looked up from the paper and resumed watching the FBI agent.

Or what she assumed was an FBI agent.

Frank never gave Darren much information, just simple instructions for simple tasks. Frank didn't know about their violent pasts, or that their businesses weren't on the up-and-up. Frank thought they were greedy capitalists willing to do dumb errands for cash under the table, which was fine by Darren and Patty.

Frank was more forthcoming with Patty when he was in her chair, but only about personal stuff. He never discussed business.

And judging by the hardcover ledger Darren held in his lap, this was business.

Patty kept the books for her barber shop and Darren's automotive place in Kerrville. In fact, accounting is how she and Darren met. He was boosting cars, and she was handling the money for a chop shop in San Antonio, though the front was an auto mechanic and towing company that had locations throughout South Texas and the Hill Country.

Darren was close with the guy who ran the operation, so after his leg injury, the owner took pity and let him run the Kerrville shop and take Patty with him. That suited Darren just fine. He always cared more about the cars than the theft.

Patty left on the condition she help clean the organization's money, and she enjoyed finances almost as much as cutting hair.

So, when Frank asked Darren to deliver the ledger to *a man who can use it*, Patty was naturally interested. It was well-documented and formal—Frank was a banker, after all—and clearly showed how the mayor of small, sleepy Hinterbach, Texas, was on the take. And the river of cash flowed through Frank's former bank.

Despite its elegant, embossed gold lettering, the ledger was a massive pile of dirt, and Frank was either turning state's or becoming a CI. Snitches didn't fare well in Patty's world, but Frank liked throwing money at Patty and Darren, and it was enough to buy their silence.

Then Darren told her about the second half of his duties. After the exchange, Darren had to follow the man back to his house and take down the address and license plate numbers.

This fed was smart enough to keep his number unlisted, and Frank needed to know where his new snitching partner lived.

Frank was as ruthless as he was smart.

But so was Patty, which is why she insisted on tagging along. If Darren was meeting someone more dangerous than a cop working white-collar crimes, he'd need backup.

Patty wasn't big, but she could handle herself. She'd grown up fighting off her methhead mother's skeezy boyfriends. When Mom finally died, CPS took Patty to a group home. She got her ass kicked. A lot. But it toughened her up, so she doesn't complain about her time there. Patty had also learned the value of a sharp blade—a skill she'd used when collecting from deadbeat thugs.

As Patty continued to watch the agent, she shifted in the seat and felt the thin handle in the back pocket of her jeans.

Patty may have forgotten her crosswords, but she'd remembered the straight razor.

20

BECK

PRESENT DAY

I heard Shayla's key slip into the tumbler. That's how quiet Big Lake was at 6:32 PM on a Wednesday, save for the occasional honk or jake brake from the highway, which was about four blocks south.

I put down her copy of Cormac McCarthy's *Blood Meridian* to meet her at the door, but Shayla breezed in before I could stand. She was still in her uniform, purse slung over her shoulder and resting on her left hip, service weapon holstered on the right.

I had just enough time to get an update before telling Shayla about our upcoming trip to retrieve Jorge's camper. "Did you get the video?"

Shayla nodded. "Our mystery man is Chuck."

It took a moment to register. The guy with the mullet who visited Jorge in the hospital. The man who'd caught it all on Snapchat and played it for Jorge to relive the next day. The dude-bro who Veronica had soaked in beer the night before.

"That sonofabitch."

"Yep. He walked in at eight and handed the manager a wad of cash."

My face was burning, but Shayla lowered her purse onto the coffee table and leaned back in her recliner like nothing was wrong. I clenched and unclenched my fists in frustration at her cavalier attitude.

"So, did you arrest him?"

Shayla shook her head.

"Do you at least have people staking out his place?"

"We checked Chuck's address this afternoon. His truck is gone, and he's not out at the jobsite, either."

"So he's in the wind."

The corner of her mouth curled into a smirk. "If that's what you want to call it, sure. We're monitoring his credit card and bank account, but I doubt we get a hit. At least not for a while."

"Why?"

"Because he has nearly ten grand in cash."

It took me a moment to piece it together. "The bank account."

Shayla nodded. "It was set up last week by Mr. Charles Davis. Two days later, nine thousand, nine hundred dollars was wired into the account. He withdrew everything on Friday and closed it."

"And that didn't raise any red flags at the bank?"

"Transactions under ten thousand dollars don't have to be reported."

I opened my mouth to ask the obvious follow-up, but she held up her palm. "We haven't traced the wire transfer yet. But it probably came from a dead-end offshore account."

A picture was emerging. Chuck is approached by someone working for Schuhmacher, who somehow knows Jorge is working here. Chuck is offered ten thousand dollars to make sure Jorge has an *accident*. Then he withdraws the money and pays, say, ten percent of the cash to Alfredo.

"I have a line on Alfredo." The words came out as a single utterance, as though saying it more quickly would make up for the time I'd spent stewing instead of informing the one person who could use the information.

"How?"

I broke down my conversation with Jorge earlier that day.

"Your friend's kind of a mess, isn't he?"

I thought about the state of Jorge's camper the last time I was a resident. The electric jack stands no longer worked correctly, and he'd resorted to creative western engineering to set up his travel home.

"You have no idea."

Shayla's purse vibrated. She ignored it at first, but when it buzzed again, she reached in and pulled out her phone.

"Christ almighty, did you tell Jorge to text me the address or something? Even if I delete the texts, the phone company still records the sender and timestamp. That's just one more thing I'll have to explain away."

The phone lit up again while it was still in her hand. Shayla swiped and started reading.

Ten seconds later, she was sprinting to the front door.

21

CASE KELLEY

FEBRUARY 21, 2000, 2:56 PM

As a younger man, Case would've had an ashtray full of butts, one in his mouth, and another cigarette at the ready.

But as he waited near a quiet construction site outside of Hinterbach, Case settled for the coffee stirrer he'd used at the Love's in Comfort.

The cup's contents would've been Irish back then, but Judy made him quit smoking and drinking early in their relationship. He was her training officer when she started with the San Antonio PD. He's not proud of it now, but it didn't take long for them to start sleeping together. When they started getting serious, Judy told Case he needed to quit, and he agreed without much fuss.

The love he got in return for kicking his habits was worth so much more.

Case was reminded of this as he looked at the dash of his truck, where Judy had left a sticky note.

Don't forget to pick up rolls of snuff for your mother. The Sam's across from her nursing home has them. XOXOXO

The note evoked both love and guilt. Judy left him reminders like that because she knew his schedule. Case didn't keep secrets from her anymore. Not on the big stuff, anyway.

Until now.

He checked his watch. Two minutes to three.

Case knew he shouldn't get out first, especially in such an open area with nothing to readily hide behind other than his truck. Then again, Jones was a banker, not a hardened criminal, so his Guy Friday probably had no idea how this was supposed to work.

He weighed getting this over with against the risk of stepping outside the relative safety of his pickup.

Case thought of his kids, the beautiful boys he and Judy had adopted after the fertility tests came back. As a career law enforcement officer, Case knew there were plenty of troublemakers who came out of the foster system. But the picture frames on his wall were proof that the negative narrative wasn't the only one, or even the most common.

Case eyed his watch again. Thirty seconds past three.

He couldn't get an ID for the man he was meeting. Jones only gave him a first name, Darren, which wasn't on the list of Jones's known associates. Or of Schuhmacher's.

Case hated meeting an unsub with no backup in a place that, while not the middle of nowhere, was far enough from town that nobody'd hear the gunshots.

But the reward outweighed the risk.

Case reached into the glove compartment and pulled out his holstered Glock, which he'd snuck into his truck during his morning walk. He made sure the magazine and chamber were full, put the pistol back in its holster, slid it onto his hip, then hid it underneath his untucked button-down.

After shutting the door and taking five steps, Case saw a man approach his position from fifty yards north, walking along the county road as though he lived in one of the crumbling shotgun houses nearby.

Shaggy brown hair, scruffy face, a bit overweight. A slight limp favoring his left leg.

A long, black book in his left hand.

The man waved and held up the ledger as he got within ten yards. "Hey there. You here for this?"

Case nodded and calmed his right hand.

Darren smiled and presented the book to Case, who accepted it without taking his eyes off the man who, now that he was closer, was at least six-four and weighed three bills, which explained why the walk left him slightly out of breath.

"You got a smoke?" Darren said.

Case worked hard to keep his face still despite the irony. Instead of laughing, he shook his head.

"Just as well," Darren said. "My old lady hates it."

This time Case let the smile form. "Mine too. We done here?"

Darren held up his hands, palms out. "I get it. Not trying to waste your time. Just giving the leg a minute. Had a car fall off the blocks once. Docs couldn't get it to heal quite right."

Case watched Darren turn and start walking back down the road. When he disappeared around the old house, Case backed up to his truck and got in.

He laid the pistol on the seat, keeping it at the ready, though he was in no danger of getting ambushed by the man.

Then he turned his attention to the ledger.

It only took a moment to realize he was holding the real deal. The record showed money coming into Jones's bank from several businesses with hinky names like *AAA Finance Inc.* The money then left and was sent to several other real estate LLPs, including one that might as well be a blinking marquee: *Schuhmacher Enterprises.* That, Case knew, was the umbrella corporation for the mayor's real estate firm, his billboard advertising company, and—no joke—a dry cleaning service, though that business wasn't publicly affiliated with Schuhmacher.

Then there was the name that made this book one of the biggest pieces of evidence he'd ever seen.

Flynn Consulting.

Case looked up. He'd hoped for this, but seeing it made Case realize he couldn't just toss it behind his seat and spend the day entertaining his mother.

He took Judy's note off the dash, folded it in half, then marked the page with Flynn's name. Now Case had to lock it, and the gun, in his safe back home, which meant coming clean to his wife about how his afternoon had started.

Judy hated when he lied to her about work. She knew how dangerous it was. She'd been a LEO until the day he joined the Bureau. The adoptions happened in Washington, DC, which is why his kids didn't have the same love for Texas he did. He'd tried to talk them both into becoming Aggies and joining the Corps, but neither even applied to A&M.

Judy didn't demand he avoid danger. She just asked that he not lie to *protect* her. It was a bullshit cliché that she wanted no part of, so they talked about most everything he did at work.

He did keep some things from Judy, of course, though most of the deception was during his counter-intel work after the World Trade Center bombing in '93. After that, he rose quickly until getting the opportunity to run his hometown field office.

They had a nice life, so the fight probably wouldn't last long.

Then it hit him. She was out with her friend Darcie.

There would be no fight at all.

Case smiled and started the truck. Thank goodness for those Presidents' Day sales. Though he liked to think of himself as a somewhat modern man—and his wife was nothing if not progressive—Case couldn't help but notice that women were powerless when presented with a day of discount shopping.

As he drove south on the 87, Case thought ahead to visiting his mother.

If only she were young enough to go shopping, too.

Dorothy Kane was born just before the Great Depression, and her own young parents never fully recovered. It wasn't until her shotgun wedding to San Antonio businessman Joseph Kelley that she had more than two dresses.

Still, she never outgrew the hardscrabble upbringing, especially after Case's father came back from the Second World War. He was volatile and drunk most of the time, and Dorothy always fought back. There was little room for love in their house, but she kept it stable enough, and Case didn't remember wanting for anything.

He owed her the same treatment now that she couldn't live on her own.

She'd lived with Case and Judy at first, but soon his mother was begging to move to *the old folks' home.* Case had the money, she argued, and everybody would be infinitely happier.

That was five years ago. Case hated the thought at first, but lately he felt more comfortable with the situation. His mother now puttered around and called every Sunday after the home's Baptist services. She didn't demand much face time with her son, except on long weekends.

She seemed happy with the arrangement, too, especially after a new nurse started working at the facility last fall. Case had gotten to know Leonard during a Christmas Day visit, and he seemed caring enough. Leonard was a good-looking kid—she said he looked like a young Rock Hudson—and seemed to care about the residents. His mother's only complaint: Leonard was part time. He could only work a few days a week. He spent the rest at local hospitals, where the pay was much better.

Case passed a sign that said Comfort was only a few miles away. He needed to stop and let Jackson know the meet had gone as planned.

He downed the last of his cold coffee. Maybe he'd get another cup of joe, too.

His wife was indulging herself.

Why shouldn't he?

22

BECK

PRESENT DAY

Jorge's habit of never charging his phone or keeping it on his person had never been so enraging.

"Voicemail again," I said. It was the fifth time I'd called him from Shayla's phone as she drove to the RV lot.

"Doesn't matter. We're here."

Ostrich Road bent to the right, and we saw the yellow overhead lights from a row of campers. There were also two sets of truck headlights less than a quarter mile away.

One of them was illuminating a camper near a barbed-wire fence separating the flat, barren lot from an overgrown pasture. The other was three rows to the north.

I hoped neither belonged to Chuck.

The first text Jorge sent was a mistake. The next two sent us speeding toward the edge of town.

> *Hey stop bangin ur old lady and help me get my camper*
>   *u fuckr*
> *Sry that was 4 my buddy chuck hes gonna help us*
> *Gittin started c u in a few*

That's the last we'd heard from him. And if Chuck had

shown up while Jorge was unhooking the water or electricity, he might already be dead.

Shayla's new Bronco threw up gravel as the pavement turned into a rough patch of caliche. When she slammed the brakes, rocks sprayed so far they pelted Jorge's traveling mansion.

"*La verga*," Jorge yelled as we hopped out and ran toward the camper's overhang. "What the hell, man?"

Shayla rushed to his side in full deputy mode, checking around the corner of the camper and gripping the pistol that had still been on her hip after her shift. "Where's Chuck?"

Jorge wiped his hands on his shorts. "He's not here. What's up with you two?"

Shayla crept down the side of the fifth-wheel, gun raised, so I answered.

"Chuck caused the explosion. He's the one who hurt you."

Jorge looked confused. "You said Alfredo did it, and he's in Vegas. Plus, Chuck was driving when it happened. You saw the video."

Shayla returned to our side, so Jorge started pleading his case to her. "Didn't he tell you all of this already?"

She holstered her weapon, apparently satisfied we weren't in immediate danger. "He did. But they're working together."

Jorge shook his head. "Look, bro, I get that you don't like him. And I know I was giving you shit about being too important to visit us and all that, but you don't have to be all butt hurt about it."

"You're right, I don't like him. But that's not what this is about. You remember how Paul's dad is a congressman? He paid Chuck—"

"We don't know it was Schuhmacher," Shayla said. "But someone paid Chuck ten grand last week, then he helped Alfredo disappear the day after the explosion." She put her hand on Jorge's shoulder. "I know Chuck, too. And I saw him on video today, at the hotel and the bank where he withdrew the cash."

Jorge mumbled under his breath, then winced and adjusted his back brace. "I don't know if I believe you. But Chuck texted me back and said he couldn't come help after all."

"We think he skipped town," Shayla said.

Jorge didn't look convinced. "Guess we have time to get this done, then."

Everyone relaxed a bit, though I still wanted to get Jorge back on the road in case we were wrong. He hadn't fixed anything in the years since we'd worked together, so I opened the side compartment to retrieve the hydraulic jacks and wooden shims we'd need to get the camper onto his truck's gooseneck hitch.

I walked over to hand a set to Shayla, who didn't look happy she'd been roped into helping. She dropped the jack and looked at Jorge, who was pulling the sewer hose toward the camper. "Can I see that shot of Alfredo in Vegas?" she asked.

"Oh, right." He took a few soft, waddling steps in his flip-flops. The physical exertion was obviously wearing him down, so Shayla hustled to meet him and disappeared around the camper. As they discussed Alfredo, I got my side ready.

"You know," I called out to Shayla, "this goes faster if we do it at the same time."

They told me to shut up in unison, then started laughing.

The next sound I heard was gunfire.

23

BECK
PRESENT DAY

Shayla sprinted toward the fence like she'd seen where the shots came from. After a moment of disorientation, Jorge's screams invaded my ears. With Shayla running down the shooter—Chuck, I assumed—I crawled around the camper to help.

Jorge was laying on his side, attempting to reach his right calf. He was still in the truck's headlights, so I could see the hole in his leg and the blood leaking out.

I jumped again at two more shots, though from much farther away this time.

My only medical training came from television hospital dramas, but instinct told me to raise the leg and pack the wound. I pulled off my T-shirt and tore away one of the sleeves.

I was about to touch the leg, but then thought about the old westerns I used to watch with my family as a kid.

I slipped my belt from the loops of my jeans and held it up to Jorge's mouth. "Bite down. This is going to hurt."

He screamed in Spanish, then did as I asked.

I grabbed the back of Jorge's knee and lifted it with my right hand. Jorge bucked and cried bloody murder through the leather between his teeth, but I gripped tighter and poked my sleeve-covered left index finger into the wound.

Jorge's yelling was now louder than I'd heard in the explosion video, but I kept folding in more of the cloth, all the while looking away so I couldn't see my slick hands or Jorge's agony.

After I ran out of sleeve, I put Jorge's leg down momentarily and reached back for the rest of my shirt to use as a makeshift tourniquet. He was no longer screaming, and the belt had fallen to the ground.

I didn't know if that was good or bad, but I tied the shirt around his lower leg anyway.

Shayla ran to us as I tightened the knot.

"How is he?"

"I don't know. I plugged the hole and tied something above the wound."

She bent down to inspect Jorge. "I think he's going into shock. We need to get him to the hospital."

She stepped to the other side and we lifted Jorge's upper body, which made him murmur something about his back. I offered an apology as we slipped our necks underneath his armpits and got him standing on his good leg.

I assumed Shayla had killed Chuck, but I felt the need to clarify as we shuffled Jorge toward her SUV.

"You got him, right?"

"Yeah. He was running to a house maybe half a mile away. I found his AR on my way back. Good thing he's a terrible shot."

Shayla opened the back of the Bronco and we muscled Jorge inside. The hospital was only a mile or two away, so I had hope we could get him there in time.

Then glass exploded from the driver's side window.

I fell and put my back beside the front passenger tire. Shayla emerged from beneath the vehicle and sheltered behind the other.

"Did you check to make sure he was dead?"

"Of course." Shayla shuffled to the back of the Bronco and

leaned around the bumper. "I can see the shooter. I'm going to run out and cover you. Get in and haul ass to the hospital."

"You sure?"

She tossed me her keys. "No. But we don't have a choice. On my go."

Shayla got on her knees like a sprinter settling into her blocks.

"Go."

She sprinted into the darkness and I reached for the door handle above my head. I crawled over the passenger seat and center console, a bull trying to escape a rodeo chute and bucking with each gunshot until I fell into the driver's seat.

Another rang out as I put my foot on the brake and punched the ignition button.

I glanced out the empty window and saw Shayla bending over her kill about ten yards past the barbed wire.

24

BECK

PRESENT DAY

The sound of my palm slapping the counter was louder than I'd anticipated. The receptionist and I were the only two in the hospital lobby this time, and I'm sure he was following protocol.

But he also wasn't listening.

"I need to tell my friend's wife that her husband is possibly dying on a surgeon's table right now," I said. "To do that, I need your phone and a web browser."

He didn't look up from the computer screen. "Look, I've been more than accommodating. You're going to have to fill out those forms for your friend before I can do anything else."

It had been more than twenty minutes since I carried Jorge through the doors and yelled for a gurney. The guy ran out from behind his desk and helped me get him secured. Jorge had blacked out on the ride over, but he was still breathing as two nurses wheeled him into the back. The one who came back out brought a set of sea green scrubs—I only needed the top—and said using my shirt to pack the wound was smart.

But I'd gotten no news since.

I was about to raise my voice again when Shayla walked through the automatic doors.

I jogged to meet her. "Thank God. I need to borrow your cellphone."

Like she had at the Pumpjack, Shayla shook her head. She was still in her uniform, though in the fluorescent light I could see patches of red mud. Jorge's blood had transferred to her pants and mixed with caliche from the RV lot.

The two men behind her wore matching khaki shirts and pants, though theirs were much cleaner.

Shayla reached behind her and retrieved a set of handcuffs. "Beck, we need you to come with us. I'm going to put these on. Please don't resist."

My hands and nose felt like pincushions and I turned around, contemplating a move toward the double doors that led into the ER. I tried remembering the layout from when I visited Jorge less than a week ago.

"Don't do it."

I was still thinking about running when the same surgeon who'd operated on Jorge's back walked into the waiting room.

"Mr. Beck, right?"

I took a step toward the doctor, but Shayla grabbed my arm.

"Is he going to be okay?" I asked, needing to get the headline before Shayla took me to the county jail.

"We think so," the doctor said. "The bullet traveled through his leg and didn't hit anything major. But that's not my biggest concern. I've already talked to his wife and gotten permission to operate on his back again. He'll be walking in a few days, but he should never have left home. Your friend is looking at months of limited mobility and the possibility of never fully recovering. He's being prepped for surgery now."

Of course the hospital had Grace's number. She'd been here with me and filled out his paperwork the first time.

I didn't have time to feel embarrassed. I thanked the surgeon, then turned and held out my hands.

As she slowly tightened the cuffs, Shayla leaned closer. "I'm sorry," she whispered. "They showed up a minute after you left.

I said I was there looking for you. It was the only excuse I could think of."

She finished and started leading me out.

"Will there be a lawyer at the jail?" I asked.

"No. You should call yours."

Veronica was supposed to be finding one for our civil cases, but I didn't think either of us had a criminal lawyer in our contacts. "I don't—"

Shayla dug her fingernails into my arm, which I took as a sign to shut up.

As we crossed through the doors, she told the other deputies to go ahead to the SUV while she checked me for weapons.

When they were out of earshot, she dropped to a knee and ran her hands down my inseam. "You do have a lawyer."

As her hands ran up the outside of my legs, I heard the crunch of paper on denim, then felt her fingers slide into my front left pocket. "That's Caitlin's number. I texted her on the ride over. She's expecting your call."

"She's okay with that? I don't know what all she told you, but our breakup wasn't exactly cordial."

Shayla finished the fake pat-down and stood. "I know. But she'll do it for me."

25

TERRY JACKSON

FEBRUARY 21, 2000, 4:32 PM

Terry wasn't sure how to feel as he buttoned his jeans. Judy was still in the shower, and he'd wanted to join her. Instead, Terry reached for his shirt, which he'd tossed onto the carpet.

They'd been in bed for hours, but only the last few minutes had been spent sleeping together. Judy had led him to the bedroom and used him as a sounding board. He'd obliged, playing the role of big spoon, his hands locked on her shoulder and his own elbow while she told him about her dual life of privilege and pain.

Judy spoke warmly about her youth as an only child in a cop family. She watched her dad work his way up through the SAPD, from a detective in the financial crimes unit to captain of the special investigation section. He might've made it all the way to deputy chief, but instead, he pulled the pin after twenty years.

Judy was seventeen at the time. With no brother to do it for her, she set her sights on continuing the family legacy. But instead of helping and championing his daughter, retired Captain Neal Gentry all but disowned her. Judy Gentry lived with a friend between graduation and entering the academy.

They only repaired their rift after Judy retired to follow

newly sworn Special Agent Case Kelley across the country to Washington, DC.

Judy told Terry she missed being a cop, but Case almost always treated her like one, letting her in on confidential investigations and acting on some of her hunches. She recounted her highlights, and how Case had angled for this post so she could be near her mother and ailing father, who'd just been moved to a hospice.

"He let me live in both worlds," she'd said. "I got to be my father's daughter again and said goodbye to him, and I got to help serve, even if it was in a roundabout way. That's why I can't leave him for you."

Terry said he understood. Then he asked why they were naked in her marital bed.

She answered by rolling over onto him. The kiss was deeper than any he'd experienced, but it was accompanied by tears falling from her face to his.

He hadn't known someone could cry and make love at the same time. But she did. Then he did, realizing it would be the last time they expressed their love.

With the moment now over, Terry scanned the floor for his beeper. He'd heard the buzz an hour ago but ignored it. If something had gone wrong, Judy would've gotten a call by now. Or another agent would've called Terry's mobile phone, a technology Case refused to adopt.

Terry ducked lower and found the beeper under the bed with the message from Case.

10 24. Assignment completed.

When he stood, Judy was standing in front of him in her robe.

He searched for the right words. A simple goodbye was probably best.

Terry didn't get the chance to say anything before hearing the exhaust of an old truck near the front of the house. Terry grabbed his shoes and ran to the living room, where he pulled a curtain to the side and confirmed what they both knew.

Hard Case Kelley was parked outside.

Terry turned to find Judy back in her underwear, scrambling to put on her pants, a shirt slung over the side of the loveseat. He knew there was no hiding what happened. Judy had plans and was supposed to be gone, but both of their vehicles were in her driveway.

Terry walked to the door and, despite Judy's screams to wait, stepped onto the porch shirtless.

Case was still in the truck, which was parallel to the house but directly behind the drive, blocking in his Corvette and Judy's Chevy Metro.

"Come on, Case," Terry said as he walked down the porch steps. "Let's talk this out."

The truck door squeaked as Case pushed it open with his left hand. After a moment, he turned off the ignition, removed his gold-framed aviators, and carefully laid them on the dash. It took another long second for him to look to the left, palm something from the passenger seat, then finally slip out of the cab.

Case made brief eye contact with Terry before shifting his gaze to the front door and marching across the lawn.

Terry stepped in his path. "It's not Judy's fault. Take it out on me, not her."

Case stopped dead and burrowed his eyes into Terry. "I would never hit my wife. And for you to think I'd react that way says a lot more about you than it does me." He held up his left hand, which was holding the evidence he'd procured in Hinterbach—an accounting ledger. "I need to lock this up."

When they were on the job, Terry trusted Case with his life.

But Terry had also been a cop before joining the Bureau. He knew anybody was capable of violence when they caught a cheating spouse red-handed.

Case started walking again. When he tried to brush past, Terry grabbed his left bicep.

Before Terry could speak, Case twisted and hit him in the temple with the spine of the ledger.

Terry loosened his grip and held the side of his head. "That's it. Get it all out now."

Case raised his fist but stopped short, so Terry turned and saw Judy standing in the doorway.

"It's not what you think," she said.

Dammit. The last thing she needed to do was lie.

"He knows." Terry turned to Case. "But we're over. We just agreed to end it."

Case laughed. "You two are terrible liars. Her hair's wet again. There's only one reason she'd need another shower."

Case nudged Terry's shoulder as he stepped toward Judy, who was frozen in her doorway.

"Get inside and lock yourself in the bedroom," Terry said. "Hurry."

Judy didn't move, so Terry took two steps and tackled Case. The old man fought hard, but Terry had Case subdued in a few seconds.

Then he heard footsteps and turned just as Judy lowered her shoulder.

Terry was on his back before he could react. When he looked up, Judy was leaning down and whispering in Case's ear.

Until that moment, Terry had hoped Judy would change her mind one day. But watching her worry over his body, Terry knew. Judy would never leave Case.

Terry scrambled to his feet as Judy helped Case to his. The couple turned to Terry but didn't say a word.

They didn't have to.

Terry turned to get in his car, but Case's truck was still parked behind it. Case came into view a few seconds later and slid into the cab.

Before he fired it up, Case put on his sunglasses. And after the ignition caught, he sat for at least ten seconds before finally lowering the column shifter and driving forward.

But instead of stopping a few feet later, he accelerated and turned right at the end of the block.

Terry spun around to look at Judy, who appeared just as stunned.

He took a step in her direction but stopped when she pointed a shaky index finger.

"Get the fuck out of here. Now."

26

BECK

PRESENT DAY

I tried hopping to when the portly deputy called my name, anxious to leave after what had to be more than twelve hours in a concrete cell.

But county jail is no place for someone pushing forty.

The night shift had given me a thin crash pad—pieces of a wrestling mat cut about six inches too narrow and a foot too short. That small piece of comfort didn't do much, though. I made it to one knee but had to stop when my side began cramping.

After making it to my feet, I was led to a tiny interrogation room with a wooden table, four matching chairs, and drywall painted gunmetal gray. The air conditioner was turned to eleven and my skin felt like one giant goosebump.

The deputy pointed to a chair on the far end of the room. "Sit there. They'll be here in a minute."

As I sat, I noticed a small video camcorder on a tripod in the corner.

He left without explaining who *they* were, and the minute felt like twenty, though there was no clock to help me gauge. I shut my eyes and rested my head on the table, exhausted. One night in the place had me reeling. How was I going to spend the rest of my life in prison?

Caitlin entered first, her copper hair longer and her features fuller than I remembered. She'd been in law school when we dated, surviving on caffeine and stress. But now she was a criminal defense attorney working at a law firm in Dallas.

She was also the inspiration for my novel. And she knew it.

Caitlin took a seat beside me and silently opened her briefcase.

Another figure from my past entered next: Caroline Walker, the Texas Ranger who started all of this by re-investigating Summer Foster's murder.

I dropped my chin, waiting for my comeuppance.

Walker took off her tan cowboy hat and started the proceedings. "Good to see you again, Beck."

The words were barely out of her mouth when Caitlin spoke. "Let's stick to questions only."

"Fine," Walker said. "I need your client to tell me what really happened on the night of July Fourth, nineteen ninety-nine."

"My client will be asserting his right to remain silent."

Walker pursed her lips, then nodded. "Understandable. But perhaps he'd like to listen."

Caitlin remained stone faced but nodded for Walker to continue.

"We already know her murder didn't go down the way you said it did. During your taped interviews with investigators, and later at trial, you never mentioned Ms. Foster's head hitting the corner of a picnic table. But blood spatter analysis proves it happened. Then there's your fingerprints in that blood, which indicate an attempt to wipe it away. That's what we call consciousness of guilt."

I looked at Caitlin, who remained focused on Walker.

"If all you're going to do is repeat news reports," Caitlin said, "we're done here."

"I think your client will want to hear what I have to say. You see, I'm not convinced he killed Ms. Foster."

I sat up straighter. "What?"

Caitlin leaned over and spoke to me for the first time in five years.

"Let me do the talking."

She turned back to Walker. "Then why is my client here?"

"That's above my pay grade. All I know is the Nimitz County DA brought charges and a judge signed the arrest warrant. Last night I got a call from a source saying you were in custody, and since I'm the one who re-opened the case, I was sent to get a confession."

I wasn't sure who the Nimitz County district attorney was these days, but he had to be working for Schuhmacher, either for cash or because the congressman had leverage. I made a mental note to tell Caitlin when we were alone.

"What I know, without a doubt," Walker said, "is you lied about that night." She leaned forward. "I also know you're a magnet for dead women, and the ones in your life are the worst I've ever seen."

Caitlin let out a dramatic sigh, but Walker continued.

"But I also know Butch Heller was caught with Foster's blood on his hands, and he confessed to the murder before being executed for it. That's hard evidence I can't ignore, which is why, in the report I handed to my superiors last week, I said I didn't feel there was enough evidence to charge you with murder. Someone obviously disagrees."

Walker leaned back. "But, if you can give me a story that explains the discrepancy in your account of her death, I'm sure we can clear all of this up right now."

I looked at Caitlin. She didn't react for a few moments, then she smiled and started clapping.

"That's an impressive trick, playing both bad cop and good cop." She stopped clapping and her face returned to its previously affectless state. "Now, if the theatrics are over, I need some time alone with my client before the arraignment."

Walker obliged, picking up her hat and turning off the camera before stepping out of the room.

As soon as the door closed, Caitlin turned to face me.

"Shayla told me everything last night. I'm not saying I believe everything she said, but it does sound like you're getting railroaded."

Her tone was mostly matter-of-fact, but I caught a tinge of the old Caitlin. She still cared, and she was ready to fight for me.

She deserved to know I wasn't innocent.

"I need to tell you something."

Caitlin shook her head. "Save it. You're going to be arraigned in Nimitz County, and they're coming to get you in"—she checked her watch, gold with diamonds around the face—"thirteen minutes. And before we go, I need to tell you something about Jorge and the guy who tried to kill you."

My confession would have to wait.

"Is Jorge okay?"

She leaned in closer, turning from attorney to friend. "He made it through surgery and is resting. The doctors say he's not paralyzed, but he won't be able to feel much of anything for a week. They expect a full recovery, though it might take a year."

"Jesus."

"Yeah, but Shayla said his wife made it in last night. And if I do my job tomorrow morning, you'll be out on bail and you can go visit him before finding a place to stay with your parents. I assume they're coming down to help you through this."

"Actually, they're not. Dad nearly died from a stroke last year, so Mom and a nurse stay at the house in Montana full-time. If anything were to happen while she wasn't there, I don't know if I could live with that, so I told her to stay put."

Caitlin put her right hand on my forearm. She let me squeeze it for a moment before pulling away and digging into her briefcase. "Now, as for the assholes who shot at Shayla, we have IDs. She said you both knew Charles Davis."

"Right."

"She didn't have much on the second guy"—Caitlin emerged with a piece of paper—"Darren Butler."

"Never heard of him."

"He lives in Kerrville, so we thought there was a chance."

That did pique my interest. Kerrville was close enough to Hinterbach to do a little more digging.

"Has she made any connection to Schuhmacher?"

Caitlin shook her head. "All we know right now is he owns A1 Automotive and Towing and has a wife, Patricia."

The names didn't mean anything to me, but the nature and location of his business did.

"Let me see your phone?"

"We don't have time for a call."

"It's not for that. I need to look something up."

She pulled out a tablet and unfolded the keyboard built into its case. "What are we looking for?"

I stood and looked over her shoulder. Being that close to her reminded me of the last morning we spent together, but I shook it off.

"Go to the *Lone Star Ledger* website and search for my name, Summer Foster, and twenty years."

When she clicked on the link, I told her to scroll until she found a PDF embedded in the story. I knew it was the invoice from work done on a BMW belonging to Franklin Jones.

The name at the top of the document was A1 Automotive and Towing.

"Who's Franklin Jones?"

"Summer's piece of shit ex-boyfriend."

Caitlin skimmed the story. "Says here he used to be the president of a bank."

The same bank from the ledger sent to Agent Jackson? I read over her shoulder.

When I found the name, I tapped the tablet so hard the case collapsed. "Hill Country Bank and Trust of Kerrville. Franklin Jones was handling Schuhmacher's dark money."

"You know that from the financial documents Shayla told me about?"

"Right. So now we have this Darren Butler, who connects to Franklin Jones, who connects to Grant Schuhmacher, who's out to get me after I killed his son."

"So you're saying US Representative Grant Schuhmacher reaches out to his old partner in crime, Franklin Jones?"

"Exactly.

"And this Franklin Jones hires Darren Butler, a guy who once repaired Jones's car, to, what, whack your friend?"

This line of questioning wasn't going to end the way I wanted, but I nodded anyway.

"And this hit is supposed to be carried out by a mulleted redneck and his gambling addict sidekick? And when they fail— the most predictable outcome ever—this old man tries to finish you off himself?"

She was right. It all sounded insane.

But she didn't know that Jones saw me in Summer's yard that night before Butch Heller drove up, drunk and easy to frame.

And now Jones and Schuhmacher, the personification of rich and powerful, had formed a pact to ruin me for killing people they loved.

The only way it made sense was knowing I was guilty of the charges, but before I could tell Caitlin, Deputy Portly knocked and told us our time was up.

"Don't talk to anyone, and let me focus on getting you bail," she said. "Then I'll give back your tin foil hat."

27

PATTY BUTLER

FEBRUARY 21, 2000, 4:47 PM

Patty watched as the woman's shirtless boyfriend drove away in his blue 'Vette. Witnessing that blowout made Patty feel even more thankful for Darren. He checked all her boxes. And, while she felt bad for thinking about it in such blunt terms, Patty was the catch and knew in her heart Darren would never stray.

Neither would she, but if a man with that body had propositioned her, the temptation would certainly be strong.

Darren handed her a small notebook that now contained the agent's address, the make and model of his truck and its license plate number, the same for his wife's white hatchback, plus the boyfriend's car and plate, just in case.

Patty tossed it back in the glove compartment and shut it, her eyes never leaving the wife. They were parked too far away to hear what all was said, but close enough to see everything—including the ledger, which had flown out of the agent's hand during the fight and ended up just underneath the wife's ride at the top of the driveway.

Darren reached for the ignition, but Patty grabbed his hand.

"Hold on."

"Why? I thought you were in a hurry to get home."

Darren was smart. He could fix anything and was great with people. His weakness, however, was reading and exploiting a situation to its fullest.

So, while he'd completed the day's mission and was ready to get back to his cars, Darren didn't see the opportunity sitting a block away.

"If she doesn't pick up that book, I'm going to walk over and get it."

"But Mr. Jones wants the guy to have it. Why would we—"

Patty leaned across the cab and kissed Darren.

She hoped one day they could stop hustling. Frank had already given them the cash infusion they needed to have a few days off a week, but in return, he was asking for more of these personal errands.

And if the FBI wanted that ledger—and Frank couldn't risk mailing or delivering it himself—it was valuable enough to steal back.

Patty left the truck before Darren had a chance to object and started walking down the sidewalk across from the house.

The wife was staring out of her large living-room window, her arms crossed in front of her chest and head hanging as though she was inspecting the perfectly manicured lawn. Patty strolled casually, like she belonged in such a high-class neighborhood.

She'd lived near this part of San Antonio once, with the same foster mother who called her *Patricia* and sent her to a private school. Of course, that parental unit only knew about the shoplifting she'd done with the horrible creatures in plaid skirts she was forced to see every day. At first, it was kid stuff. They'd sneak into the city's southwest Sam's Club, by following a large family and pretending they belonged. They could walk around for hours while eating chips and candy. They never took anything because the thrill was enough. That, and there's no market for stuff like cheap, comically large boxes of toilet paper.

Soon she moved again and graduated to shoplifting at malls.

Those girls kept the shoes and bags, which is how she got caught. Patty fenced her items using old group home friends, but the other girls named names.

She was booted from that school—and the house—for kicking their asses. And in that case, kicking their asses meant breaking one girl's nose and cutting another's cheek so badly her mother sued Patty's foster parents and the state. The pissed-off CPS guy said she wanted reimbursement for the plastic surgery and compensation for *emotional distress.*

Those rich bitches didn't know the meaning of distress.

She assumed the same of the fed's wife, who stood frozen in the same position as Patty pulled even with the window. Her plan was to get to the end of the block, then cross the street and use the car and trees to block the wife's view from inside the house.

As she passed the wife's field of vision, Patty glanced her way. The woman lifted her head, eyes red, cheeks flushed. She looked mortified when she saw Patty and scurried away.

Patty was torn. The wife had seen her, which was always a problem. On the other hand, her world had just come crashing down. If her agent husband came back and wondered where the ledger was, would the wife remember seeing Patty? If so, could she describe Patty in any meaningful detail, other than a white woman with brown hair wearing jeans and a black leather jacket?

It was worth the risk, even if the wife could see her clearly through the tears. Patty reached the end of the block, looked both ways, and crossed. As she headed back toward the driveway, Patty noticed how the houses weren't as cookie-cutter as the suburb she'd once occupied. The home she passed now wasn't brick like the FBI agent's, but covered in off-white tin siding. The porch was much larger, though, with a grill and patio furniture that most people put in the backyard.

Most importantly, there were no vehicles in the driveway.

They might be in the garage, but nobody around here used garages for storing cars, except in severe weather.

Patty slowed as she reached the end of the neighbor's lawn. The white hatchback was too low to the ground to reach the ledger from her side, so she jogged to the back bumper and crouched for a moment, making sure neither the wife nor the neighbor opened their doors. If they did, she'd say she saw a cat and wanted to pet it. Women were easy enough to dismiss, especially when they were expressing *girly* emotions like wanting to love on a pet.

Satisfied she was in the clear, Patty stayed low as she crept around the car, picked up the ledger, then retraced her steps. She took a moment to wedge the ledger between her waistband and the small of her back, then stood and tried to look casual as she strode down the driveway.

Patty fought her adrenaline as she turned right to continue down the sidewalk. It had been a while since she'd done something so daring. Her days were now spent cutting hair, getting hit on by her creepy clients, and doing math.

Patty kept walking past Darren's pickup. He knew the drill.

When she reached the end of the block, Patty turned right and kept walking until Darren approached, having circled the block in the opposite direction.

Another man might've been upset that Patty left him in the middle of a conversation for a potentially dangerous grab like that. Instead, Darren reached across the cab, opened the door, and kissed her after she buckled herself in.

"It was nice to see you at work again," he said. "Now what?"

Darren trusted her, a rarity in a world where Rule Number One is *Don't trust anybody.* Maybe that's why she loved him so much.

"We go home, stay patient, and see how this plays out," Patty said. "Blackmail's like whiskey. The longer it sits, the stronger it gets."

He nodded and put the truck in gear. As she assessed the

ledger again, Patty noticed something new. A yellow piece of paper sticking out from the top. The agent had bookmarked a page, though she wasn't interested in that.

His bookmark had been a sticky note with a message written on it.

Before Darren turned toward the highway leading home, Patty smiled.

"On second thought, let's stick around town," Patty said. "We're not done with this guy just yet."

PATTY COULDN'T BE sure she had the right place. But that Sam's from her childhood was across the street from a row of medical facilities, so it had been worth checking out. If nothing else, maybe she could pick up a few things for the house under her shop's business account.

When she saw the nursing home sign, Patty was sure, so they parked and waited. And waited some more. After twenty minutes, she wondered if somehow there existed two of the club stores across from nursing homes.

Then Darren spotted the fed's truck.

They'd parked in between two other pickups at the edge of the lot. They ran the risk of the agent seeing Darren, but it was unlikely. He couldn't park nearby, and they wouldn't be in his path to the front door.

Still, she told an impatient Darren to slide down in his seat.

"I still don't understand why we're doing this," he said like a petulant teen, though she knew his leg was hurting, too. "We've done everything Mr. Jones said and more. You know he won't pay us any extra, right?"

Patty knew that. But the more valuable they became now—especially Darren, who was getting the more meaningful jobs—the more money they'd make long-term.

"You have to look ahead," she said as their target parked.

"Frank wanted to know more about this guy. That's why he wanted the address and license plate numbers. But Frank probably didn't know about this guy's mom. So, if we bring him that information, Frank has more leverage in case their deal goes bad. And if we do that now, without him asking, Frank will give us better jobs in the future. And that's when we make the money."

Darren grinned and put his hand on her thigh. "I love it when you get like this." He slid his hand farther up.

Patty giggled but playfully slapped his hand away. "Focus. We'll have plenty of time for that later."

28

BECK

PRESENT DAY

Energy poured through the doorway and into the Nimitz County courtroom. Even the old bailiff was impressed.

"I've never seen it this packed," he said, "and I've been here for ten years now."

I'd seen the space that electric. You just had to go back another decade or so.

He touched my elbow, which was tucked to my side above shackled wrists, and led me into the two-story hotbox. It had gotten a makeover since the last time I was there, but all the changes were cosmetic. New varnish here, new table there. In all the ways that mattered, though, it was still the place where I'd testified against Butch Heller.

If Grant Schuhmacher got his way, I would suffer the same fate.

Though it was just an arraignment, every seat in the historic courthouse was filled. Even the aisles in the upper deck were filled with standing gawkers. Though it was mostly a faceless mass, three stood out as I approached Caitlin, who was already seated at the defense table, head buried in her briefcase.

Caroline Walker was seated just behind the prosecutors, her

collared white shirt pressed, beige dress hat resting on her right knee. She gave a slight nod of recognition as I passed.

Veronica sat directly behind Caitlin. She'd driven down with the understated suit I was wearing after convincing my building manager to let her in. Though her eyes floated above dark bags, she was at attention with a bouncing right heel.

To her right was Shayla, wearing civilian clothing dressy enough to pass for one of Caitlin's paralegals.

Her presence was a surprise. She sucked in a deep breath and motioned with her hands, telling me to do the same. I obliged.

Caitlin looked up while I waited for the bailiff—whose nameplate read R. McCollum—to remove the handcuffs. I was in my chair for two seconds before standing again as McCollum announced the presence of the honorable Judge Douglas Grantham, an older Black gentleman with a shaved head and a neatly trimmed moustache.

"Be seated," Judge Grantham said. "And who do we have with us today?"

A short, skinny guy in a navy suit stood at the table across the aisle. "District Attorney Jeremy Wolff for the state, your honor."

"Caitlin Parks for the defense." She remained standing, while Wolff took a seat.

"Very good," the judge said, his baritone echoing off the rafters. "Does the defendant wish to have the indictment read aloud?"

"No, your honor," Caitlin said.

"Excellent. Mr. Beck, how do you plead?"

I'd gone through this with Caitlin an hour ago. Though it seemed simple enough, Caitlin said she'd seen too many of her clients freeze and annoy the judge by hesitating or speaking too softly.

I stood, took another one of Shayla's deep breaths, and made sure to project.

"Not guilty."

"Okay then. I have a motion from the state requesting I deny bail for the defendant."

Wolff stood, joining Caitlin. "That's right, your honor. The defendant, who has admitted to killing at least one person—"

"Objection. Relevance."

Before the judge could respond, Wolff walked out from behind his table and began creeping toward the bench. "Your honor, the defendant has been arrested on a charge of second-degree murder. His past homicides—"

"Objection—"

"—are crucial to showing—"

"—your honor—"

Grantham swung his gavel. Its crack hushed the lawyers but elicited whispers from the crowd.

"You two will not speak over each other in my courtroom." He was calm but stern. "Now, the past homicide you're referring to, Mr. Wolff, was ruled justified and took place twenty years after the death of Miss Foster. Objection sustained."

Caitlin smiled and nodded.

Wolff clenched his jaw. "Bartholomew Beck is charged with a violent felony and poses a danger to the public. He's also a man with considerable means, which makes him an obvious flight risk. He must be remanded to custody pending trial, your honor."

I didn't know if Wolff hadn't run my financials or was lying to the judge. Either way, it wasn't looking good for me so far.

The judge turned his attention to Caitlin. "Ms. Parks?"

"Thank you, your honor." She stepped out from behind our table. "It's true, my client has some money. But Mr. Beck has no criminal record and vehemently denies these charges. It's in his interest to cooperate fully and clear his name quickly so he can resume making a living. We also strongly object to the district attorney's claim he's a danger to the public. His career has been about freedom and justice, and he wants nothing more than to continue turning a spotlight on real criminals."

As Judge Grantham considered their arguments, the court-house was treated to a harmony of caws and yips from a pair of mockingbirds just outside an open window. My eyes drifted there, jealous of their freedom.

When Judge Grantham cleared his throat, even the birds went silent.

"Unlike the district attorney, I don't believe Mr. Beck poses an immediate danger to the public."

I took a deep breath and heard one escape from Caitlin's lungs.

"That said, I cannot ignore the fact that he's facing serious charges that come with a long prison sentence if he's found guilty. That's enough to make any man, let alone one with disposable income, think about fleeing."

I looked over at Caitlin, whose lips were pursed. She probably knew what was coming. I had no idea.

"Therefore, I am setting bail at one hundred thousand dollars and ordering the defendant to stay within the bounds of Nimitz County until the commencement of a trial or the charges are dropped. This will require a GPS tracking device, to be paid for by the defendant. We're adjourned, pending further pretrial motions."

The crowd erupted before Grantham's gavel hit its block.

Caitlin leaned over. "You're going back to the cell now until we bail you out."

A bail bondsman would need 10 percent up front. "How are you going to cover ten thousand?"

Before she could answer, the bailiff was beside me, telling me to stand and present my hands for cuffing.

As we walked to the side door that led to the courthouse's interior, I made eye contact with Veronica, Shayla, and Walker. Then, just as I was about to disappear back into solitude, I noticed another figure.

The slick, almost white hair of Parker Mallory was floating above his phone. I couldn't see behind the black device, but I pictured him smiling at my imminent demise. It didn't matter, but I tried to decide whether he sought out the job of ruining my reputation because he was jealous, or whether his disdain for my existence came after he learned more about my past.

I was still working through the thought exercise when another face made me cough up bile.

The still-boyish face of the Hinterbach Rams' star quarterback now belonged to a forty-year-old wearing a cerulean suit and pink power tie; he was unmistakable, standing all of six-foot-four in the front row.

Samuel Clemens Foster.

I was somewhere between asleep and awake when Bailiff McCollum said my name.

It had been at least an hour since I saw Sammy, which had made me freeze until McCollum pushed me forward and led me to a changing room. Then it was down the hall to county lockup, where the concrete felt cool against the back of my head, and the only other inmate was still passed out from the night before.

McCollum led me back to the changing room, where I signed for my possessions. The ones I had on me when I was arrested, that is, not what I'd left behind at the Pumpjack Hotel.

Caitlin, Veronica, and Shayla were waiting for me in the courthouse foyer.

"So, who do I need to make the check out to?" I asked, smiling like a lunatic despite the aching back and sleep deprivation.

Veronica rushed to me and squeezed. "It's on my card. But we'll settle up after you're done paying your lawyer."

On cue, Caitlin walked up with Shayla in tow. "Before you leave, Bubba over there has to put on your ankle monitor." She pointed to a heavyset man with a blond beard and tattoos for sleeves.

"His name really Bubba?"

Shayla laughed. Caitlin didn't.

After the digital ball and chain was attached and turned on by the man—I didn't ask his name, and he didn't utter a word—I walked out, shielding my eyes from the sun.

"Can we go to Fern's?" I pointed across the square to a German café that had been owned by Hinterbach elder Fern Falkner, may she rest in peace. "I need a caffeine infusion and food that didn't come from a can."

They agreed, and we started walking.

"Has anyone heard from Jorge's wife?" I asked.

Veronica answered. "I got ahold of her. As of yesterday afternoon, he was healing on schedule and should be able to go back home early next week. She's going to keep calling me with updates."

Next on my list was Shayla. "Why aren't you in Big Lake?"

"I'm on administrative leave for two weeks," she said. "It's standard anytime we fire our service weapon, let alone kill two people. At least I'm still getting paid."

I'd been so focused on me, I'd forgotten about what she went through. We both knew what it was like to watch someone die, but the second time wasn't any easier.

"You look like you're holding up all right."

"Smoke and mirrors." Her mouth smiled, but her eyes didn't. "That's the first time I've had to use my gun on duty."

My stomach twitched with guilt. "Really?"

"Look at where I've worked. Weatherford and Big Lake aren't known for their gunfights."

I sped up as we approached the door, making a show of holding it open for them. Every head had turned our way, and they weren't pleased. Veronica took the initiative and led us to a somewhat isolated four-top in the corner.

We were still looking at our menus when a woman, who looked like the restaurant's namesake but sixteen years younger, approached.

"Y'all need to leave."

Caitlin the lawyer came out swinging. "And why is that?"

The woman's eyes took aim. "Because we have the right to refuse service to anybody. Especially murderers."

"First, he's not a murderer," Caitlin said. "Second, we resent the implication that we've done anything wrong."

Fern's daughter put a veiny hand on her hip and looked down at my ankle monitor. "I don't care what you resent, missy. You're disturbing my customers, and the sheriff hates when you city folk cause a scene."

Shayla laughed, probably at the thought of being called *city folk* after her childhood on a North Texas ranch and her current residence in the West Texas oil patch.

That was the last straw for our not-so-friendly proprietor. "Look, if all y'all aren't gone in one minute, I'm calling Sheriff Wolff. I have his cell number on speed dial."

I nearly had to push Caitlin out, but we left and started walking back to the courthouse parking lot, where I recognized Veronica's Benz—its windshield still cracked—parked beside a Porsche Macan SUV.

They fit right into the rest of Hinterbach's traffic, which were all snowbirds now that fall's last gasp was turning into snow up north. After Butch Heller's trial, then-mayor Grant Schuhmacher led a campaign to rehabilitate the town's reputation and transform it into a German-themed tourist trap, a plan that included the publication of *Cold Summer*.

The Porsche's headlights flashed, and I turned to see Caitlin holding a key fob.

"At least now we know how Schuhmacher got to the DA," I said. "Where to now?"

"We set up shop at Mom's old house," Veronica said. "Took me all day to clean out her crap, but it'll work for now."

29

BECK

PRESENT DAY

The old McDonough house had me longing for Shayla's place. Veronica's mother, Ethel, had been a prostitute with a severe drinking problem. She died of cirrhosis just before the book came out. Veronica wasn't a match for a partial liver transplant, and even that would've been a longshot since Ethel waited until she was nearly dead to tell her daughter.

As she got sicker, Ethel stopped keeping up with the place, which was already two steps from being condemned when Veronica moved out at eighteen. It was tucked around the corner from a strip mall built behind County Road K. Veronica kept insisting she was going to fix it up for rent, but her only investment had been paying the utility bills.

Veronica pointed down the hall lined with yellowing wallpaper. "I packed you a suitcase. Second room on the left."

It was obvious after opening the door that I'd walked into Veronica's old room. Though the corners were curling in, posters of Pink, Miley Cyrus and Katy Perry were on every wall. My suitcase was on the twin bed, below a hand-drawn poster pinned to the wall where a headboard would've been. It read V is for Verna—the name her mother used to call her—but stylized to look like the Vendetta comics.

I changed into a gray T-shirt and jeans. When I walked back out to the front half of the house, which included the living room and kitchen, Veronica and Shayla were seated at a dining table, two legs on matted brown carpet and two on cheap linoleum.

"Where's Caitlin?"

Veronica looked up from her phone and tossed her head to the side. "Out back."

Unwilling to walk through the master bedroom to the back door, I exited the front and descended the rotting porch steps. It was a quick trip around the house, and I found Caitlin cupping her elbow as she smoked, staring at two piles of rust, one of which used to be a Volkswagen Bug.

"I always figured you'd quit after law school."

She spoke without turning to face me. "I did, but I'm more stressed than usual."

I felt bad, but I was glad to have her on my side. I'd never met a more driven person, and when we were good—me working on the manuscript humanizing her mother, Caitlin working with a team of lawyers to get Mistress Samantha's sentence commuted to life—I had envisioned a power couple righting the world's injustices. But when it became clear I didn't have her work ethic, our relationship started to crack.

As I settled in beside her, I considered whether I should go through with it. Then again, Caitlin was my lawyer. If she was going to argue on my behalf, she deserved to know the truth.

"There's something you should know before we get any further into this. I—"

"Don't." Caitlin tossed her cigarette and ground it into the dirt with her shoe. "I don't need to know about what you did or didn't do."

She turned to look at me. "My team back in Dallas is working on a motion to dismiss based on insufficient evidence. For the hearing, I'll have that Walker woman who interviewed you saying she recommended no charges. The case won't go to trial, so I don't have to know anything about that night."

She didn't want to know, which meant she suspected I was guilty of the charges, even if the circumstances were far from what Grant Schuhmacher wanted everyone to believe.

Before I could decide whether to respect her wishes or blurt out the truth, Shayla opened the back door so hard it threatened to come off its hinges.

"Y'all are not going to believe this," she said before waving for us to follow her back into the house.

I was stunned at the drive-by announcement, but Caitlin reacted quickly, ascending the cinderblock pyramid that led to the door like a pro. I trailed behind, weaving my way through stacks of boxes and broken furniture, then jogging down the hall.

We gathered around the dining room table, where Veronica was ending a phone conversation.

"That was Agent Jackson," she said. "He just told me the pistol found with Darren Butler is the one that had been issued to Agent Casey Kelley."

As Caitlin and I searched for the appropriate reaction to this news, Shayla left the house to take a call of her own.

I took a step toward Veronica. "How does he know?"

"Serial number on the gun. Nobody'd even tried to get rid of it."

"So that means, what? This Darren guy also killed Hard Case Kelley?"

"Jackson thinks so," Veronica said. "What other explanation is there?"

Caitlin's heels crunched on the cheap kitchen flooring as she walked toward the fridge. She pulled out a longneck and tipped it back as though it might erase her decision to help. "This is all interesting, but none of it helps me."

Veronica reached under the table and came back up with her laptop. "Not in a courtroom. But I can hurt Schuhmacher's credibility by publishing a story tying him to what happened in Big Lake. Jackson said the FBI is opening an investigation now that they have new evidence. He's also turning in the ledger he got in the mail. If the sheriff and DA think Schuhmacher's going down, they may drop the charges."

Caitlin took another long pull from her beer as she considered Veronica's logic. "I don't know if it'll be as easy as that, but it wouldn't hurt."

As Veronica started typing, I had another question. "Aren't you still on suspension from the *Ledger*?"

"I am," she said, not looking up from her computer. "But Emily at *Manhattanist* is always asking me to write pieces for their dot coms. She'll convince her bosses to run this."

As she pounded her keyboard and Caitlin finished off her beer, Shayla opened the front door, looking deflated. "That was the lab tech in Austin. He said the DNA Jackson gave us was a bust."

Veronica wanted clarification. "No matches?"

Shayla shook her head. "No. Not anyone in CODIS. Not Darren Butler, either. I asked him to do a familial DNA test for CODIS and Interpol, just in case. But that'll take a few more days, even as a favor to me."

I sat down beside Veronica. "So now Darren Butler didn't kill Agent Kelley?"

Caitlin twisted off another bottlecap. "Not necessarily. If I understood Shayla correctly, we don't know the provenance of the blood, which means we have no idea if it belongs to the person who actually killed that FBI agent."

Caitlin and I turned to Shayla, who nodded. Veronica kept typing.

"But we do know Butler shot at y'all with the gun that was stolen from Kelley." Caitlin took a drink. "That's circumstantial, but it's pretty damning."

"But if the blood's a setup," I said, "what about the books proving Schuhmacher was using Franklin Jones to clean his money?"

Caitlin walked toward the dining table. "It could be a forgery. But even if it is, Butler's still tied to Schuhmacher through

Franklin Jones and the body shop. Combine that with the gun and new FBI investigation, and Schuhmacher looks like he's part of a conspiracy. And people eat that shit up."

"Don't I know it."

"But I'll say this," Caitlin said. "It's a damn good thing your freedom doesn't depend on us proving what really happened to Agent Kelley."

30

CASE KELLEY

FEBRUARY 21, 2000, 5:18 PM

Case's second cigarette was pure pleasure. The one he lit after exiting Sam's wasn't pleasant, but he'd choked it down out of spite.

Now that he was in the nursing home parking lot, sitting in his truck and staring at the aging building where he'd quarantined his mother, it was like he'd never quit.

Judy would be pissed when she smelled it on him later that night, though Case wondered if she had the gumption to say anything. She'd always held the moral high ground. With good reason.

She'd given up on her dream for him.

She'd done nearly all the adoption work.

She'd stayed home and raised their sons.

In return, he'd done his job well, provided her with a great life—or so he'd thought—and lived the way she'd asked.

Picking up old habits may seem like a small punishment for infidelity, but Case could think of nothing more intimate than blowing smoke in her face and talking to her with lips numbed from a few glasses of Jack or Jim.

Some men might cheat on their wives to get even. But that would be too tit-for-tat. Too transactional. Plus, Case didn't have anyone in mind. He didn't have some young secretary or subordinate he wanted to seduce. He'd done that once. Then he'd married her.

And without an immediate mark, what man had the time for an affair? Maybe once he was retired. But he'd do what, pick up women at a bar? At fifty-seven? Case kept himself in shape and Judy said the mostly bald buzzcut suited his face, but he wasn't barfly bait, at least not the kind that would attract something worth taking to a motel.

That whole scenario made Case feel dirty.

Instead, he'd go home and make sure she knew he was done listening to her. Hell, he might just make *her* sleep on the couch. How's that for a twist? She could move out, but to where? Her parents were both gone, and she'd been an only child. A hotel, perhaps, but he wouldn't shell out a goddamn dime to finance that.

No. He'd walk in, light one up, and sit down on the couch to catch *RAW*. She could try and talk things out with him, but Case would pretend to be far more concerned with what happened between The Rock and Triple H than what was going on between his wife and Terry.

And what of Terry, who was at once a supremely talented agent and a backstabbing sonofabitch? Case had the clout to punish him at work, relegate him to a desk, flag his file, and make sure he pulled some crap detail the rest of his career. But that would be a waste of an agent and make Case just as big a chicken shit.

Case pulled a fresh smoke out of the pack and lit it with the last. As he flicked the butt out of his window, Leonard, the nurse his mother was so impressed with, walked out of the front in a flashy black leather jacket and jeans. He pulled out his own pack and lit a cigarette as fast as he could.

Having his mother live in a no-smoking facility had been important to Case not that long ago, even though she hated it. Rather than use a walker and drag her oxygen tank outside, she'd taken up dipping. The home claimed to be tobacco free, but nobody was going to fuss over an old lady trying to get through her last days.

As Leonard walked, Case smiled at the sight of a nurse, someone purporting to keep people healthy, sucking down the same tar he was using to get back at his cheating wife. He also took a moment to laugh at Leonard's goofy name and the fact that he'd chosen a life doing women's work. Why would a young, strapping man choose to feed pills to dying old ladies?

It wasn't the politically correct thing to think, and if he were to say it around Judy, she'd slap him on the arm and tell him to get with the times. Maybe he'd tell her all about his feelings toward Leonard while cheering on The Rock.

Case took a final drag, tossed out the half-smoked cigarette, and reached to take his keys out of the ignition.

Then it happened again.

Like he'd done after his scuffle with Terry—one he would've won, even without Judy's help—Case decided to leave. He looked at the rolls of snuff in his passenger seat. Case could bring those to his mother some other time.

She was just one more person with expectations.

Case usually didn't mind putting others before himself. It's what good guys do. But today was his day off, and Case was going to be selfish for a change.

His truck started with a cough, and Leonard looked his way. The nurse knew Case's pickup. He sometimes helped Case's mother out of his cab after she and Case went for walks at a park around the corner. He'd also spent some time with the old lady, Case, and Judy when they stopped in to celebrate Christmas a few months back.

Leonard waved, a ribbon of smoke trailing from his right hand. He smiled, and Case saw what his mother saw. Hell, Case would even buy a pretty boy like him trying to make it in Hollywood instead of shooting up old farts with feel-good drugs.

Of course, being spotted meant he had to make Leonard

think he's going through with the visit, so Case slipped on his aviators and pulled out of the spot. He'd give the guy a vague work excuse, then pull back around and wait until Leonard cleared the parking lot.

Then Case would go back to his favorite dive bar for old time's sake and reminisce, maybe have a few before his date with the World Wrestling Federation.

The path out of the parking lot led him past Leonard, who was crushing his cigarette next to a Beamer when Case drove by.

"We'd given up on you, Mr. Kelley," Leonard said.

"Yeah, something came up at work. How's she doing?"

"She just fell asleep, actually."

Perfect. Now he doesn't have to make up an excuse. "Well, I won't disturb her, then. Have fun on your night shift."

"Actually, I'm off early today. I'm not sure what to do with myself."

"Oh, I'm sure you'll find something fun to do."

Case winked, then waved as he put the truck in gear.

Leonard returned the gesture, a devil-may-care smirk on his face.

31

BECK

PRESENT DAY

I'd gotten spoiled over the past few years, drinking hot English breakfast tea dispensed from K-cups.

I thought about that while pouring a glass of iced Lipton into a Mason jar. Not one sold at craft and hobby stores with fun lids or write-your-own labels, but one that had been filled with jam when Ethel McDonough purchased it during Veronica's childhood. Or maybe it was one Ethel herself had inherited. Perhaps, like the kitchen I was standing in, it had been passed down three generations, re-used to jar homemade jam, then relegated to the cupboard after receiving the chip that marked where I had to stop pouring from an equally antique pitcher.

Thanks to our efforts yesterday, those items were at least clean. The tub and showerhead I'd just used were not. Instead of a full shower, I'd settled for hanging my head and shirtless torso over the side and using Veronica's surprisingly subtle shampoo. That and extra deodorant—which Veronica had remembered to pack, along with my toothbrush—would suffice until Caitlin could do her magic.

As I drank, I surveyed the opposite side of the table. Veronica's laptop was still open, but its keyboard was covered with loose pages. A few were from the ledger Agent Jackson had given us. One was a printout of the invoice from Darren Butler's body shop, which had taken a trip to a copy place in the strip mall down the road.

Veronica had stayed up late writing and, presumably, emailing the story to her friendly *Manhattanist Magazine* editor by using the wireless hotspot on her cell. Before I called it a night, she'd given me the seven-digit code for the phone and the password to her computer. I tried not to read into the fact it was *ButchHeller1990!*, an ode to the man who used to sit and drink at this table, plus her birth year.

She'd also left her keys on the table and told me to use the car if I needed, but to leave a note. I had no idea what time she'd dragged herself to Ethel's old bed, but when I'd peeked in, she was snoring in her clothes.

I chugged the rest of the tea, picked up her phone, and tapped the numbers. Next was the green dialogue bubble, which brought up her messages. The last one was sent to *Emily M, Manhattanist* at 4:23 AM.

Emailed you the story. Let me know if you have any Qs.

The next conversation was with Caitlin. It just contained a reply with the name of my ex-girlfriend-turned-attorney from when they traded numbers.

I thumbed a message to Caitlin.

It's Beck. Can I come over? Talk strategy?

She texted *K* almost immediately and provided the address and room number.

I shoved Veronica's keys into my left front pocket out of habit, feeling half-naked without a cellphone on the other side. Next came a light jacket to protect against the autumn morning. Then, before leaving as quietly as was possible on the creaky floor, I turned over a sheet of copy paper and grabbed Veronica's blue pen.

Went to meet Caitlin. Call her cell if you need me — Beck

———

CAITLIN, dressed in sweatpants and a baggy sweatshirt, sipped coffee out of a blue mug on the balcony of a Main Street bed and breakfast. She didn't seem to recognize the car as I parked, so I waited a beat. She used to wear the same clothes while we read the *Dallas Morning News* in our apartment.

She caught me watching through the windshield and waved me up to her perch on the second floor.

The door was ajar, but I knocked just to be on the safe side. The room looked barely slept in, including the bed, whose cream comforter was tucked in and looked freshly smoothed.

"Did you make the bed this morning?"

Caitlin stood and turned before I could make it out to the balcony. "Shayla and I sampled all the local breweries and wineries, then took a couple bottles to her room." She walked toward a small desk and motioned for me to sit on the leather chair. "We passed out there. She'll be hurting when she wakes up."

I took my seat before she handed me a tablet with a document filling the screen. It took a moment for me to realize it was the motion to dismiss my case. Caitlin's team took nearly a dozen pages to say Grant Schuhmacher had manipulated the DA into filing the charges, which were nothing more than retaliation for my justified killing of his son.

While it was all true, the argument wasn't going to play well coming from an outsider like Caitlin.

"Please tell me you haven't filed this already."

She took another sip and glared over her mug—a look I'd

nearly forgotten. "Most clients trust me to handle pre-trial motions."

I took a deep breath and was about to explain my frustration when she held up her palm.

"But you're not most clients, which is why I have two versions for you to choose from."

Caitlin sat her coffee on the desk and took the tablet from my hands.

"I think you'll find this one bland enough," she said before returning to the black office chair.

She was right, and I nodded while skimming through the document. "Judge Grantham will probably appreciate this one much more. Not that it'll do much good."

"Schuhmacher may have the sheriff and DA in his pocket, but I think the judge liked us. I really think you should consider letting me make the case that Schuhmacher is railroading you."

Maybe she was right. Caitlin was a hell of a lawyer, after all. Even after I'd failed to sell the manuscript about her mother, Caitlin fought and won an appeal to get her mother off Death Row.

That was the last conversation we'd had. We hadn't been together for a year, and I was preparing to go to work with Jorge for the first time. She surprised me with Chinese from a place just up the road from my shitty East Fort Worth apartment. Between her glowing face and the smell of restaurant food, I couldn't say no, despite how badly we'd left things.

"Tell you what," I said. "You order us some breakfast and I'll think about it."

She picked up the black receiver and ordered a fruit plate for her and a Western omelet for me, along with a carafe of hot water and bags of English breakfast.

"You remembered," I said.

"You ate it every Sunday for more than a year," she said. "You'd've needed another credit card just for brunch if we'd stayed together much longer."

I was desperate back then, too. But not just desperate for money. Desperate for recognition. For affection. And, after spending time together mapping out the manuscript, for her.

Most of my memories of our courtship were pleasant. Time does that, they say. But there are moments that I will never forget about the night it ended.

The thud of a champaign bottle after dropping it to the cheap carpeting of a law student's apartment floor. Her black bra draped on the back of a beige futon next to a green graphic T-shirt that wasn't mine. Thick cologne mixed with sex as I crept toward her bedroom.

Still, I smiled. "We did have some good times."

Caitlin downed the rest of her coffee, then dropped her eyes to the mug, perhaps hoping the leftover grounds contained a message about how to get out of the conversation. "A few, maybe."

I shifted to face her more directly. "Look, I know things ended badly, but—"

Her head shot up, eyes wide. "Badly? You threw a bottle of cheap wine into the wall in my apartment. I lost my deposit, and they charged me for fixing the hole and new carpeting because the stain wouldn't come out."

Maybe it was wine, not champagne. And maybe I had thrown it through the sheet rock rather than dropping it. But those details shouldn't have mattered.

"I did catch you with some fratboy douchebag." I took another calming breath. "That doesn't erase the rest of the relationship, though."

Caitlin put the mug down and cleared her throat. "I'll admit, the first month or so was great. Seeing you excited had me excited, and I got caught up in it with you. But then you went down into your hole and never came out. Every time I tried to ask if you were okay, you were either sullen or angry. You didn't even want to sleep with me anymore."

I focused on a spot on the floor. There was no use denying

any of that. But it was still beside the point. "Then why didn't you just leave me? Why'd you lie and say you were studying at the library that night? I came over to set up a surprise romantic dinner."

"Yeah, to let me know you were done with the manuscript. It was always about you and that goddamn book."

I clenched my teeth and fought the anger, but it had taken hold. "I was writing that *goddamn book* for you. And I wrote knowing I probably couldn't sell it because I had to lie for you and Shayla. Maybe that's why I was in such a bad mood all the time."

Though I was almost yelling, Caitlin remained calm. "There were a lot of things wrong with us. And to answer your question, I didn't leave you because I thought you might hurt yourself if I did. That's why I came over that day to let you know my mom's sentence had been commuted to life. I felt sorry for you, Beck. I still do."

We were interrupted by a knock. Caitlin stood to get the room service but turned after a few steps. "I am glad you remember us so fondly. Maybe when I'm your age, I will, too."

I slumped in the chair and looked back down at the tablet. The words hadn't changed, just my mood.

I'd been hated. Mistrusted. Lied to and lied about.

But this was the first time I'd been pitied.

I was still staring into my lap when Shayla's voice brought me back to the present.

"Why don't you look hung over?" she asked Caitlin.

"Three cups of coffee. And I drink more than you."

I looked up and found Shayla in athletic shorts and a gray tank top. She smiled, so I forced one and nodded. "Morning."

Shayla yawned in response before turning back to Caitlin. "So, what's on the docket today?"

She smiled at her own pun. Caitlin shook her head. "You and your lawyer jokes."

Caitlin motioned for me to hand her the tablet. "Today I'll file a motion to dismiss, then drive back and wait for the judge to set a hearing date. You should go home, too."

Shayla shrugged. "I'm on leave for at least another five days, and the DNA tech has my cell. This is a cute town. Maybe I'll see if Veronica will let me crash with her. Make a vacation out of it."

She turned to me, and I got the feeling she was about to ask for permission. But before either of us could talk, Caitlin got a call.

"It's Veronica." She looked at me. "She did give you permission to take her car, right?"

"Yeah. She probably just wants us to go pick her up."

Caitlin greeted Veronica, then let loose a string of expletives.

"Don't let them in until I get there. If they break down your door, I'll pay to get it fixed." She put the phone on the desk and tapped the screen as Shayla and I squeezed beside her. "You're on speaker now. Tell them what you just told me."

"A guy who claims to be the sheriff is outside banging on my door. He's got a few other guys in uniform with him, and a guy in a suit. I think it's the DA from yesterday, but I can't tell."

We could hear the banging in the background, adding to the panic that was creeping from my stomach to my lungs and heart. "They must think I'm in there."

"I'm not sure," Veronica said. "All they've said is my name and that I need to open the door because they have a search warrant. They haven't said what for or mentioned anyone's name."

"We're on our way," Caitlin said. "But before they force their way in, hide your phone and computer. If they find it, oh well. If not, they won't know what we have on you-know-who. If they try to ask you questions, tell them you're waiting on your attorney."

32

BECK

PRESENT DAY

Veronica had been right about the guy in the suit, and I had no doubt the lean mustachioed man standing next to Jeremy Wolff was his father. They were still outside, while deputies were inside searching the house. We could see them tearing the place apart because they'd propped open the front door with one of the cinderblocks that littered the overgrown McDonough land.

The younger Wolff stepped forward to meet Caitlin after we slammed the doors to her Porsche, which she'd parked on the road next to a jet-black pickup with tinted windows.

She didn't wait to hear his argument.

"You have no right to—"

"And good morning to you, too, Ms. Parks." He flashed a smile, though it was far from disarming.

"I'm Ms. Stein's attorney. Where is your search warrant?"

"Your client has her copy. You're welcome to join her inside." He stepped to the side and motioned for her to proceed, which she did while telling us to stay put.

I waited for Caitlin to enter the house, then started toward the man trying to put me away. But before I could get to Jeremy Wolff, his father stepped up and stuck out a calloused hand.

"Stop right there," he said through a dip so large I could see the tobacco rising above his bottom lip. "This don't concern you."

"The hell it doesn't. You're harassing my friend to get to me." I took a step back and opened my arms wide. "It worked. I'm right here."

Jeremy Wolff stepped even with his father. "Mr. Beck, I don't think you've been properly introduced. This is my father, Nimitz County Sheriff James Wolff, though most folks call him Jimbo when he's not in uniform."

Jeremy mumbled something to his father, who pointed toward me and mumbled back. I stepped forward to hear their conversation, but Sheriff Wolff turned and started walking inside.

I continued my advance toward Jeremy but held up my palms. "Look, I know this isn't your idea. I've known Grant Schuhmacher a long time—long enough to know that he gets his way. So I want you and Jumbo to get a message back to him."

His blue eyes didn't blink as he nodded for me to continue.

"Tell him if he stops coming after the people I care about, I'll give him what he wants."

Wolff's lips tilted into a crooked grin. "And what does he want?"

I wasn't entirely sure, but I knew what *I* wanted.

I wanted to stop the fight. To stop getting calls about my friends being hurt and harassed. To stop defending myself against barbs in the press and bullets from a dead FBI agent's gun.

Most of all, I wanted to sleep without knocking myself out every night and to wake up without wondering when everything was going to collapse.

I'd rather stand in the ruins.

"A confession," I said. "In open court, then to his lapdog Parker Mallory."

Wolff's smile widened. "I'm happy to take that right here. Save everyone the trouble."

"No. I want plenty of witnesses. And tell him I'll be telling the truth, not that horseshit he had Parker write."

His eyes moved from mine and focused on a spot over my shoulder, where I imagined Shayla was giving him her meanest go-to-hell look.

"I can deliver your message, but I don't see that working out for you." Wolff stepped back, his eyes still trained on Shayla. "But congratulations on the new girlfriend. She's one hot piece of—"

He was interrupted by two thick deputies as they emerged from the house on either side of Veronica, her face red and hands cuffed behind her back. Caitlin wasn't far behind. She was talking fast and holding what had to be the search warrant.

I caught up with the group as they reached one of the two sheriff's SUVs parked in the driveway. One of the uniforms was holding a gallon-sized bag.

"We'll get you out soon," I told Veronica just before the door shut.

When I turned, Caitlin was reading the document.

"What the hell?" I asked.

"They had a search warrant for drugs and drug paraphernalia due to the increased activity at a suspicious residence." She was still reading the document. "And one of the deputies said he found a gallon-sized bag of meth. That's enough for a distribution charge."

The SUV peeled out next to us, sending gravel and dust so thick we had to retreat toward Shayla, who was leaning against the Porsche.

"So?" Shayla asked.

"They planted drugs in the house," I said.

"They're claiming the property is under surveillance because it was known for prostitution and drug use when her mom was there," Caitlin said. "When they saw the cars and multiple people in and out, they suspected criminal activity had resumed."

"What a crock of shit," I said.

"I've seen judges sign off with a lot less probable cause," Shayla said.

Caitlin folded the papers and stuffed them into her back pocket. "Me too. And proving that a sheriff's deputy planted evidence is next to impossible."

They looked at the ground. Neither of them wanted to tell me what I already knew. The charges were going to stick, and Veronica might do serious prison time.

Schuhmacher was going to win.

33

TERRY JACKSON

FEBRUARY 21, 2000, 5:26 PM

Terry cracked open another Diet Dr Pepper and surveyed the mess of paper spread across his coffee table.

He'd spent an hour driving around after the blowup at Case's house. Terry's first instinct had been to tail his boss and confront him when he stopped. He hated leaving the situation unresolved.

Then he put himself in Case's shoes. While Terry was confused and hurt, Case was probably livid. Terry had been worried he'd hit Judy, and perhaps Case drove off to allow himself time to cool down.

So that's what Terry did. And after his hands stopped shaking on the Corvette's steering wheel, Terry returned home to do the other thing that would keep his mind occupied with anything but Judy and Case.

Work.

He'd read the documents dozens of times already, though he was an expert skimmer. And he never considered the investigation his responsibility. The federal government already had an entire branch of law enforcement dedicated to working drug cases. Why should the Bureau waste resources like Terry doing work that the DEA should handle themselves?

On the other hand, Terry had taken his appointment to the Organized Crime Drug Enforcement Task Force as a major atta-boy from Case, even if he was at the bottom of the local unit, known as a strike force. Confusing? Yes. Effective? That remained to be seen.

The government formed the OCDETF in the '80s to fight its war on drugs and roped in every branch—even the Postal Service. Then came the permanent strike forces, including the one in Houston, which handled the coast and South Texas. Terry wasn't on the regular roster, but when Houston called Case needing help investigating new drug activity in San Antonio, Terry was traded to the strike force for a favor to be named later.

Case was running out of time to cash in that favor. Plus, after what he'd done, giving Case closure on this project felt right, even if all it did was sooth Terry's guilt. And all Terry had to do was help find the asshole stealing fentanyl for the heroin dealers.

Terry picked up the largest of his files, which documented a series of street busts performed by undercover SAPD officers. Getting H in South Texas was easy, and junkies overdosing was nothing new. But lately, there'd been a spike in deaths from its much stronger cousin.

The narcotics detectives went in and asked if the usual dealers could get them this superdrug. After the undercovers finally got one to bite, the SAPD flipped him, giving the task force a valuable confidential informant.

Terry found a different folder. This one contained affidavits, mostly from DEA agents. The strike force had been hopeful after the initial bust, but they'd been working for more than a year, making their way up to the main connection. They'd also been tracking missing doses of fentanyl from local hospitals and their in-house pharmacies. Most were barely statistically significant, but local dealers could make a small amount of the stuff go a long way. It was at least fifty times stronger than morphine.

Since it was such a localized issue, Houston wanted more San Antonio resources.

Enter Terry.

Though he wasn't fully invested, he'd made some headway. About six months ago, Terry got a nickname from a supplier-turned-snitch. *Pretty Boy.* He didn't have a Christian name for the guy, and the description was about as vague as they come: white, about six feet, dark hair. Maybe a cleft chin. Kind of reminded the CI of the actor from the asteroid movie. Not Bruce Willis, but the younger one.

The lead had gone nowhere. When Terry reported the progress to Case, he went to some of his old informants from his SAPD days. But Case swore he'd talked to everyone he knew and had still come up with nothing.

Terry thumbed through more documents but couldn't focus. This wasn't the investigation he needed to be working, no matter what Case said. If he really wanted to help, Terry should be trying to connect Schuhmacher to Flynn.

He needed to stop looking at these files and start reading that ledger Case had gotten from his source in Hinterbach.

HE WAS PREPARED for the worst. But after leaving three messages on her machine, Terry had no choice but to return to Judy. Once again, he'd prepared a speech, but he didn't know if it would work this time.

As he opened the door to his car, she opened the door to her house. One hand was occupied by the doorknob, while the other gripped a mini baseball bat, the kind marketed to children at minor-league games.

"You've got some nerve," she said, barreling across her front porch and down the steps.

Terry opened his palms but kept them at his side, ready to protect against the wooden baton with a sketch of the Alamo near the top. "I'm not here for you. I'm here for Case."

Judy didn't slow her advance. Instead she leapt forward and

raised the bat above her head. As it arced toward his face, Terry palmed it with his left hand and used his right to secure Judy's free wrist.

After struggling and realizing she couldn't escape his grip, Judy relaxed for a moment.

It was just enough.

As Terry began dropping his arms, Judy bared her teeth and swung her shin squarely between his legs.

He doubled over, tears stinging his eyes and lungs unable to hold air. Between gasps, Terry tried explaining that he'd returned for the ledger Case had brought back from his meeting that afternoon.

"Huh?" Judy asked after retrieving her bat.

"The ledger," he managed. "The black book he hit me with."

"What about it?"

Terry coughed and got to his knees. "It's part of a major investigation we're working, so I wanted to read it. To help Case. That's why I was calling. Nobody called back, so I came over. But just to look at the ledger, I swear."

Judy let her bat-wielding arm drop. "What makes you think it's here?"

"IT'S MY FAULT," Terry said. "Not yours."

They'd looked everywhere and agreed on two points. Case never made it into the house, and neither Terry nor Judy ever took possession of the ledger.

Neither could remember whether Case had taken it with him.

That's why Judy had called the nursing home. Terry had hoped someone would put Case on the phone. Then Case could tell Judy he had the thing, and they'd move on with their new lives the next morning.

Instead, the news had gotten even worse.

"If he didn't go there, then what the hell is going on?" Judy asked.

He thought she was speaking rhetorically, but when she looked up from the phone and slapped his arm, Terry knew he had to say something.

"We'll send a 911 to his beeper, but I'm sure he just went to blow off some steam. He'll be back to watch wrestling."

"Case doesn't blow off steam. He comes home and talks to me."

Terry knew that wasn't always true, but now was not the time to argue with her. "Where else does he go on the weekends?"

Judy shook her head. "Nowhere. If we're not together, he's either visiting his mother or with you, working when he shouldn't be."

Terry knew Case would be back in a few hours. He wouldn't jeopardize a career, pension, and the Schuhmacher case. And despite the affair, he still loved Judy. Terry had seen that in Case's eyes before he left.

But Case had Judy worried, and she was going to go crazy staring at that phone until someone called with news. So, Terry made a plan.

"How about this," he said. "I'll drive to the nursing home, talk to some more folks, maybe see if they have video of the lobby."

Judy stood up so fast the couch slid across the hardwood.

Terry rushed to get between her and the door. "You need to stay here in case he comes back."

"Screw you. I'm not going to just sit here and wait like some useless goddamn housewife."

Terry had anticipated her reaction and developed a counter-argument. "And what's Case going to think if he comes back and your car's here, but you're not? That you ran off with me? That someone else has you? He'll be worried, just like you are now."

She stood still for a moment, processing, then turned and pointed a finger in his face.

"Call me the second you know something."

34

BECK

PRESENT DAY

Veronica's house looked like someplace FEMA might've set up shop after a coastal hurricane, down to water flowing onto the linoleum.

Shayla emerged from the bathroom after rushing to shut off the bath and sink faucets. I met her at the edge of the kitchen, where the sink had been on full blast with both drains plugged. We slopped toward Caitlin, who'd remained near the front door, declining to expose her expensive-looking shoes to the filtered creek water.

"Assholes," Shayla muttered.

I toed an ancient copy of *National Geographic,* one from the rickety bookshelf that had been tossed onto the living room floor. "So that's not standard procedure when executing a search warrant?"

Shayla let out a throaty laugh, which seemed inappropriate for the circumstances. Then again, my life had been held up to a funhouse mirror, so maybe seeing the humor was a natural reaction. The restraint Veronica showed while watching those sheriff's deputies set out to ruin what remained of her late mother's life was beyond my comprehension.

"I should get to the jail," Caitlin said. "After she's booked, I'll let her know you're cleaning up. Then I'll stop by Wolff's office and see what I can work out with him."

Though I knew the law was no longer governing his actions, I let Caitlin leave. She'd feel more in control of the situation, which might keep her in our corner. Otherwise, she had no reason to keep helping.

Shayla's version of taking control was cleaning. She slipped out of her flats and power walked to the hall closet for the mop and bucket. "You get started in the bathroom."

I obeyed and took a cue from her, untying my sneakers and balling up the socks before tiptoeing into the other flood zone. With the mop in use, it was probably a six-towel job, and that included wringing them out and re-using them.

The towel I used that morning wasn't draped over the shower curtain, so I opened the slightly off-kilter cabinet door in the corner. No towels there, either.

I splashed to the bathroom door and peeked out at Shayla. "Where'd you put the towels yesterday?"

She looked at me like a five-year-old being told to clean their room. "The cabinet in the bathroom. Where else?"

I opened my mouth to explain but thought better of it. Instead, I walked across the hall for the next best thing: blankets. As I took a step into the closet in search of the light switch, my bare foot sunk a fraction of an inch into the carpet. I stopped and tested the floorboard again.

A hidden door.

I flicked on the light, knelt to the ground, and found a seam in the carpet. It came up easily, which meant Veronica had used it earlier.

Before pulling on the exposed floorboard, I called out to Shayla. "Could you get me a—"

She tapped me on the shoulder with a flashlight.

I nodded my thanks and hesitated for another moment before opening the door.

IF IT'D HAPPENED ten minutes earlier, we might have missed the sound of Veronica's phone buzzing on the coffee table.

We'd finished sopping up the floors—which were probably as clean as they'd been in years—and had the house mostly put back together when the sound brought us to the living room.

I relaxed a bit when I read *Emily Dreyer Manhattanist* on the damaged screen, its hairline fractures now outlined in dank mud. Veronica had been in such a hurry that careful placement wasn't an option, and the phone had bounced loose from the towels that she'd wrapped around her cell and her computer.

I wasn't sure how much to tell Emily. She was the media elite and would probably barter with her appendages to get a few million clicks. Then again, Veronica trusted her. And right now, using her publication to put pressure on Schuhmacher was our best bet to get her out of jail—and keep me from going back.

I tapped the green receiver and the speakerphone icon so Shayla could add law enforcement insight if necessary.

"Emily, this is Beck. Veronica's been arrested."

"Holy shit."

"Yeah. It's all pretty effed up."

"Well, I was calling about the story she emailed last night. Our editors wanted to run it in the morning on both *Culturist* and *Ingelligentsia,* if we could get a few things checked. But it sounds like—"

"I can help you out. I'm also sitting next to the woman who shot the men in Big Lake, so she'll have whatever answers I don't."

Shayla gave me a what-the-hell look, so I added, "On background only. Not for attribution." I smiled. "But I also have the cell number for Veronica's lawyer, so I can conference her in for on-the-record quotes."

We heard a chuckle from the slightly fuzzy speaker. "Yeah,

that'll work. Good thing, too. My bosses can't wait to stick it to Parker Mallory."

35

BECK

PRESENT DAY

A jolt of adrenaline hit me as the email popped into Veronica's inbox.

Re: Schuhmacher / Mallory takedown

The attachment was Emily's edited version of the piece, which I opened and began reading, with Shayla squeezing in beside me.

It was obvious from the headline and opening paragraphs that Veronica had forgone all notions of objectivity. She'd written an opinion piece dripping with her voice.

I loved it.

Did this US congressman have an FBI agent killed 23 years ago? If so, he also tried to kill my friends.

By Veronica Stein @vsteinscribe

Grant Schuhmacher is as crooked as they come, even for a member of Congress.

Until this week, however, the rumors had circled around tax evasion schemes and money laundering. His rise from mayor of a two-bit Central Texas town to chair of a major House committee was fueled by a massive campaign war chest, one that seemed to have no bottom despite a merely lukewarm reception in most national Republican circles.

But then a man named Darren Butler tried to kill my friend last week in a West Texas shootout that also involved a sheriff's deputy and a man who went by the nickname Chuck D.

Butler died in the exchange, but he left behind the key to unlocking Schuhmacher's dark past.

Next, Veronica recapped the background on Butler and his use of Agent Kelley's old service weapon, the alternate-history version of Summer Foster's death, and the life and death of Butch Heller.

This is where Emily needed some reassurance.

"The main issue we have is the part about Jim Flynn. I know Veronica said she's seen the ledger, but even after everything that happened, he's still got enough juice to put up a fight if we're not a hundred percent on that."

I understood her point—especially after finding myself on the receiving end of two bullshit lawsuits—but taking out those facts would gut the story. I scanned that section.

"It says she's seen the ledger's pages, which is true. We saw a photocopied set together when her anonymous FBI source gave them to us, then reviewed the copy ourselves. Flynn Consulting is referenced several times."

"Where's that copy now? Can I see it?"

I looked at Shayla, who reached down and muted our end of the call. "They have everything in evidence lockup. I couldn't leak them even if I were in the office, let alone from here."

Emily would have to take my word for it. And as I unmuted the call, I thought of one more way to ease her mind.

"I don't have immediate access to the documents, but the FBI agent has the original. After he makes the arrest, Veronica will have access to it again. I'm sure she'll be able to get photos for you to use if Flynn sues you."

After a few moments of silence, I had an idea.

"How about you quote me as saying I saw Flynn's name in the pages. That way you have some deniability."

"No, I love her voice and don't want anyone else's in there. You'll be a second source, and I'll count her federal agent as number three if anyone asks."

Emily typed for a few seconds then cleared her throat. "Now, since I have you, I might's well ask: Is her timeline for the shootout right? And did she really post your bail?"

Veronica had been straightforward, so a simple *yes* did the trick.

The rest of her story was pretty much a character assassination of Schuhmacher and Mallory, which Emily said the *Manhattanist* executives had already signed off on, especially since Veronica wasn't giving me a free pass, either.

It's true that the Texas Rangers found evidence that contradicts Beck's testimony. But then Schuhmacher accused Beck of several murders in a libelous story written by a smarmy excuse for a reporter (Yes, Parker, I'm talking about you), and now a district attorney in the town Schuhmacher once ruled is preparing his opening remarks.

Doesn't it make more sense, though, that Schuhmacher would have helped cover up the fact that his friend Franklin Jones killed Summer Foster all those years ago?

Yes, that means Beck was part of said coverup and lied under oath. But he was a teenager, and that's a hell of a jump from being put away for murder.

And since Schuhmacher is one to engage in a coverup, what are the chances he at least helped cover up the murder of Agent Kelley?

Or, since Kelley was investigating Schuhmacher's involvement with a man we now know was almost as shady as Schuhmacher himself, was the good congressman more directly involved in Darren Butler's dirty deeds?

I don't have the answers.

Yet.

The FBI is investigating all of this. They're also looking into connections between Butler and Chuck D, who may have helped plan and cause an explosion that severely injured a close friend of Beck's and mine.

And where Butler is, a trail will lead back to Grant Schuhmacher, like a slug crawling across your back porch.

So now you're asking yourself, why would Schuhmacher wait until now to execute this grand scheme of smearing Beck's name and trying to kill him and his friend?

Veronica answered the question by recapping the events that led to Paul's death, and a dig at Parker that made me grin.

That part of Parker Mallory's story was actually true.

"Well, I think that's all I needed," Emily said.

I was about to say goodbye when I realized what would give Veronica's column a bit more punch. "Since this is all about her, why not add that Schuhmacher had her arrested?"

"I don't think we can. What you're reading is as risky as my editors are willing to get with Schuhmacher and Parker."

I muted the call again and turned to Shayla.

"If it comes down to it, will you go on the record saying you were here and there were no drugs? That the sheriff's deputies must've planted them?"

"Oh yeah. I'm gonna report that shit anyway."

I unmuted the phone. "Me and the law enforcement source were there for the arrest and were with Veronica in the days leading up to it. We'd love to testify that they planted evidence. Plus, the district attorney intimated to me that Schuhmacher was the one pulling his strings."

Emily was so quiet I could hear her nails clicking on the desk until she spoke again.

"Fine. We'll put something in after she asks why Schuhmacher waited until now, then let them decide."

I typed up a couple of sentences and emailed them to her.

(And have me thrown in jail on a trumped-up charge. That's right, someone else wrote this sentence because I was arrested before the story could get published.)

"What do you think?" I asked.

"I think it sounds just like Veronica. You've been working together a long time."

I frowned. The way things were going, I didn't know how long our partnership would last. But rather than worry about it, I focused on the next step.

We had to get Veronica out of jail.

36

BECK

PRESENT DAY

I recognized the smile on Veronica's face. It's the same one I'd worn upon my release from an overnight stay at the Nimitz County Jail.

"Just be glad your bail wasn't as high as mine," I said as she wrapped me in a hug. "Otherwise I might've had to think twice."

The joke worked, though her laugh was accompanied by tears. "Thank you so much." She looked over my shoulder to Caitlin and Shayla. "All of you."

Veronica squeezed one more time and stepped back. "I'm just glad they didn't find my phone and computer. They're—"

Shayla held up her phone. "We found the trap door."

Veronica took two quick steps and had the device palmed before we had a chance to answer her next question. "Did you get any word about the story?"

All three of us smiled.

"It's up," I said. "Shayla and I answered some questions yesterday, and I wrote a couple of sentences about them arresting you before the story was published."

Veronica tapped the device to life, pausing for a moment to

notice the new mud embedded in the glass before opening a browser and finding the article. "Any response from Parker or the *Post*?"

I hadn't thought to look, though I wasn't waging my own personal media war with a Pulitzer winner.

Veronica shook off our blank stares and went to work on her phone. "Nothing from him. The paper put out a statement on Twitter, sticking by the story. The article, quote, went through the same rigorous fact-checking process as all stories published by the *Post*, and Parker Mallory is among the most respected journalists working today."

While Shayla and Caitlin attacked Parker, I looked around the courthouse, remembering his presence at my trial. Assuming the Wolffs were after Veronica on behalf of Schuhmacher…

I stepped closer to the circle and lowered my voice. "Don't react."

They froze but did as I asked.

"He hasn't posted anything because he's here. Sitting on the bench beside the DA's office."

Veronica's face turned pink, then began to darken. "Is he videoing us?"

I nodded. Though he was known for his prose, Parker would tell you after a few drinks that his endgame was on-camera work. After my arraignment, he'd edited my perp walk and posted the footage on his social media with his own narration. The video was retweeted and shared tens of thousands of times and shown on all the major cable networks.

I took two steps and put myself between the camera and Veronica's beet-red face. "I'll stand back here. You three start walking toward the front. If he chases us, he'll have to deal with me."

As we moved, I tried listening for Parker's steps behind me, though the echo of our own shoes in the cavernous foyer made that nearly impossible. When we hit the cool October air, I wheeled around.

Nothing.

I stood guard for a few more moments before feeling confident Parker's cowardice had won out against his need for impressions and social reach.

Still, we hustled to Caitlin's Macan, then her tires squealed as she turned toward the highway that led to County Road K.

Veronica leaned forward so her face was nearly beside Caitlin. "When am I due back in court?"

"Monday." She found me in the rearview mirror. "You'll be waiting a few months. At least."

The SUV went nearly silent, a gentle hum of the road our only distraction from an increasingly helpless situation. Caitlin had the power to argue on our behalf in court. But against those aligned with the likes of Schuhmacher and Jones? Hope was in short supply.

Caitlin didn't know it yet, but I was going to demand she put me on the stand for my trial.

Before that, I had to convince Veronica to let me stay in her house. I'd have to sell my condo in Austin—perhaps to her if she wanted it—but all that money would go to paying Caitlin.

Then there was Shayla. She'd saved Jorge's life that night in Big Lake. Saved my life. And for her troubles, she'd been put on leave, though she'd probably head back in a few hours.

Unless I asked her to stay.

But that was the talk of a crazy man, one looking ahead to months of solitude and then a lifetime in his own personal hell. Shayla was nearly ten years younger and had a good job waiting for her.

A string of colorful curse words from Veronica pulled me out of the pity party.

"Schuhmacher's here," she said, holding up her phone to reveal the *Daily Times* headline. "He's campaigning hard now that the election's only two weeks away. He has a town hall in Kerrville tomorrow, then another one in Hinterbach on Monday afternoon."

Shayla took the phone. "Which means—"

Caitlin finished. "Schuhmacher'll be at the courthouse for your hearing, ready to give interviews to anyone with a pen or a camera."

That a congressman was campaigning in his district in the days before an election shouldn't have been surprising. But Grant Schuhmacher had shied away from the public and media since I'd killed Paul. The *Post* had even run a piece last year about his absence. The story quoted two anonymous staffers as saying he'd fallen into a depression following Paul's death.

I'd been skeptical given the fact he'd disowned his felonious embarrassment of a son, but his lack of bravado in the media and on the House floor had been noticeable.

Shayla was still reading the *Daily Times* story when Veronica's cell started vibrating.

"It's the FBI guy," she said. "Agent Jackson."

WHEN THE LIGHT finally appeared at the end of my tunnel, I didn't react.

Veronica did, spilling out the good news as fast as she could, then immediately calling Emily to file another story.

Caitlin did, absorbing Veronica's chatter then using the SUV's Bluetooth to call her team back in Dallas.

Shayla did, putting a hand on my knee, then updating her supervisors.

When the conversations ended and Caitlin finally parked, the group turned to look at me. Nobody said anything for a few excruciating beats. Caitlin and Shayla eventually turned to Veronica and silently appointed her their spokeswoman.

"Beck, you know what this means, right?"

"It means the last week was nothing compared to what's coming."

Veronica opened her mouth, then shut it before finding the right question for what must've sounded like a nonsensical response. "How do you figure? We're this close to clearing your name."

I shook my head. "When the FBI raids Franklin Jones's compound, what do you think they'll find? These aren't the kind of guys who leave evidence. And I've seen Jones at his worst. He won't confess to anything."

"You don't know that," Veronica said. "At least things are moving in the right direction."

I opened the Macan's door. "Not fast enough. I'll be convicted before the FBI can prove anything."

"Thanks for the vote of confidence," Caitlin said before grabbing her purse and throwing open her door. "You're a real piece of work."

Veronica also left in a huff, muttering something about me being a prick.

Shayla cleared her throat. "Beck, I know you're a dark guy. And I understand why better than any of them." She paused for a moment to let me read between the lines. "But you have people putting their asses on the line for you. You could at least pretend to be grateful."

We stared at each other for a few long seconds. I should've known she'd figure it out eventually. Shayla was one of the smartest and most capable people I'd ever met, and she's heard all the evidence.

My mouth was slack, waiting for a thousand things to come out.

I should've said I didn't set out to kill Summer. Yes, the guilt had turned me dark, but I had a plan. I was developing feelings I knew she'd never reciprocate.

In the end, I mustered the one thing I absolutely owed her.

"I'm sorry."

I was halfway to the house when I heard Shayla answer the

phone behind me. I heard *hi* and *uh-huh* before an excited *holy shit* made me stop and turn.

"That familial DNA test came back," she said. "And if this doesn't put a smile on your face, I don't know what to tell you."

37

PATTY BUTLER

PRESENT DAY

Patty opened and closed the front door with care. Not because she wanted to surprise Frank. He had security cameras and alarms that sounded when someone got close to the house. But he hated slamming doors, and Patty didn't want to put him on edge.

She needed him calm.

"What are you doing here?" he asked from the den.

"It's First Friday."

Patty walked through the never-used living room. Every month for decades, she'd gone out to Frank's land, driven her increasingly more expensive cars the mile-plus up to his ranch-style McMansion, and turned his master bathroom into a private barbershop.

He'd installed a chair opposite the mirror years ago and offered to buy a set of tools to leave there, but Patty insisted on bringing her own.

She snapped on a pair of red nitrile gloves and was unpacking the black bag when Frank finally shuffled in.

"I'm surprised you came today, considering all you're going through," he said. "I didn't even wash my hair."

All you're going through. By that, of course, Frank meant the death of her husband. Shot by a Reagan County sheriff's deputy, according to the news sites. The man who called on the phone had said Darren *died during an official sheriff's office operation.*

"That's all right, Frank. I brought the stuff I use at the shop. You remember those days, don't you?"

He smiled, and Patty gave it right back to him while motioning to the chair.

"You're handling this really well," he said in that pretentious way Frank said everything. "What have the authorities told you?"

She folded his collar into the white shirt and draped her cover over him. As she sprayed water onto his blond hair—which was thinning but plentiful enough for a man in his late fifties—Patty told him what little they'd conveyed, including that, per procedure, Darren's body was undergoing an autopsy and would be unavailable to bury for at least another day or two.

"That's terrible," he said. "Let me know if I can be of any help."

Patty forced a smile. It was that or wipe away his. Frank could've *helped* by never sending Darren off to play hitman.

But she kept her cool and started her stainless-steel hair clippers, their familiar buzz calming her enough to focus.

Patty remembered that she was at least partially responsible for what happened to Darren. After the FBI agent's death, Patty saw a way to make her husband even more valuable to their new benefactor. She'd convinced Darren to return the ledger to Frank, explain what happened—the truth, though in his version Darren was the hero and not Patty—and ask for a raise and more important duties. And, in the process, Patty was invited to do the more menial tasks.

Tasks that included dropping off Frank's mail in town.

"I also wanted to thank you for helping me again with Congressman Schuhmacher," he said over the shears. "Our exchanges at your salon are invaluable."

Patty smiled and nodded into the mirror. After the FBI agent's death, Frank started using her shop as a place to deliver information. The exchanges used to be small envelopes. As technology advanced, she was given CDs and then flash drives—a sign that Frank trusted her, though they both knew she couldn't de-crypt whatever information they were passing like schoolboys in English class.

Frank never looped her in. But when Patty was alone with Darren, he would relay Frank's ever evolving plans. Patty would give her husband ideas to bring to the table, and soon she was in the business of setting up a sitting US congressman.

Patty replaced the clippers with scissors and tipped Frank's head. "He asked why you didn't have anything for him yesterday. Do you think he's suspicious now?"

"Maybe. But it doesn't matter. Thanks to recent events, I can only assume the FBI will arrest him any day now." Frank chuckled. "At least he'll have a fresh haircut in all the papers."

A deep, steadying breath kept Patty from skipping ahead. *Recent events* included the firefight in Big Lake. It had served its purpose by putting the FBI agent's gun into play, which caused them to reopen the investigation and give Jackson the opening he needed to take down Schuhmacher.

But Darren's death was never part of their plan.

After a minute of cutting what remained of Frank's hair, Patty carefully laid down the scissors. "Almost done."

He nodded and leaned back, melting into the chair. "Few things in this world compare to a close shave from you."

She used to enjoy his flattery, but lately, every word out of Frank's mouth made her want to scream.

But rather than ruin her plan, Patty countered with some flattery of her own. "I have to hand it to you—you really did think of everything. I mean, having me nick him while shaving so we could give DNA to the FBI was the work of a true genius."

She wasn't lying. After all, she'd told Darren to suggest it.

Patty unfolded the razor. Under normal circumstances, Patty

would've laid the blade down and started lathering his face and neck with that awful minty shaving cream—his preference, even though she told him unscented worked just as well. But she took a moment to relish the smile on his face.

"Well, you were the one who got the ledger back, ensuring I kept my unlimited and unending leverage over him," he said, eyes still closed. "And the gun was the key to this whole operation. Truly excellent instincts."

This caught Patty off guard. "Darren did those things."

"Oh, come on, Patty. You just said I was a genius. Did you really think I believed Darren was capable of that kind of reasoning?" He opened his eyes for a moment to wink at her in the mirror, then closed them again and returned to his comfortable smugness. "I pretended to be fooled because it made you feel in control, and that kind of confidence is what's made you so valuable to me."

Patty felt the tension in her right arm and hand relax despite herself.

"But," Frank continued, "your talents would be wasted without me."

"Fuck you, Frank, you narcissistic piece of shit."

She'd never spoken to Frank like that. Sure, she busted his balls when they were younger. He still flirted with her like the gross old man he was, and she ignored it or playfully gave him shit for it.

But to let him know how deeply she hated his control over her and Darren had never seemed possible. She despised the insidious nature of Frank's money and how he wielded it, how he inserted himself into their marriage and made unimaginable the mere thought of telling him to fuck right off.

But now Darren was gone, and she finally saw how weak Frank was.

He reacted to her insubordination by shifting in his seat, sitting up a bit straighter. But he kept his eyes closed, secure in his invincibility. "I mean, you put some of the pieces together, but only I could've devised a plan to take out the one man still powerful enough to ruin us. Only *I* could've taken Agent J's contempt for Schuhmacher and paired it with the physical evidence needed to secure a conviction."

"And who brought you the evidence," she said, restraining her anger just enough to keep him from cutting short their conversation. "Not to mention the information about young Agent Jackson screwing his friend's wife."

Frank smiled. "I said you were talented. But as you may recall, it was my idea to put that gun in the hands of Bartholomew Fucking Beck. I was also the one who got Schuhmacher to help hang himself."

Patty hated to admit it, and would never do so out loud, but Frank's plan had been beautiful.

First, Schuhmacher and his pet reporter had to turn the public against the author. And if the media could be believed, Beck had killed his neighbor and lived with the secret for decades. Then he'd killed his old high school friend. Add his arrest for murder, and suicide would be easily believable, perhaps inevitable, in retrospect. They even had the perfect person to stage the suicide—Summer Foster's son, a former Marine who would've just learned that Beck killed his mother. If they provided the weapon, suicide note, and enough cash, Schuhmacher was sure he could talk Samuel Foster into it. If not, they'd hire a pro. Both had connections to bad men.

When Frank approached Schuhmacher with that plan, the mourning father was enthusiastic. But he didn't know Beck would die from a bullet fired out of Agent Kelley's old gun. Or that the suicide note would explain how Beck was using a gun given to him by his old friend Paul, who said it originally belonged to Grant. Beck would end the note with an apology to Congressman Schuhmacher, and it would read like poetic justice had been served. Beck was a writer, after all. Case open and shut.

But as good as Frank's plan had been, it had one major flaw. And it was a big one.

In keeping his Girl Friday in her place, Frank had left Patty an opportunity. She was still in charge of the mail duties, which gave her unquestioned access to his study, where she'd seen him hide the ledger all those years ago.

It also meant she packed all his envelopes and flat-rate boxes.

He'd made it too easy to slip out with the thin book in the small of her back. All she had to do was combine it with the bloodstained tissue and a new note, providing the feds with everything they'd need to take down both horrible men. That'd finally leave her and Darren free to enjoy their retirement in peace, something Frank and Schuhmacher would've never allowed.

And her plan was going perfectly.

Until it wasn't.

Frank had gotten greedy. Killing the writer wasn't enough. He wanted to make him suffer first, which is why he located Jorge Hernandez and tasked Darren with finding a way to kill Beck's best friend before Samuel Foster staged his suicide. When Hernandez ended up in the hospital instead, Frank should've abandoned the stupid, unnecessary scheme. Instead, he instructed Darren to find another opportunity, then personally oversee both deaths. That would also cut out Foster, keeping the conspiracy circle even tighter.

Patty tried to convince Darren to say no. She even argued for letting her do the deed instead of Darren, but he refused to listen. The last thing Patty said before her husband picked up the gun and left was, *If you go, don't bother coming back.*

Patty held that image in her mind as she leaned down, her lips nearly grazing Frank's earlobe. "You know, before Darren died, I just wanted them to arrest you."

Frank's eyes shot open, and Patty took pleasure in knowing the last thing he saw was her smile in the mirror.

THE WARMTH of fresh blood had shocked Patty the first time it flowed across her skin, as though she'd expected the guy's sangre to be cold just because it looked like beet juice. Only her right hand was stained that evening, so she wiped it on his shirt and walked away, tossing the blade in a dumpster down the block. The thrill didn't come until she relived it later that night while cutting into a rare steak, its red juices spreading across a white plate.

That's what Frank's blood looked like on his creamy bathroom tiles. Patty wondered if there was enough bleach in Texas to remove the stains. Thankfully, cleaning up wasn't her problem. Patty only needed to hide enough evidence to avoid a premature arrest.

After changing in Frank's unsullied shower, Patty packed the clothes and tools into her bag and mentally revisited the plan to dump it all in the Guadalupe.

Before closing his front door for the last time, Patty felt for the razor in the left back pocket of her jeans, then pulled her phone out from the right and thumbed her way to the web browser.

After pulling up the story about a pretrial hearing in Hinterbach, Patty zoomed in on the photo and centered it on a woman with black hair pulled into a ponytail. She hadn't bothered with makeup—not that she needed it—and was standing beside a fancy-looking lawyer and a harried woman who'd just been released from jail. Schuhmacher's journalist, Parker Mallory, captured the image.

Patty used her index finger to push the photo off the screen and read the end of the caption.

Standing to the left of Stein is Shayla Hickman, a deputy with the Reagan County Sheriff's Office who arrested murder suspect Bartholomew John Beck following a deadly shootout in Big Lake, Texas.

38

TERRY JACKSON

PRESENT DAY

The body didn't look quite the same. This one was bloated and beginning to decompose, a sure sign he wasn't killed the night before. Jones was also slumped over in a chair, not lying on the ground.

But his throat had been sliced. And that was enough.

Terry pulled out his phone. Her name was second on his list of recent calls.

"He still there?" Terry asked.

"Yeah. But we're in recess right now, so he walked to a café across from the courthouse. Is Jones in cuffs yet?"

Terry looked around, knowing he shouldn't have this conversation within earshot of the other agents. Two were talking into radios, likely helping direct crime scene techs to the Jones homestead, so he wandered into what looked like a study.

"No. He's dead."

The line went quiet as she processed the new information. After waiting forever to get an arrest warrant for Jones, things had moved quickly. They were still planning the raid when Veronica called to say the lab in Austin had matched the DNA on the tissue to a male family member of Paul Schuhmacher. It didn't take long to confirm what Terry knew instinctively.

Problem was, that piece of DNA had been tested off the books. Terry couldn't bring the information to anyone in the Bureau.

"You won't be able to charge Schuhmacher without a confession from Jones," she said. There was no doubt in her voice, which could be a problem if he didn't calm her down.

"It'll be okay." Terry looked around again, just to be sure he was alone. "You should see this body. It'll be easy to convince everyone the same guy did him and Case. And we may hit the jackpot and find out Schuhmacher killed Jones himself."

Terry heard the unmistakable ding of an open car door. "If he killed Jones, it was before I got to town," she said. "Either way, I don't trust the Bureau or the DA to lock him up."

Terry had to say something to keep her in line.

He felt responsible for whatever Judy might do.

Terry had left her to mourn Case's death for decades, but he called Judy after receiving the ledger. She wasn't as hostile as he'd expected, but she showed little interest in speaking with him.

Then Terry told Judy he needed her help to nail Schuhmacher.

She was all in.

Terry sent her to attend one of the town hall meetings and track him from there, just so they'd know where Schuhmacher was when it came time to arrest him.

He'd told her to leave her registered 9mm at home, but he wasn't sure Judy would obey that order.

Schuhmacher would deserve whatever she did, but Terry couldn't live with himself if Hard Case Kelley's widow spent the rest of her life in prison because he brought her into this.

"Judy, listen to me. I feel guilty over Case's death, too." He took a steadying breath. "We'll arrest Schuhmacher. You just have to trust—"

"They're starting to file back in."

Before he could tell her to stay outside, the line went dead.

39

BECK

PRESENT DAY

Guilt and cigarette smoke hit me as I sidled up to Caitlin, who'd spent most of the recess making phone calls next to her Porsche.

"Sorry I got you started again."

"You didn't. I lied before. I'm always stressed." She took a final drag then checked her watch. "We better head back in. Everybody and their mother is here for this because of Wolff's stunt."

On a low-level drug case like this, the defense and county DA would've negotiated a plea deal by now. But Wolff was only bringing charges to screw with me, and in trying to get Judge Grantham to throw out the bogus case, Caitlin had given him exactly what he wanted.

We walked toward the front door of the courthouse, where a line had already formed outside. It was mostly retirees or bored housewives, though there were a few soccer moms from Kerrville who looked underwhelmed by their live episode of *Nancy Grace.*

None of them would've been there if Wolff hadn't sent a news release about the pre-trial hearing, complete with a witness list.

"Any word from Jackson?" I asked.

Caitlin reached into her pocket and checked her cell. "No. I'm sure Veronica will let us know as soon as she hears something."

Veronica had stayed inside, not wanting to go through the metal detectors again. I'd bought her a vending machine lunch and sat with her for a few minutes, but I didn't want to be inside when Schuhmacher returned.

He and his aides had made a show of walking to Fern's, waving at the old-timers and shaking hands with potential voters. If his paunch was any indication, that was the longest walk he'd taken in years. Schuhmacher had also lost much of the hair he'd once kept so perfect, and what remained had gone white.

Heads turned in unison as he approached from the other side of the parking lot. He tried smiling again, but it wasn't quite right. The corners of his mouth were turned upward, but his eyes remained quiet, almost lifeless.

Then he turned to me, and they lit up. Though he'd already displayed his anger through trying to kill my best friend and ruin my life, Schuhmacher's hate for me had been abstract until that moment.

I was about to fake a phone call to avoid standing in line when Bailiff McCollum opened the second of the courthouse's double doors and kicked down the stop.

"C'mon in," he said, motioning like a traffic cop. "Can't keep the judge waiting."

Almost nobody stayed in the line with the metal detectors.

BEFORE WOLFF BEGAN QUESTIONING ME, both attorneys approached Judge Grantham.

"Your honor," Wolff began, "Mr. Beck was at Ms. Stein's house when the sheriff—"

"You mean Daddy?" Caitlin asked.

Wolff swung his arm in her direction. "I don't know what judges in Dallas allow, but this behavior is uncalled for."

Grantham held up his right palm and cleared his throat. "Ms. Parks, he's right. On both counts. I understand you are currently representing Mr. Beck in a separate case before this court, but he is clearly a relevant witness." He turned to the district attorney. "You may proceed."

Wolff winked at me before gathering a yellow legal pad. He thought he had me.

And after this was over, Wolff would probably think he'd won.

Arrogance often blinds those who are getting manipulated.

"Mr. Beck, how do you know the defendant?"

I leaned toward the mic and smiled at Veronica. "We first met in 2019. She contacted me as a source for a story about the Summer Foster murder."

Wolff flipped to the next page in his notebook, which was probably just a prop. "And later that year, did you invite her to work with you on an oil pipeline as part of a scheme to cover up another murder?"

"Objection—"

"I'll rephrase," Wolff said. "Did Ms. Stein come to work with you on an oil pipeline later that year?"

"Yes."

Wolff asked a few more benign questions to establish my close working relationship with Veronica. I stuck to one-word answers but knew the attack was imminent.

"Going back for a moment to the day you killed Paul Schuhmacher—"

"Objection," Caitlin said. "Prejudicial."

Wolff took a step toward the judge. "Your honor, I was simply stating a fact that has been established."

"It's like déjà vu all over again," Grantham said. "Only this time, I agree with Mr. Wolff. Overruled."

"But your honor—"

Grantham's swung his gavel. "Ms. Parks, you'll find that arguing with me will do nothing to help your cause, especially when you're asking me to rule in your favor on what are some pretty serious charges."

The judge motioned for Wolff to continue.

"On that day, Mr. Beck, did you save the defendant's life?"

Caitlin had started to stand as soon as he began speaking, but the question caught both of us off guard.

She sat.

"Yes," I said.

"So, she owes you one?" He flashed a toothy smile. "Maybe more than one."

I looked at Caitlin. We'd prepared for this as soon as the news release went out. Wolff would try to corner me into saying something on the record that could be used against me later.

She shook her head, which meant I didn't have to plead the Fifth.

Yet.

"Yes."

"And coming to Hinterbach and staying in her old house while you sorted out your own legal matters, that was part of repaying the debt?"

Caitlin shook me off again.

"I believe so, though you'd have to ask her."

"So, it's fair to say you two have a give-and-take relationship then?" Wolff turned to Veronica. "Like most friends do."

With Caitlin's attention occupied, I assumed she'd be okay with me answering. "Yes."

"Then it stands to reason that, if there were something in that house she wanted hidden or destroyed, you'd help her out?"

I expected Caitlin to object, but instead she nodded.

"Upon the advice of counsel," I said, "I am asserting my Fifth Amendment right against self-incrimination and decline to answer."

Wolff grinned. "To be clear, you're admitting that there was something in that house that could incriminate you."

Caitlin stood but Grantham cleared his throat before she could object.

"Your point has been made, Mr. Wolff. Let's move on."

"Sorry your honor." He turned and placed his legal pad neatly beside an assortment of documents. "Going back to your relationship with the defendant—"

Caitlin nearly screamed her objection. "Relevance, your honor."

"I am trying to establish the kind of friends the defendant keeps and the kind of activities they're involved in. Goes to her character."

"Overruled," Grantham said. "But get there quickly."

Now we were getting to it.

"Is letting you crash at her place the first big favor Ms. Stein has done for you?"

Caitlin nodded.

"No."

Caitlin's face hardened at my insubordination. Even Wolff paused a beat when I didn't plead the Fifth again.

But Veronica knew what I was doing. Her face was chalk white.

"What other favors has she done for you?"

Veronica mouthed *no*.

"Despite being a journalist, she never thoroughly investigated—"

I stopped at the sound of Caitlin's chair as she pushed it back. Her hip glanced off the corner of the defense table as she hustled toward the judge.

"Your honor, my client—"

"He's not your client right now," Wolff said, cutting her off, both verbally and physically. "He's my witness."

Grantham swung his gavel while they bickered.

"Enough," he yelled. "Ms. Parks, you'll get your turn. But if the witness wants to answer the prosecution's questions, he is free to do so."

Caitlin looked at me. She was more upset than during our worst fights and more flushed than when I'd caught her *in flagrante*. "May I at least have a brief recess to confer with ..."

She trailed off because, as the DA again pointed out, I was not in the court as her client. Caitlin fixed her posture and took her seat. But instead of looking at me or the judge or Wolff, she stared out one of the windows.

Beside her, Veronica was holding back tears.

40

BECK

PRESENT DAY

I'd memorized my confession the night before. I would mechanically recount what happened that night in Summer Foster's back yard, describe the fireworks scoring my crescendo of misguided vengeance and rage, detail the crack of her skull and the blood on my hands, explain the coverup and hiding while Butch Heller sobbed over her body.

But before I could start, a middle-aged woman in a red shirt put her purse on the ground beneath her feet and came back up with something in her hand.

Then she reached for Shayla's hair.

I yelled and hopped over the short wall that cordoned off the witness stand. The floor came fast and one of my ankles gave way, but I scrambled to my feet and did my best to sprint toward them as the gallery began flooding the aisles.

I wasn't going to make it.

The woman had Shayla's hair and was pulling her head back. The blade was at her neck and I still couldn't reach them. I was still five steps away when Shayla jerked her head away and reached for the woman's wrist. She didn't gain control of the blade, but Shayla broke free of her attacker and ran to the aisle.

But so did the woman in red.

When she raised her arm and charged at Shayla, I buried my shoulder into her exposed side.

We were both on the ground when someone in a beige uniform landed on top of me.

That's when I felt blood on my neck.

WHILE FINISHING HER STITCHES, the Kerrville doctor explained that the blade had been scalpel-sharp, based on the smooth incision. It was far too shallow to do much damage, though.

"The scar won't look terrible, but it's going to be sore when the local anesthetic wears off," she said. "So will your side. I'll write you a prescription for some non-narcotic pain killers. I suggest you stop taking your sleeping medication temporarily. Or live with the pain."

As the doctor brushed past the white curtain that led to the rest of the ER, another woman's voice asked if she could have a few minutes.

"Shayla." I sounded too excited but didn't care. "Why are you here?"

She pulled up a chair. "I was nominated to drive you home. Caitlin and Veronica are still at the courthouse with the judge and DA. Apparently Grantham is done with this bullshit case and wants them to work it out before suppertime, as he put it."

That meant I was done on the stand. But it meant Veronica wouldn't have to deal with Wolff anymore.

"I'm surprised they let you back here."

"It's all over Facebook and Twitter. I told the staff I was the one who got attacked and wanted to congratulate my hero. It's close enough to the truth." She slid forward to get a better look at my neck. "You gonna be okay?"

"The doctor said there was almost no chance of permanent nerve damage. Did you find out why the hell that woman was trying to hurt you?"

Shayla nodded. "The deputies here gave me some information while they took my statement. Professional courtesy. Her name is Patricia Butler."

I reacted so violently the new stitches tugged at my skin. "Big Lake. That was her husband."

"Bingo. Veronica's FBI friend also showed up. At first, he asked if the *shooter* was in custody. But after the deputies read him in, he said Butler was part of an ongoing federal investigation, and he was going to stick around to interview her."

"So they got Jones. Good."

"Sure," she said. "I guess you could say that."

41

PATTY BUTLER

PRESENT DAY

The bitch was still alive. Instead of being in a body bag, the pig who killed Darren was out there getting drunk or laid or whatever girls do these days to blow off steam.

Thinking about it made her even angrier. She'd expected the cuffs and the interrogations. The arrest was part of the plan she'd set in motion from the moment Darren died.

But the bitch was supposed to be dead.

Patty was still stewing when the handsome fed walked in. They were older now, but she recognized him instantly.

"Before I begin," he said, "I want to state for the record that you've been read your Miranda rights, including your right to have an attorney present during this interview. Do you understand?"

Patty looked at the camera in the corner. "Yes."

He leaned back and clicked his pen. "You're in a lot of trouble for that stunt earlier. Assault with a deadly. Maybe attempted murder. But that's for the local DA to decide."

Part of her wanted to get this over with. Confess to every-thing he wanted so she could get to one of the many cells she'd call home until her execution date. But the admissions would feel more authentic if she let him lead.

Then all the charges would stick.

"You're not here for that. You're in here because we went to arrest someone earlier today. Instead, we found this"—he slid a photo of Frank's corpse across the metal table—"and I thought you could help us out."

She studied the picture. Frank was discolored and nearly unrecognizable, but the photographer did capture her handiwork well. When she was done, Patty looked back up and stared blankly at Jackson.

"Before you deny anything," he said, "we know you had a longstanding relationship of some kind with Franklin Jones. We're gathering fingerprints at his house right now, and I'm certain we'll find yours there. In that bathroom. Maybe in his bedroom."

He was reaching. Then again, they all lie to get confessions, something she'd learned a long time ago.

"We're also testing all the blood that leaked into the hinge and handle of your straight razor. I expect to find a match to Jones unless you were smart enough to bring a different one today. But my guess is you didn't." He leaned forward. "You tried to kill that woman in public. You're not worried about getting caught."

He was almost there.

Jackson pulled another photo from the file. Though she'd prepared to see it, the image of Darren laid out on the dirt turned her stomach to stone. His eyes were open and his lips parted, begging for her help.

She swallowed and clenched her teeth to keep from spitting in his goddamn face.

"The woman you attacked today killed Darren. That's the easy one. Figuring out why you blame Franklin Jones for his death is a little harder, so I was hoping you might just tell me."

Jackson let her go another minute without speaking before getting frustrated. He stood, gathered the photos, and slapped them back into the file before turning for the door. "I guess you need a little more time to decide whether you want life or the needle."

Now.

"Agent J."

He froze. "What did you call me?"

"Did you end up getting back together with your girlfriend? You know, Agent K's widow."

Jackson turned, and for a moment Patty wondered if he might attack her. When he remained standing across the room, she continued.

"That was one hell of a fight y'all had. If it makes you feel any better, I'd've chosen you over him. Especially with your shirt off."

The hate in Jackson's eyes turned to panic. But that was the only giveaway as he walked back to the table and returned to his seat.

"You've mistaken me for someone else," he said.

"No, I haven't. What did you think happened to that ledger? And who do you think sent it to you all these years later?"

Jackson's eyes shot to the camera.

Patty had guessed right. He hadn't told his fed bosses about that. Or the bloody tissue. Otherwise, they'd have gotten to Frank and Schuhmacher before Darren was killed. She blamed Jackson for that. But she needed him for a while longer. The hate he'd get from colleagues for the affair would have to be punishment enough.

"Don't worry, Agent J, I'm sure you'll still get all the credit for finally catching me."

She stared at Jackson, who appeared to be working to keep calm.

"Don't be shy," she said. "Ask me."

Jackson pretended to look through the file. Pretended to straighten out the photos. Pretended like he wasn't playing catch-up.

When he finally looked up, Jackson was back in interrogation mode. "Did you kill Franklin Jones?"

"Yes."

"Why?"

Patty leaned back and smiled. "We'll get to that in a minute. But first, ask the other question."

Jackson stared at her for ten full, gloriously awkward seconds before sucking in a breath.

"Did you kill FBI Supervisory Special Agent Casey Kelley on the evening of February 21, 2000?"

42

BECK

PRESENT DAY

Shayla tossed her phone onto the couch cushion. "They're almost here."

The doctor was right about the pain, so I'd taken two of the pills and settled into the recliner. "Perfect timing."

"You ready for Caitlin to bite your head off?"

We'd done the drive from Kerrville and spent half an hour at Veronica's old house without talking about it. There was no time now, so I settled for the short version.

"Yeah."

I stared at nothing, hoping she was done with the conversation and we could move on.

It was quiet enough to hear car doors slam outside.

Caitlin walked in first, head buried in her phone. Veronica followed close behind and rushed to inspect the bandage on my neck. "Jesus."

"It looks worse than it is. I'd rather talk about why Wolff didn't drop the charges."

"Caitlin can explain it better."

Caitlin looked up from her phone at the mention of her name. "He was being a real prick and wanted Veronica to plead to possession. I told him we weren't admitting to anything and he and his daddy could go screw themselves."

"You said that?" I asked.

"You're damn right. I was in no mood to be fucked with after what you pulled."

The room fell silent except for the fridge door opening as Shayla pulled out a fresh longneck.

"Anyway," Caitlin continued, "we got a day's continuance. You'll have to take the stand again."

She started walking across the living room. "We need to talk in private. Now."

Caitlin closed the door to my temporary room as I sat on the bed. "I need to know that you're not going to try that again. If you are, I'll drive you over to the DA's office so you can confess straight to him and leave me out of it."

Her phone rang before I could speak. Caitlin put her palm up and answered.

"Those pointy ears of yours burning?"

Wolff.

"Uh huh… Why the hell did you wait until now to call me? … Oh bullshit, nothing's changed in the twenty minutes since I left your office… Whatever. Copy me on everything."

She ended the call, mumbling to herself. "Well, we won't have to worry about it for now. Wolff's dropping the charges against Veronica."

She said it so matter-of-factly, no excitement for the win or joy for her client. Was it the stress of the day? Or me?

"Look," I said. "We need to talk about—"

I was interrupted by Veronica bursting through the door.

"I just talked with Agent Jackson. You won't believe this."

43

TERRY JACKSON
PRESENT DAY

Terry's nose and fingertips pricked with adrenaline. It was risky. But this was the only way to keep Schuhmacher from controlling the narrative.

The crowd, which had gathered in and around the pavilion in downtown Kerrville, clapped as Terry and two other agents finished navigating the packed parking lot. Terry sidled up to an *Express-News* reporter he recognized while the others bookended a row of television cameras.

The journalist's eyes went wide. He was about to open his mouth when Terry put an index finger to his lips.

"I'd get your phone out. You'll want video of this."

As Schuhmacher stepped in front of the cameras, Terry walked into the shot, holding up his badge and credentials.

"Grant Schuhmacher, I'm Special Agent Terry Jackson with the Federal Bureau of Investigation."

The other agents moved in and engaged with the congressman's panicking aides.

Schuhmacher didn't appear flustered, fully aware that the cameras had started rolling. "And what can I do to help the FBI this afternoon?"

Terry saw himself punching that bastard square in the nose, then climbing on top of his reeling body and throwing haymakers until he was torn away. And when the reporters asked him why, Terry would say because the venerable Congressman Schuhmacher is a lying, thieving piece of shit. Because that old man with blood dripping down his face was at the center of the investigation that led to his mentor's death.

Because if it weren't for Schuhmacher's corruption, Case and Judy would still be in his life.

But Terry didn't do or say any of that.

His superiors had been gracious in letting him make the arrest for sentimental reasons. For starters, Terry hadn't taken a suspect into custody since cuffing Lenny Floyd, a wannabe gangster who called himself *Pretty Boy* after the 1930s bank robber. In reality, Floyd was a fucking nurse, one of several who'd been stealing fentanyl and selling it to local H dealers. And the charges didn't even stick.

Then there was the fact Terry had copped to withholding evidence and running an off-the-books investigation using civilians, one of whom was out on bond with a pending murder trial.

Anything less than a straight arrest—especially in front of news cameras, a setting he'd chosen against the advice of those same superiors—and Terry would get an early retirement with none of the benefits.

"I'm placing you under arrest on charges of conspiracy to commit murder in connection with the death of FBI Supervisory Special Agent Casey Kelley." Terry motioned toward the parking lot. "I'd appreciate it if you could come with me, please."

Schuhmacher's mouth kept smiling. "There's been some kind of misunderstanding. I'm sure if you get your boss on the phone, we can clear this up."

A smile crept across Terry's face. "There's been no misunderstanding, congressman. We have the person who killed Agent Kelley in custody." He pulled out his handcuffs. "If you don't come willingly, we *will* restrain you."

Schuhmacher's eyes betrayed his otherwise calm expression, flashing the same glimpse of confusion and fear Terry had seen during dozens of arrests. But Schuhmacher was a smooth sonofabitch and choked those feelings down after looking around at the cameras and cellphones pointed his way.

"That won't be necessary."

The congressman began walking toward the parking lot while Terry and the other agents made a path through the journalists as they swarmed and shouted questions. Adding to the commotion were Schuhmacher's lackeys. One was screaming into a phone, likely soliciting the services of a top-notch criminal attorney.

As Terry closed the rear door to a Bureau SUV, he hoped the impromptu perp walk was enough to combat Schuhmacher's own media machine. Though the DOJ would have a strong case, he'd have to be found guilty in the press first.

Only then would there be enough pressure to send a sitting congressman to prison.

TERRY DID A DOUBLE TAKE. Her house had been blue, not this pastel yellow. The driveway had been paved over again, and it was now covered by a carport.

Terry was still a bit unsure he had the right place until Judy stepped out.

"I saw the news. What now?"

"Can I come in?"

She hesitated. "I'm not sure that's a good idea."

Terry looked around. He understood why she was uncomfortable, but what they were about to discuss required privacy. "We're going to attract attention out here."

"Fine." She stepped aside. "Where does Mrs. Jackson think you are right now?"

Terry wondered for a moment if she'd kept up with him, too.

But she was probably assuming he hadn't remained a bachelor this long. Otherwise, she'd have known. "She died a few years ago. Cancer."

Judy's expression softened, but only for a moment as she let him silently cross her threshold. The house was different on the inside, too. Everything was new. Terry should've expected that, but he still longed for the past, wished he could step back in and fill the void he'd helped create.

She led him to the kitchen and the strong aroma of fresh coffee. Without turning to him, Judy took two mugs out of a cupboard.

"Is he in jail?" she asked.

Terry took a seat at the kitchen table. "No. He was, but the lawyers had him out in an hour."

Judy picked up the mugs and started walking toward him.

"You know this thing's going to take a while, right? I'm talking years."

Judy set one mug in front of Terry, then paused before hurling the other at her own kitchen wall. Terry flinched out of instinct, then stood to console her. But as her screams turned to sobs, Terry knew there was nothing he could do. He couldn't fix what was broken. All he could do was stand beside her and watch the coffee spread down the muted green paint toward her kitchen floor.

"He's going to get life. Maybe the needle. You just have to be patient."

Judy didn't believe him. And why should she? Even with Patricia Butler's testimony, no prosecutor wanted to take on Schuhmacher and his legal team. The risk of losing was too high. They'd settle out of court, and Schuhmacher would walk away free, his only punishment an early retirement from politics.

"How long do you expect me to live like this," she said. "All that guilt over his death was dead and buried until you called. But now, all I can think about is the life I could've had with Case if it weren't for you and me."

As he watched Judy gather her strength, Terry thought about the note he'd received from the Butler woman, the one that had brought everything back to the surface.

I can't live knowing nobody was punished for his murder.
   Can you?

44

PATTY BUTLER

FEBRUARY 21, 2000, 5:43 PM

Their field trip was getting risky. When the agent had sat in his truck for more than ten minutes, she and Darren had been worried they were made. Then he didn't go in to visit his mother, so Patty demanded Darren follow him again. He did as she asked, though he was firmer in his dissent.

What could they possibly gain by continuing to tail him? Patty didn't know.

But the opportunity to take back the ledger had come because they'd been nearby. If they were diligent and saw this through, they'd find more.

Then they watched the fed's truck turn into the parking lot of a dive bar, and Patty knew Darren was getting pissed.

"That's it," he said. "We're not going to wait out here while this guy gets loaded before going home to confront his whore of a wife."

As he reached for the gearshift to speed up, Patty grabbed his hand. "Look, I know this seems stupid. And you're right, we're not going to wait here if that's all he's doing. But please, let me do one thing first."

When she let go of his hand, Patty wasn't sure if he'd downshift and turn to the bar or upshift and tell her he was *putting his foot down*—or some other macho euphemism he'd heard other men tell their wives.

Like any couple, she and Darren argued. Every relationship benefits from the occasional round of makeup sex. But his buttons were hard to push, which was part of his charm. So was Darren's physicality, though it was also a consideration when deciding how far to push him. However, Patty was confident he'd never hit her, no matter what she did.

She was still calculating when Darren slowed and turned into the bar.

"Okay, but you better have a good reason, or we're outta here."

"Don't I always?" She smiled wide and batted her eyes, Patty's way of playing innocent for him. "But seriously, here's what I'm thinking. What would make a guy skip seeing his own mother? My money's on work. He probably got a page from an informant and is meeting that person here. So, let me go check it out. If I'm right, I'll remember what the informant looked like and what I heard, if anything. If not, and he's just at the bar drinking by himself, I'll come out and we'll go."

Darren shook his head. "That's even more dangerous than what we've been doing. I don't want you going anywhere near the guy. I mean, he's a cop, for crying out loud."

"It's not like I'm wearing a sign that says, *Hey, I'm a criminal, arrest me,*" she said. "Besides, I have a way to make this fun for you, too."

He narrowed his eyes but didn't shoot her down, so Patty turned and started digging behind Darren's seat. "While he's inside and I'm being a lookout, you can break into his truck and see if there's anything useful in there." She held up Darren's Slim Jim. "C'mon, you know you want to."

He smiled despite himself and grabbed the tool. "Fine. But the second he either settles in or looks like he's about to leave, you come out and we haul ass. Got it?"

"Yes sir." She leaned over and kissed him again. "Now go get us something good."

They got out of the truck. Darren strolled to the agent's vehicle and pulled out his key ring, acting like standing next to the door was no big deal.

Patty weaved through the parking lot, then fought her adrenaline as she stepped inside the bar.

45

JUDY KELLEY
PRESENT DAY

This was her last chance. Tomorrow he'd be surrounded by his sycophants all day and night. Then, after winning re-election in a landslide, Grant Schuhmacher would be wheels up on his way back to DC.

But as she stood in the Kerrville crowd that evening, the lying, cheating, murderous bastard who was responsible for decades of pain was ripe for the picking.

This was Schuhmacher's last campaign stop, his last chance to plead innocence and swindle his constituents. He told them his accuser was deranged. Mentally ill. Not to be trusted—especially when compared with his record of public service.

That he was spreading these lies was bad enough. But he was doing so after his public, disappointingly uneventful arrest. All Schuhmacher had to do was pay a criminally low bail. That was it. They fucking had him on the murder of a top federal agent, but now he was free.

Some animals refuse to stay caged.

Judy clapped along with the crowd, just another middle-aged woman fawning over the once-handsome congressman. She plastered on a smile like the rest and solidified her place at the edge of the rope.

As Schuhmacher descended the platform, he walked over to the crowd to shake his last hands and kiss his last babies. Until his arrest, the papers had run a decades-old photo of the congressman, before his hair turned white and his teeth yellow. His booking mugshot was the truest representation of the man. Though he tried to smile for the jailhouse camera, the emotion never reached his eyes, which were forever cold and detached.

Judy's face was red as he approached her position, and she hoped Schuhmacher blamed the day's chill and her excitement at meeting him.

When he was a few yards away, Judy reached into her pocket. The disposable camera had been hard to find. Ordering online would create a paper trail, but the third dollar store she tried had one in stock. She didn't want a photo with him, nor did she want anyone to later prove she was there via her cellphone.

Judy put her left arm low and raised the camera high.

"Can I get a picture with you?" she shouted.

Schuhmacher leaned down. "I can't remember the last time I saw one of those."

She was repulsed when his cheek made contact with hers but smiled anyway. She needed him that close so he could hear.

"I know where Patricia Butler was that evening. And I can prove it."

After pretending to take the photo, she turned to him.

"Meet me behind your house at midnight."

JUDY SHIFTED HER WEIGHT. The hiking boots were uncomfortable —new and loose despite her thick socks—and it was getting hard to stand.

While she'd been tailing Schuhmacher, Judy had discovered a secret that could ruin him politically. Though he'd vowed that afternoon to keep Texas marijuana free, the esteemed congressman liked to light up every evening at a firepit behind his home near the Pedernales River. And while she'd hide among the trees and light shrubbery that surrounded his McMansion, Schuhmacher would remove a photo from his wallet and stare at it. Sometimes he'd sob for a few minutes. She could never get close enough, but Judy would bet money the photo was of his dead son.

In those moments, Grant Schuhmacher almost seemed human.

Then she'd remember her mission.

And his secret had given her the perfect opportunity now that the law had failed.

Judy's watch read two minutes to midnight when she saw a dot of light approaching her position. She pressed the button on her flashlight and aimed it his way, revealing Schuhmacher holding his phone. Judy reached for her own out of reflex, then panicked for a moment before remembering she'd left it back in San Antonio.

"Who are you?" Schuhmacher said as he neared.

"Someone who knows the truth. Someone who hasn't been able to sleep since all this happened."

Schuhmacher edged closer. "You're doing the right thing."

Judy coughed into her free hand to hide her smile.

"So, what can you tell me?" he asked.

"I saw her that day."

That part was true. Terry had told her about Patricia Butler and how she'd seen the fight in front of Judy's house. How Butler had stolen the ledger and mailed it to Terry after it had collected dust for more than twenty years.

Terry thought Butler had taken the book from Case's truck after slicing his throat and leaving him to bleed out, but Judy had been staring out of her living room window after Case had driven away from their fight. She remembered thinking the woman walking across the street had seemed out of place. She didn't think about it again until seeing Butler's photo in the paper.

Schuhmacher pressed his hands together and looked to the sky, as if Heaven would let in a vicious monster like him. When he began praying and ranting to God, Judy tiptoed closer to hear him, though she also considered kicking him square in the balls.

"I knew she wouldn't get away with it," Schuhmacher mumbled. "How could she? I didn't hire her to do anything. She didn't kill that insufferable agent and she didn't steal his gun. And now I can finally prove it."

Case's gun was the linchpin holding together the DOJ's case. Terry said they'd matched DNA inside the pistol to Schuhmacher. The problem, though, was proving Patricia Butler was there that night. Otherwise, she wasn't a credible witness.

Judy could help with that by confirming Butler was following Case that day.

But she wouldn't.

Though Terry and the DA would jump at the chance to put Judy on the stand, it wouldn't be enough. Even if the jurors believed her decades-old testimony, what did it prove? That Patricia Butler had been walking in front of their house hours before the murder?

And what if the defense attorney asked why that moment was memorable enough to recall all these years later. She'd have to explain the circumstance. She'd have to tell the jury that the federal agent who arrested Schuhmacher had been sleeping with one of the state's key witnesses, who also happened to be the victim's unfaithful liar of a wife.

And say twelve people could see past the conflict of interest. Judy still couldn't place Butler in the alley where Case bled out. Any good criminal lawyer—and Schuhmacher had the best— would easily cast enough doubt to hang a jury, if not secure a verdict of not guilty.

But there were no jurors out in that field. Just Judy Kelley and Grant Schuhmacher.

"I have been wondering," Judy said. "If Patricia Butler wasn't there, how did she and her husband get a hold of that *insufferable* agent's gun?"

Schuhmacher looked down at her, his face no longer plastered with his fake, punch-me-in-the-mouth smile. "I wouldn't know. But it doesn't matter. You know she wasn't there to take it from him. That's what we should focus on."

He closed the gap between them, and Judy realized just how imposing Schuhmacher could still be, despite the years and added emotional stress of his son's death. Under normal circumstances, she'd be no match for him. But Schuhmacher wanted something from her, so he'd play nice for now.

"No," she said. "I think we should talk about that gun. See, I said I knew where Butler was that day. I saw her following Case around that afternoon."

Schuhmacher frowned. "I don't see how that's possible."

"Sure you do. You knew Jones was giving you up to the feds, so you bought off one of his lackeys, one who had a violent record but didn't look threatening on the street. You told Patricia Butler to follow Case around until she found an opportunity to kill him. That way you could steal back the evidence and have the *insufferable* lead investigator out of your hair."

By the time she was done speaking, Schuhmacher's face had gone from confused to sinister. "I'll admit, Agent Kelley's death proved beneficial, but I swear I had nothing to do with it. Whatever Patty did, she did on her own, or for someone else."

Patty. Schuhmacher did know her.

That was the opening she needed.

"The FBI sent me and I'm wearing a wire. If you admit to everything, they're willing to help you cut a deal. But only if you confess to me right now."

She wasn't wearing a wire. What she did have was an unregistered revolver lodged in the back of her waistband, a six-shooter with a pearl grip handed down to Case from his father.

It still worked.

Judy thought she'd sounded convincing enough, but when

Schuhmacher replaced his sour face with a crooked grin, Judy knew she'd been wrong.

"You watch too many movies," he said. "Who are you?"

Schuhmacher grabbed her left arm and pulled her close. She dropped the flashlight, which landed pointing toward them, giving her just enough light to see his eyes. If she didn't act now, he'd never let her leave that meadow.

Her right hand was on the gun when another light flashed on from over her shoulder.

He tightened his grip but shielded his eyes.

"Let her go," a voice called out, "or I'll have you on assault, too."

Schuhmacher did as told. Judy let go of the revolver's grip and backed away slowly until Terry put his hand on the small of her back.

"What the hell is this?" Schuhmacher asked. "A sting? Well, I call it trespassing and trying to interrogate me without my lawyer present. I'm going to have your badge for this, *former* Special Agent Jackson."

"You may be right. But if I get the truth out of you tonight, it'll be worth it."

Terry moved his fingers farther down her back until they hit pearl. "You're already on tape admitting to obstruction of justice." He took his hand away and stepped forward. "You might's well give us the rest."

Judy didn't know how Terry had gotten to the meet. But he'd been there, listening, letting her have at Schuhmacher. He'd backed her play.

Now she'd see how far he was willing to go.

Patty reached back and pulled the gun.

Schuhmacher smirked. "And what're you fixing to do with that, little lady?"

Judy walked up to Schuhmacher and pointed it right at his smug face. "I'm going to blow your goddamn head off."

He didn't look impressed. Terry stayed put, still pointing his flashlight at them.

"You keep asking who I am." Judy cocked the gun. "My name is Judy. Judy Kelley. Widow of the late Casey Kelley."

That got Schuhmacher's attention. He turned to Terry. "Agent Jackson, aren't you going to do something?"

Terry shrugged. "I didn't bring my gun. Or my badge. If I were you, I'd start talking."

Schuhmacher's eyes were wild, bouncing between Judy, Terry, and the gun. "If you're looking for revenge, you've come to the wrong place, lady. I had nothing to do with your husband's death. Yes, I know Patty now, but only because she gives me a haircut and a shave when I'm in town. Franklin and I occasionally used her place to pass information to each other, but your husband was already dead before all of that, I swear." His eyes shifted from Judy's eyes to the gun. "You should put that thing down before doing something you'll regret."

"Bullshit," Judy said. "I saw her. I saw that awful woman outside my house that day. She was there, following Case around, waiting for her chance."

Terry stepped forward far enough to get in Judy's periphery, careful not to take his eyes or the light off the revolver before turning to her. "That's great. Now you can be a witness—"

"He'll still walk." Judy raised the gun higher and stepped toward Schuhmacher. "His lawyers will come up with some loophole. You know they will."

She was still focused on Schuhmacher when Terry grabbed the gun. She resisted, but soon realized he could easily take it from her. She replaced the hammer and lowered the revolver to her side.

Schuhmacher breathed deeply. "Thank you, Agent Jackson." He turned to Judy. "I understand your grief. Truly, I do. But I don't know where Patty was or wasn't that day. Or how she got ahold of that ledger and your husband's gun."

He'd lost a son, so Judy knew he was telling the truth about grief. Perhaps that's what made the rest sound truthful.

But she wasn't going to take him at his word.

"Then why is she lying?" Judy yelled. "What's in it for her?"

Schuhmacher sighed. "I assume that, like you, she blames me for her husband's death. But I didn't send Darren Butler to kill anyone. Franklin did that all on his own. The only person I wanted dead was Bart Beck."

Judy stepped back and composed herself. She didn't want him to make sense. That's not how this night was supposed to go.

"I don't care how you rationalize it," she said. "They killed Case because he was investigating you. And now you're going to get a life sentence for it."

She nodded at Terry, who pulled a set of handcuffs from his back pocket as though they'd planned this.

"Turn around," he said. "I'm placing you under arrest. We'll work out the charges later."

Schuhmacher froze. "You're kidding, right? This impromptu, highly illegal operation of yours won't make it past a judge."

Terry stepped closer. "Maybe not. But we're going to make a hell of a scene out here. And you're not the only one with a reporter on speed dial."

He handed Judy the flashlight and grabbed Schuhmacher by the arm. She kept them illuminated while Terry cuffed him, hands behind his back, one arm on Schuhmacher's shoulder and the other on his wrists.

"Hand me your phone so I can call this in."

"I didn't bring it."

Terry's gaze bounced between her and Schuhmacher. Then he looked at the nearest bench.

"Walk," he told Schuhmacher. "Sit there."

Judy recognized the opportunity instantly. There was enough space and time if she acted quickly.

As Terry lowered him onto the bench, Judy tightened her

grip on the revolver. She dug the hammer into her thigh and cocked it, hoping Schuhmacher's protests had covered the sound.

When Terry stepped back and reached into his front pocket, she moved. Two long steps—clumsier than she'd expected in the boots—before pressing the barrel to Schuhmacher's temple and squeezing the trigger, remembering to adjust for the extra recoil from a revolver.

Her ears were ringing, but she heard Terry curse as he rushed toward Schuhmacher's body. Then he turned his phone's flashlight on her.

She didn't resist when Terry grabbed the gun out of her shaking hand. "What the fuck? We had him. We had a confession."

"You knew why I came out here. No phone. These clodhoppers. That old six-shooter."

Terry looked around. "Someone's bound to have heard that, so we don't have much time."

Was he acting out of selfishness? Or did he care whether she spent the rest of her life in prison? That discussion—and so many other ones—would have to wait.

He yanked the flashlight away from Judy and turned it off.

"Do exactly what I say."

46

PRESENT DAY

Embattled congressman dead, authorities suspect suicide

By Veronica Stein @vsteinscribe

HINTERBACH, Texas – United States Rep. Grant Schuhmacher was found dead early Tuesday morning near his Central Texas home.

The longtime Texas politician was discovered at about 12:30 AM by his wife after hearing a gunshot behind their house, according to a news release from the Nimitz County Sheriff's Office.

The statement didn't reveal the cause of death, but a law enforcement source said Schuhmacher died of a bullet wound to the head that appeared to be self-inflicted. The source, who spoke on the condition of anonymity, also said drug paraphernalia was found at the scene.

Schuhmacher, R-Texas, was out on bail after pleading not guilty to murder conspiracy charges last week.

"We're still investigating and will have to wait for the medical examiner's determination, but given the evidence we have now, I expect us to consider Special Agent Casey Kelley's murder solved in a matter of days," FBI spokesman Terry Jackson said. "I think I speak for

everyone in the FBI when I say we are disappointed Mr. Schuhmacher won't have to answer for his role in that heinous crime."

Jackson said Schuhmacher was also expected to be a key witness in an unrelated murder charge against bestselling true crime author Bartholomew John Beck.

After learning of Schuhmacher's apparent suicide, Nimitz County District Attorney Jeremy Wolff said he will be meeting soon with Beck's attorney, Dallas lawyer Caitlin Parks, but added no further details on the case.

No funeral arrangements for Schuhmacher have been announced.

Veronica Stein is a freelance reporter and columnist for Manhattanist Magazine.

47

BECK

PRESENT DAY

Veronica had been the first to leave her childhood home. With the amount of writing ahead of her, she wanted to get back to WiFi and better coffee. The *Lone Star Ledger* called to inform her the suspension was lifted, and they'd like to have her back. Plus, Emily at the *Manhattanist* was starting to plan a cover story.

Caitlin hadn't stayed after Veronica's case was dismissed, but she returned to Hinterbach for my final court proceeding. Wolff dropped the charges because he now had no witness to testify. That left Walker's evidence, which was not—and never had been—enough. Wolff also had no pressure to prosecute.

"He didn't put up much of a fight," Caitlin said. "Did you see how pissed he was? He looks like a fool now."

Though I was eager to resume my life, I took no great pleasure in Schuhmacher's death. Not that I felt sorry for him. Schuhmacher had always been an arrogant prick, something I experienced firsthand when he pressured me—via my parents and favorite English teacher—into writing *Cold Summer* as part of a city reformation effort. I wasn't sad when Veronica shook me awake in the middle of the night to recount her conversation with Agent Jackson before returning to her laptop.

His death would not be the end of things, though.

Authorities would no doubt cite the uncovering of his role in Hard Case Kelley's death and his ties to Jim Flynn as reasons for his suicide. All that on top of losing a son. They probably wouldn't look for any other explanation. He was a cop killer, after all.

But there's no way in hell Schuhmacher offed himself. He was executed. And no matter who killed him, a body and a coverup only leads to more death and more lies.

I was proof of that.

Caitlin turned just before closing the door. "Call me when you get a phone. If I need you before then, I'll call Shayla. I still have to work out the lawsuits. It won't be a problem, but it might take a little time."

She drove off, leaving the driveway empty. Shayla and her rental car were out getting supplies for dinner. Neither of us wanted fast food again, so she offered to cook a celebratory dinner before I locked up the old McDonough house and we drove to Big Lake.

We planned on leaving at nine the next morning.

THE SPAGHETTI WAS DELICIOUS. I had no part in making it that way, nor the tossed Caesar or breadsticks. Shayla had banned me from the kitchen, so I found an old Louis L'Amour paperback in what had been Ethel's bedroom.

Shayla assured me the wine was also phenomenal, but I passed, not wanting to mix alcohol with my pain medication.

"For someone who's spent his whole life lying," she said, "you sure are a rule-follower."

"Says the sheriff's deputy who arrested me for murder."

She nearly spit out the local merlot. "Fair enough. But you know what I mean. Don't you ever loosen up?"

I lifted my tea as an excuse not to respond right away.

"Besides," she said, "I'm not going to be one for very much longer."

"Really?"

"Yeah. I'm going to tell them next week. I wasn't kidding when I said it was all smoke and mirrors." She drained the bottle into her glass. "I mean, I've killed three men. Were they bad guys? Of course. But you know what? The second and third weren't any easier." She took a gulp of the wine. "But you already knew that."

Shayla was getting louder. The alcohol had something to do with it, but so did her anger. A change of subject seemed best.

"What'll you do now?"

"Caitlin says I can crash with her, and if I get a PI license, she can hire me to investigate some of her cases. That'll be enough to get me started."

I pushed my paper plate to the side and leaned back. "I'm glad you two stayed so close. Jorge and I are that way. Well, you read the book. You know."

"But how much of that book can I trust?" She stood and downed the rest of her wine. "You know what? Don't answer that. I don't want to know."

I dropped my gaze, embarrassed, waiting for her to get to the bedroom before I started throwing everything away.

48

TERRY JACKSON

PRESENT DAY

Terry made it to the porch this time, but Judy opened the door before he could knock.

This time she looked around and waved him in.

"Were you followed?"

She was paranoid, and for good reason. But meeting at her house was safer than leaving a trail of phone calls or text messages, even from burner phones. Records of unusual numbers in odd patterns were suspicious, too.

"No. And even if I was, I'm just an FBI agent following up on a case we closed."

Judy didn't look satisfied with that answer. "You put us both at risk, showing up out there. I had it all planned out. It wouldn't've looked like a suicide, but they'd've never solved it."

She was right.

And he'd nearly let her do it.

Terry had been attending all of Schuhmacher's public appearances, waiting for Judy to take matters into her own hands. When he didn't see her car in the parking lot for Schuhmacher's final stop, he was relieved he'd been wrong. He waited through the end to make sure he didn't hear any shots ring out from Judy's 9mm. And when the crowd started returning to their vehicles, Case put his truck in drive and was about to pull out when he spotted her.

But instead of unlocking her expensive SUV—a birthday present from her sons—Judy hopped into the cab of a restored pickup. Case's old truck, which he hadn't recognized out of context.

Terry knew Judy could still tail someone. But could she spot one?

He followed her from Hinterbach to Kerrville, where she bought the pair of cheap, generic, could've-been-purchased-anywhere work boots she'd later wear. There were security cameras there, and on the drive to the park where she sat with a book and read for hours. But police would need a reason to review the video from those places, and they'd have none.

Terry thought she might spot him on the back roads leading to Schuhmacher's place. Fortunately, he'd discovered the path to the back entrance to his land many years ago, when Case's death was still fresh.

So, rather than risk spooking her, Terry gave Judy a ten-minute cushion and arrived as Schuhmacher was walking to her. He should've busted it up the moment he got to the tree line. But part of him wanted Schuhmacher to die, so he let it play out until the moment of truth. He couldn't let Judy commit cold-blooded murder, no matter the motivation.

But after she pulled the trigger, Terry snapped into action. He had Judy take off the cuffs while he wiped down the gun. Then he placed it in Schuhmacher's palm for prints, and hopefully some trace gunshot residue. He quickly staged the body, knowing approximately how the pistol and his arms would've landed. The rest Judy had done herself by making it such a close-range shot while he was sitting somewhat naturally.

It had taken less than a minute to set the scene, and they'd been running for their trucks by the time someone turned on a light in the Schuhmacher house.

"They're still not going to solve it," Terry said. "It's been ruled a suicide and nobody's ever going to re-open the case."

Judy sat at the kitchen table, where two steaming mugs of coffee were waiting despite the fact it was after dark. "You don't know that. We were in such a hurry. What if we left behind a print on the gun, or they see all the footprints. Maybe the cuffs left bruises on his wrists."

Terry shook his head. "I'm telling you, this is over. He's dead. And now that he is, I say good riddance."

"Do you? Because I don't know. It's stupid to say it now, but I can't shake the feeling he was telling the truth. I mean, Schuhmacher admitted to setting up that writer and wanting him dead. Why would he tell us about his involvement in that, but still deny having anything to do with Case's murder?"

Terry didn't feel the need to think about what Schuhmacher had said. Then again, he hadn't pulled the trigger.

"You shouldn't feel guilty," he said. "He got what was coming to him. And if Butler didn't do it, how the hell did her husband end up with Case's gun?"

Judy nodded, but Terry could tell she wasn't convinced. If he didn't do something, she'd let it fester until telling someone was the only way to sleep at night.

"Why don't I interview her again in the morning," he said. "If she was lying, maybe she'll tell us what really happened, now that Schuhmacher's dead."

"You'd do that for me?"

"Of course. I'll call right now to set it up."

Terry reached across the table and held his hand out, palm up. Judy looked him in the eye and, for the first time in more than twenty years, reached back.

THE NIMITZ COUNTY JAIL'S coffee left something to be desired. But at six in the morning, anything with caffeine was welcome, especially after driving from San Antonio.

Terry wasn't complaining about the early interview, though. He'd asked for it, and the jailer had been kind enough to oblige. He needed to get this over with.

Butler wasn't groggy despite the hour. She thanked her escort in a strangely chipper voice before sitting across from Terry.

"Agent Jackson," she said. "I didn't expect to see you again so soon. Was my confession not thorough enough the first time around?"

He leaned toward her. "Oh, it was a hell of a story. Very complete. But I thought you might have a different one to tell now that Schuhmacher's dead."

Butler was still, offering no insight into her state of mind, so he continued. "I've never had someone offer up a confession for a crime she's gotten away with. I knew that the first time around, but I was willing to look past it to put that sonofabitch away for life."

He paused again, giving her a chance to disagree and reaffirm her original statement.

Nothing.

"But I no longer have any use for your confession, so here's what I want. No, here's what I need, Ms. Butler. I need you to tell me what really happened the day Agent Kelley was killed. Everything you know, from start to finish."

When Terry paused again, Butler cleared her throat. "It seems to me, Agent Jackson, that I'm looking at the same sentence either way. I know the physical evidence in Frank's bathroom will be enough to send me away for life. What incentive would I have to work with law enforcement? Hypothetically, of course."

He grinned. "You're not as well versed in the law as you think. See, when you said Schuhmacher paid you, you confessed to a capital crime without representation to work out an agreement for your cooperation. And since he was law enforcement, we both know they'll indict you for capital murder. You'll get the needle, no matter what your attorney argues now."

Terry had no idea if his play would work. She'd already shown a disregard for her own future. Perhaps she wanted to die and join her husband in Hell. But if that wasn't the case, her survival instincts might kick in now that Judy had already doled out Schuhmacher's punishment.

"Hypothetically," she said, "if I recant, you can make sure the death penalty is taken off the table. That's what you're saying?"

"It'll take more than that." Terry leaned back now that she'd all but broken. "See, part of what makes your confession so convincing is the fact you had the ledger and your husband had Agent Kelley's gun. So a simple *I didn't kill him* won't cut it. I'll need to know how you two came into possession of those items. I need to hear everything you know about Agent Kelley's death. Otherwise, any influence I may have on your charges and sentencing will disappear. Hypothetically."

As she set her jaw and closed her eyes, Terry hoped this would work. He needed her to keep her mouth shut and allow the case to be buried with Schuhmacher or give Terry another suspect.

When she opened her eyes, Butler also lifted her chin, as though trying to appear stoic. "I did not kill Agent Kelley. I won't go through my entire day, but I will give you everything that's relevant, Agent Jackson."

Terry nodded for her to continue. He could always get up and threaten to walk out if he thought she was holding back.

"First, the ledger. I was honest about that part the last time we spoke. Well, mostly. I did see your fight in front of Kelley's house, and since everybody scattered without remembering the book, I walked over and picked it up."

He'd suspected as much after Judy's confession the night she shot Schuhmacher.

"However," she continued, "Darren was with me. And *Frank* sent us to follow Kelley, not Schuhmacher."

"For the record, Frank is Franklin Jones."

"Yes. Now, after your tussle, Kelley drove to a nursing home on the southwest side of town."

Terry shook his head and slammed his hand on the table. "I told you we were done if you lied to me. We reviewed the tapes, and he never entered that building."

"I didn't say he went inside. We watched him park, smoke two cigarettes, then pull out of his parking spot."

Terry didn't like that explanation, but it bought her another few minutes. "Fine. What happened next."

"Before he left the lot, Kelley stopped and had a brief conversation with a handsome young man in what had to be a pricey black leather jacket. I remember being jealous because I was wearing a bargain-store knockoff, but his was the real thing."

Something gnawed on the back of Terry's brain as she continued.

"From there, he drove to the bar. This was around 5:40. I followed Kelley in, thinking he might be meeting up with an informant or another agent, and told Darren to search his truck while we were inside. The place was busy, but I found an empty stool a few feet down from him. He'd never seen me before, so the only risk was catching his eye and becoming the object of his affection for the evening. But if he were there on business, I wouldn't have to worry."

More gnawing, like a rat through cheap sheet rock.

"I got bored watching Kelley drown his marital sorrows at the bar, so when he stood to use the restroom, I did the same and started walking to the door. I was halfway there when I bumped into someone I recognized. I remember thinking how strange it was to see him again so soon. It was like he'd tailed us there."

An entire mischief of rats was now eating away at Terry's gray matter.

"My suspicions were confirmed when he followed Kelley to the back."

The gnawing stopped.

Everything stopped.

49

CASE KELLEY

FEBRUARY 21, 2000, 6:02 PM

Case had planned on being on the road home already. But after two shots chased by a beer, Case realized he had no tolerance and couldn't drive yet, so he'd asked the bartender to change the channel so he could watch the beginning of *RAW* while he sobered up.

Case ordered a glass of water and pulled the soft pack from his shirt pocket. Nobody else had lit up, but Case didn't see any no-smoking signs.

He palmed a white gas station lighter and was about to strike it when a waitress walked out from the back. Judging by her hustle and an apology to the bartender, she was running late for a six o'clock shift.

She was also at least six months pregnant.

Part of him still wanted to do it. To flout society's rules and make the girl and her unborn suck in his poison. Why should he be the only one in misery?

Then he thought about Judy. The waitress looked nothing like her, and Judy had never gotten that far along, but her smile and easy way with the regulars was enough to make the comparison.

Case stared at her and realized he wasn't angry with Judy. He wasn't angry at all. He hadn't driven away twice to go on a spiteful, juvenile quest to be his worst self. He was running out of fear. Fear he was losing Judy. Fear he was getting old. Fear of retiring and fading into obscurity.

"Fine," he muttered and replaced the lighter and cigarette, drawing a curious look from the barkeep.

It was time to go home and deal with it.

But first, he needed to sober up.

And take a piss.

The already dimly lit bar got darker as he rounded the corner to the bathroom. Singular, which meant it was a one-holer, likely in need of some serious cleaning. He tried turning the knob and got an *It's gonna be a minute* from the guy inside.

Rather than belly up to the bar again, Case decided to break the law, though he'd never heard of any man actually getting ticketed in Texas for public urination. Well, except that one time. But Ozzy relieved himself on a war memorial at the Alamo.

Case was going to go in the alley behind a dive bar.

So, instead of turning back to the left, he turned right and pushed open the back door.

The days were getting longer again and it was still bright outside, but Case found a bit of cover in the form of a nearby dumpster. He did a quick 360, then walked to the gap between it and the brick wall.

Case was midstream when he heard the door open. He reflexively leaned his pelvis forward and peeked behind him, but there wasn't much Case could do with his legs spread and his fly open.

When he heard two quick steps, Case tried to run.

When he tasted the latex, Case tried yell.

When he felt the blood on his chest, Case tried to ask why.

Though he wanted to fight while holding in blood with one hand, Case was too weak to do anything but fall to his knees. Hands rummaged through his pockets, then shoved him to the ground face-first. Case tried crawling toward the bar's back door, but he was too lightheaded.

The last thing he heard was footsteps jogging away.

50

PATTY BUTLER

PRESENT DAY

Patty enjoyed the moment he put it together. It might be the last time she'd get to watch an arrogant prick realize how monumentally clueless he'd been.

"When neither of them came out, I let my curiosity get the better of me," she said. "I figured if anyone looked at me sideways, I could play like a dumb girl looking for the women's restroom."

Patty was sure she'd found the clandestine meeting she'd built up in her head. Darren had chauffeured her all day while she chased Kelley, and Patty needed the payoff, so she abandoned the beer she'd ordered but hadn't touched.

When she didn't hear voices in the hall, Patty tried the bathroom. The guy inside told Patty to screw off in a way that told her the two men she was after had tried that doorknob already.

"Then I saw the back exit and realized they must be behind Door Number Two," Patty said.

She'd known approaching them was risky. Too risky. Unless Patty acted like she'd gone out for a smoke but forgot the cigarettes. Would either of the nice gentlemen let her bum one?

The door had obstructed her view at first. But after taking a step, Patty noticed the slick, darkened asphalt that led to Kelley's corpse.

"There's nothing I could've done for poor Agent Kelley, so I ran around the building to the parking lot. Darren was waiting for me."

"After searching Case's truck and stealing his gun," Jackson said.

Patty noticed his use of Kelley's nickname. Jackson was done with all the pretense and the games.

"Yes," she said. "In the moment, I was upset with Darren for taking it. If I hadn't just run from a crime scene, I'd've told him to put it back. Of course, he looked like a genius later when it came time to plan that writer's"—she held up air quotes—"suicide. I suppose you'll want to hear about that, too."

Jackson had a thousand-yard stare and Patty knew damn well he'd stopped listening, but she wanted to seem as cooperative as possible.

Career criminals like her tend to make their peace with doing a stretch when the time came, and Patty was no exception. There's a lot you can do in prison. Hell, people get their law degrees while in the pen.

But the needle?

Fuck that.

Patty let Jackson sit in the personal hell he'd discovered for another few seconds before bringing him back to the present. "Is there anything else, Agent Jackson? Or may I be excused."

51

TERRY JACKSON
PRESENT DAY

Terry didn't bother responding. He had to call Judy. It wouldn't be real until he heard the name.

She answered before he made it out of the interview room. "Did you—"

"What was the name of her nurse?" he asked.

"What? You sound out of breath. Are you okay?"

Terry was jogging across the parking lot, but Judy was picking up on his anxiety. If Terry was right, it was all his fault.

And not for the reason he and Judy had thought.

"Case's mom," he said. "In the home. He said she had a new nurse that she liked. Do you remember his name?"

Long pause.

"Judy, I need you to think." Terry opened the door to his truck. "What was the nurse's name."

Silence.

"Goddammit Judy, say someth—"

"Leonard," she said. "I'm pretty sure that was it. Why?"

Lenny *Pretty Boy* Floyd.

Terry had been so preoccupied with Franklin Jones and Grant Schuhmacher that he'd never considered any of the office's other investigations. Or the fact Case had spent months asking every law enforcement and underworld contact if they'd heard of a guy with the street name *Pretty Boy* who had access to fentanyl.

And all because Terry didn't want to do the work himself.

He also never questioned who'd be more likely to resort to murder, white-collar assholes or the evil men who dealt in pharmaceutical-grade opiates.

Lenny Floyd, the guy he'd cuffed. The guy who'd avoided prison time on some bullshit technicality.

How was he going to tell Judy that he'd had her husband's killer in custody without knowing it?

Terry leaned out of his truck and puked on the cracked blacktop.

"Terry, what's going on? What did that woman tell you?"

"It was the nurse," he said. "It was the goddamn nurse."

Judy must've taken the phone away from her mouth because the cuss words were faint before she resumed the conversation. "You know, this is a pretty shitty time to joke around."

It did sound absurd without the proper context. "Did Case tell you about the drug task force investigation I was working."

"I think so. Something about heroin."

"Fentanyl. It was being stolen from local medical facilities and sold to the heroin dealers."

Judy paused, piecing it together. "But you swore to me Case didn't go see his mother that evening. You fucking swore to me, Terry."

By the time he was done explaining it, Judy was equal parts sobbing and screaming, though she managed to ask how Terry planned on finding Lenny.

"I'm going to call in a BOLO right now," he said. "Then I'm going to get his most recent photo onto every website and TV screen in the western hemisphere with a bounty next to it. Either he'll try to run, or someone'll snitch."

Terry heard her take a few deep breaths, then nothing.

She'd ended the call.

He thought about dialing her back but knew it would do no

good. Their next conversation would have to start with *We got him*, or he may never hear her voice again.

AFTER EXPLAINING everything to HQ in San Antonio, Terry checked the time. Just after seven.

A little early, but he had to get Veronica moving.

"Jackson?" She sounded groggy.

"I need your help."

"At seven in the morning?"

"Yes. I need you to call your editors. Let them know you'll have a major story that needs to go out as soon as you send it. If you get it written now, when they hold the news conference—"

"You woke me up for this," she said through a yawn. "I don't do news conferences. I get the exclusive now, or I'm going back to sleep."

"Look, I can't leak anything this time. But you can send the email from your phone as soon as I step onto the podium, and you'll have a ton of extra information that nobody else will. I need you to have everything ready to post to the internet the second I start talking."

Veronica chuckled. "Oh yeah? The whole internet, or somewhere in particular?"

"Everywhere you fucking can."

He got silence for a beat, then heard Veronica clear her throat. Good. Maybe now she'd get with the goddamn program.

"What's going on?"

"It's going to take a while to explain. You'll need to be in San Antonio anyway, so for now, get on the road and make your calls. I'm about an hour away, so we should get there at about the same time. I'll text you the place. And bring Beck with you. He needs to hear this, too."

"Beck's not in Austin. And did you say you weren't at home?"

"No, I'm in Hinterbach."

Another laugh, but without the condescension this time. "Looks like you'll get to tell Beck first. He's there, too."

Telling Beck was secondary, but Terry owed him the same apology as Veronica. Terry had roped them into his cluster for no good reason.

"What's his number? I'll pick him up and explain everything on the way."

"He doesn't have his phone yet, but I'll call the friend he's with, then text you the address."

"Fine. But tell him to be ready. I'm in no mood to be screwed around with."

52

BECK

PRESENT DAY

I wasn't prepared for the violence. While Veronica had been relatively gentle when waking me up at the Pumpjack, Shayla had slapped the exposed side of my face.

She didn't stop until I batted away her wrist.

"Finally," she said. "There's been a change in plans. Agent Jackson's coming to pick you up in a few minutes."

"What?" I croaked. "What time is it?"

"It's only seven. But, like I said, plans have changed."

After pulling on a shirt and pants, I walked to the living room. Shayla was sitting on the couch typing on her phone.

"Did you say that Agent Jackson was on his way?"

"Yes. I don't know all the details, but there's been some big development and he needs to speak with you and Veronica. He was here at the sheriff's office this morning for some reason, so he's coming to pick you up and take you to San Antonio, where y'all will meet Veronica."

My brain was still foggy and trying to process the information when a heavy fist knocked on the door.

THE NEWS CONFERENCE was still five minutes away, but the area just outside the four-story FBI building was already buzzing with TV cameras, newspaper reporters, and gawkers, who'd been allowed to gather on the lawn. Though it was early November, South Texas was enjoying a day in the seventies, and there was something about an outdoor setting that made the news conference feel that much more important.

Jackson had told Veronica to use her social media reach to promote the event like it was a book signing. He wanted the reporters to feel the weight of the announcement and the TV viewing audience to buy into the hype.

The combined twenty-thousand followers on her Twitter and Instagram accounts had produced at least a hundred. Now that there was an audience, Veronica took a photo of the crowd—a mix of college kids, working professionals on their lunch breaks, and at least one bearded dude in sunglasses looking for his next conspiracy theory—and sent one more message.

Almost time. Stay tuned for a HUGE announcement re: Grant Schuhmacher and the murder of Agent Casey Kelley.

"You think all of this will work?" I asked. "This Lenny guy's been hiding for decades. I mean, the most recent photo is his mugshot from the last time Jackson arrested him."

I nodded to Lenny Floyd, who watched over the gathering from an easel next to the empty lectern, smiling even as he was being processed on federal drug charges. Perhaps he knew he'd never see a courtroom. That was Jackson's theory. In retrospect, he was sure the case was botched on purpose. As the decades had passed since Kelley's murder, stories of corrupt agents had become common.

"It can't hurt," she said. "Besides, they're offering a six-figure bounty. That's enough to make some criminals talk, even to the FBI."

Veronica and I were with the rest of the reporters on the front row. When we saw Jackson and a few other agents approach their positions, the buzzing grew louder. But instead of taking his place, Jackson stepped toward us and motioned for Veronica to come closer.

I stepped with her, but Jackson waved me off.

"I don't think he wants to be photographed with you," she said. "I know it sucks. But I'll tell you everything he says."

It hurt, knowing that my being in his presence was something to be avoided, but I nodded and watched her brief huddle with Jackson. I couldn't imagine what he still had to tell us. On the ride from Hinterbach, Jackson had spent an hour detailing his involvement with the drug task force and how he'd asked Kelley to blab all over town about Floyd's identity.

When we'd joined Veronica at a place specializing in breakfast tacos, he'd summarized his interview with Patricia Butler. The three of us discussed the best ways to get a line on Floyd, and everyone agreed on a media push and high-dollar reward.

Veronica jogged back to me after talking with Jackson for less than a minute.

"So?" I asked.

"He wants me to open up my DMs for tips and offer the same reward as the FBI. It's risky. I could get a thousand bullshit leads, and the money would have to come from me. But if it works—"

"We'll more than make up for it with the book," I said, excited about our next project for the first time.

Before she could respond, Jackson took his place behind the lectern. Veronica lowered her eyes and started typing on her phone. "Time for Emily to hit the send button."

She'd written the story in Jackson's living room, then turned it over to him to check for accuracy. I read it, too, offering some writing and editing advice. She'd been so quick, Veronica had time to take me to a store to buy a new cellphone.

After her story hit the web, Veronica would tweet out a link, followed by live video from the news conference and—thanks to the last-minute addition from Jackson—a message asking for tips.

Then Veronica and I would get eight or ten hours to tie a bow on our second insane adventure that would be printed and bound and sold to the masses.

"Thanks again for agreeing to drive me to Big Lake," I said. "You really don't have to."

"Hey, Jorge is my friend, too. I feel bad I haven't gone to see him yet, so this is a great reason."

"So I was thinking about titles for this one. What do you think of—"

Veronica shushed me as Jackson started speaking.

53

BECK

PRESENT DAY

Since she was driving, I'd been put in charge of handling Veronica's social media on the drive. I gave up after an hour of reading messages to her, though, because only two even sounded promising. Most were from creepy guys either propositioning her or threatening to kill her. I was disgusted by it all, but she said it was mostly business as usual.

I shut off her phone and we talked about Jorge after that. I tried to bring up the book we were about to start writing, but Veronica insisted we take one last afternoon off. She wasn't ready to start that marathon just yet.

Veronica had sped the whole way, and we were in the hospital parking lot by 3:45.

"They're in room 109," I said as we entered the lobby.

I looked for signs until Shayla walked up behind us. She was in dressy civilian clothes, something between her courtroom attire and what I imagined she wore on the weekends. I'd asked her to meet us at the hospital so she could take me to my car afterward, which meant getting the keys from her boss in the sheriff's office.

She took the lead, and the three of us turned into the last

room on the left. Jorge was awake and watching outlaw drag racing.

"Holy shit," he said. "What happened to your neck, bro?" He looked at Shayla and Veronica. "One of you get a little too rough last night?"

He asked the question through a grin.

"Shut up." My smile matched his. "I'm okay. How you feeling?"

"I'm so ready to get out of here, man. I'm going nuts."

Veronica walked to his side and put a hand on his forearm. "Do you know how long you'll have to stay?"

"Depends on how fast I heal. They won't let me leave until I can walk down the hall and back. Right now, I can barely make it to the bathroom."

Reality sucked the oxygen from the room. They damn near killed Jorge and it was my fault. And while he recuperated, Jorge and Grace might have to choose between their assets going into collection or feeding their kids. Then there was Shayla, who gunned down two men to save us. Now she was giving up her career in law enforcement.

Veronica and I would benefit from the ordeal, though I had a feeling Veronica would've been fine writing a book that didn't involve her friend getting shot.

The click of Grace's boots interrupted my spiral. I was only halfway turned when she wrapped her arms around me. I grunted in pain but squeezed back.

"I've been reading about you in the news," she said. "I'm so glad you're not going to jail."

Grace let go of me and reached for Shayla. "And you must be the woman who saved his life. I never got the chance to say thank you."

Shayla looked uncomfortable but returned the hug. After a few long moments, Grace moved on to Veronica, who she still called Ronnie.

They were still hugging when someone knocked on the

already open door. "I'm sorry to interrupt, but I wanted to give the Hernandezes an update."

"Is something wrong?" I asked.

"No," she said, frustrated. "Your friend will recover, as long as he stays away from dangerous people and situations." She paused and tried to let the insinuation linger, but Grace called her something in Spanish and Jorge laughed.

We listened as the doctor stressed rest and rehabilitation— advice I also intended to heed while putting my life back together.

The first step was getting my car back, so I said goodbye to Veronica. My Challenger—which was searched but not seized because the sheriff's department had nowhere to store it—had been towed to an impound lot just north of the Pumpjack. I had a hell of a tab to pay, but soon enough I'd be on the road back to Austin, so the charge on my card would be worth it.

When Shayla parked, I turned before opening the door. "I'm not sure if we were close before, but right now you're one of the best friends I have. I hope you'll give me a chance to be one to you, too."

I shifted my weight toward the door. I wasn't expecting a response, but she reached across the console and put a hand on my forearm.

"Call me when you're home," she said, her voice as soft as her touch. "Let me know you made it okay."

54

BECK

PRESENT DAY

My first call was to Shayla, but she didn't answer. Though it was after nine, I hadn't expected her to be asleep already. Lucky for me, I had something to do while waiting for her to respond.

Veronica had left a note on my door, asking for a call as soon as I got in.

"Why didn't you just text me?" I asked before giving her a chance to speak.

"You've got to be kidding." I heard several cars honk. "I missed you by less than five minutes."

"How long were you waiting at my place?"

"Just long enough to say hi to your new neighbor and write the note."

New neighbor? I made a mental note to knock on the door across the hall in the morning.

"I got a message just as I pulled into town from someone claiming to have information on Lenny Floyd," she continued. "He wanted to meet near campus, so I drove straight there and waited for thirty freaking minutes before realizing he wasn't coming. Then, right after I walked into your place, I got an apology and another place to meet that's halfway to Round Rock. I'm heading there now."

"I can't believe you're wasting your time like that."

"Normally I wouldn't," she said. "But the guy sent me a photo of Floyd in scrubs, and it looks clear enough to have been taken digitally. I think there's a real chance this source knows him."

I had a hard time believing her call for information would yield results so soon, but I'd probably get to say *I told you so* in the morning. For now, Veronica had a message to deliver.

"That's great," I said. "But I'm guessing that's not why you stopped by."

She was silent for a moment, confirming what I'd suspected.

Veronica had been trying to deliver bad news.

"Karen called on my way back from Big Lake," she said. "She'd tried calling you, but apparently you didn't answer."

I had ignored our literary agent's call. I'd planned on calling back in the morning. If Veronica had wanted to talk about Karen and our next book proposal, perhaps I'd been worried for nothing.

"Wow, she must be excited," I said. "I've been thinking about titles. What do you think of—"

"Beck, stop and listen."

So, it was bad news. I did as she asked and stayed silent.

"I've been talking with Karen since the day you were arrested. She said the editors at Gavel wanted to drop you. The fact you were arrested using evidence that proves you lied in their books was more than enough, regardless of whether you were convicted."

I tried not to jump to the worst case. "You said wanted? Past tense?"

"I told her that Schuhmacher was out to get you and that we were going to prove he was lying. She said she'd talk to Gavel and persuade them to hold off until then."

"Awesome. Thank you. I still wish you'd told me."

"Don't thank me. It didn't work."

I wish she could've seen my expression. "Why today? The charges were dropped. It's over."

"Wolff called Parker."

I looked around my office to confirm that, yes, my laptop was still in an evidence room somewhere, waiting for Caitlin to file the necessary paperwork so I could retrieve it.

"Just give me the highlights."

"He posted an affidavit from Walker that details her findings. A summary of the blood spatter and all the other evidence is in there. Everything that proves you lied about that night."

I sank into my chair, slowly deflating. "Gavel had no choice."

"No. And neither did Karen. She told me to tell you she's dropping you again. You'll have an email tomorrow."

I'd lost my agent and publisher before. But there was no coming back from this. Even if I wrote novels under a pen name, the press would find out it was me.

"I wanted to tell you all this in person, I swear."

"I know."

"And Beck, I had to …"

She took a deep breath. I knew what she wanted to say but couldn't, so I did it for her.

"You told them I lied to you, starting with that first story in the *Ledger*. Now you'll have to publicly denounce me. Write pieces about being victimized by me. Not be seen around town with me." I took a beat to steady my voice. "It's the right move. The only move."

"I'm so sorry."

"Don't be."

The tears waited until after we ended the call. It wasn't a sob or a weep, but a quiet acknowledgment of all that I'd just lost.

In no mood to talk to Caitlin or stay up in case Shayla called, I pocketed the phone and headed toward the bathroom and sleeping pills waiting in the medicine drawer.

A knock at the door froze me in my tracks.

Jorge was laid up. Caitlin should've been in Dallas. I assumed Shayla was still in Big Lake. They all had my address but no reason to be here.

I tried to ease my frantic mind with the possibility it was my mother. I tried to swat away visions of badges and cuffs, though I knew someone could've convinced an Austin DA to file new charges. I slid away the peephole cover to reveal a face I'd only seen once since graduating high school.

Sammy Foster. In a sharp baby blue suit and striped tie.

Holding something behind his back.

55

BECK

PRESENT DAY

This would hurt, but I deserved it.

Still, the deadbolt was never louder and the door never heavier. I had no idea how to greet him, so I took a step back and braced for a golf club or baseball bat. Or worse, a knife or gun. When none of those were produced, I resorted to stating the only thing I knew to be true.

"Sammy. You're here."

He smiled and revealed his hidden object: a bottle of Scotch. Good Scotch. The kind with a name nobody this side of the Atlantic can pronounce.

"I go by Sam now," he said. "Don't worry, I come in peace."

I stepped aside, still stunned and mute. He walked by and scanned the condo.

"Nice place. Where do you keep your booze? I want to crack this baby open."

I pointed to the room I'd just left. "My office. I really only drink at home when I've finished a draft or get good news about my books."

He led me through my own home and walked over to my decanters and tumblers like they were his. "Neat okay?"

"Sure."

I sat at my desk and he brought over a pair of glasses containing the smallest of pours. Apparently, whatever he'd come for wasn't worth much of his good stuff. He sat mine on the desk and remained standing.

"You're obviously wondering why I'm here."

I wondered why I wasn't bleeding out on the floor but decided not to offer that scenario. I settled on a deep breath and a nod.

"I wanted to tell you in person that I dropped all the lawsuits against you and your partner, Ms. Stein."

That had been a foregone conclusion since his client was dead. And there's no chance he'd have driven from Dallas just to tell me in person.

He read the hesitation on my face. "I also wanted to apologize. I shouldn't've believed him. But it was hard not to feel like a kid doing what Mayor Schuhmacher told me."

Had he not seen Parker Mallory's story and document dump? If not, he would soon.

Unless I told him first. All of it, starting with Butch Heller killing my sister while driving drunk and ending with me mutilating his mother's body to make it look like a violent attack by the closest thing he'd had to a father figure.

But first, another, less shameful truth. "You have to know I didn't do the things he said."

"That's why I'm here." He raised his glass. "A toast. To old friends."

I downed my liquor, which was as smooth a Scotch as I'd ever had. That was good. I'd need more of it in a hurry before the night was over.

Sammy only sipped his expensive hooch. "Before we catch up, can I use your bathroom?"

I told him where it was, and he put the glass to his lips again while walking out of the room.

It was an odd feeling, knowing I had nothing to lose. Caitlin was sure no DA would charge me after Wolff's aborted attempt.

But I was also forever branded a liar, and most would also consider me a murderer until I faded into obscurity. That may not take long since my career was now gone, too. My writing partner, who despite our violent beginning was my closest friend and ally, was about to cut me out of her life like the cancer I had become. I was no longer teetering on the edge, trying with pills and brief feelings of celebrity to hold in what I'd done, convincing myself that saving everyone from *my* lies was in *their* best interest.

"Sorry about that," Sammy said as he strode into the room without a care, not knowing it was me who'd shoved his life off course and taken the only family he had. "I drove straight through from the office. Let me pour us another."

I handed him my tumbler and he took both to the liquor cabinet.

"Thanks," I said, barely keeping myself together. "Sounds like you're past working eighty-hour weeks?"

"Yeah," he said over his shoulder as he poured. "I'm a junior associate now, albeit an old one. And even the partners are a bit deferential to a combat vet."

This time there were three fingers in each glass, and he sat on the corner as we downed our Scotch in a few quick drinks. I was glad he'd finally get a buzz, hoping it might dull the pain I was about to inflict.

But he didn't seem overly affected by the booze. Meanwhile, I felt like a freshman at my first frat party.

Sammy hadn't been in my place more than five minutes before my eyes started swimming and I couldn't quite get through my story about meeting Patterson in the men's room at a charity event.

Then, a moment of recognition. Dallas. Saturday night, after the cocktail party. Only now it was backward.

Right amount of Scotch.

Wrong number of pills.

56

BECK

PRESENT DAY

Coughing. Burning nostrils. My heart pounding and lungs sucking in air like Houdini just before the tank closed.

"Whoa, Beck. Just breathe. You're not dying. I know smelling salts are a bitch, but you'll be okay."

Sammy's voice was soothing, which only added to the confusion. My arms were being pulled from their sockets, and my knees ached from being bent. The rope around my wrists was already wearing a burn, pulling down toward my suspended feet. I kicked my legs but only managed to pull my arms even farther back.

Sammy had resumed his position, though he'd shed his suit jacket and was down to his pants and a white undershirt. "It only hurts when you struggle, and I don't advise it. Even you aren't strong enough to get out of this."

He leaned over and waved the ammonia under my nose again, causing me to jerk and curse in pain as my sutured skin pulled apart.

"I figured I'd find some Vicodin or Oxy for that"—he nodded at the bandage on my neck, which was now getting saturated with blood—"but those sleeping pills were perfect."

He'd taken his glass, which was identical to mine. Then he'd returned and poured both drinks. I was too preoccupied to notice if anything had settled at the bottom of the glass.

"You don't have to do this," I pleaded.

He reached for the edge of my desk. I followed his hand as it moved over our cellphones before gripping the scariest knife I'd ever seen outside of an action movie, its blade cobalt black, the last few inches of the sharp edge serrated before entering the handle.

He picked up the mini machete and began tapping it on the desk, counting down the final seconds of my life. When my heartbeat synced with Sammy's sinister metronome, I realized this would be the climax of Veronica's next book—infamous author Bartholomew Beck getting what he deserved from the person he wronged most.

Blood was filling the bandage on my neck as Sammy stopped tapping and pointed his blade toward my right eye. The steel got so close that my lashes brushed up against the tip as I squeezed the eyelid shut.

"There's no medical evidence," Sammy said, "but I know Mom was still alive when you put that screwdriver through her cornea."

I jerked my head to the left, and Sammy responded by shuffling behind me and palming my forehead, his left index finger finding my eyelid and sliding it open.

"If you want to keep yours, you better start talking."

His voice was disconnected from a body, like God himself asking for my final confession.

But where to start? His mother's affair with my sister, poor Ruth Ann, who was killed by Butch Heller in a car crash six months before? No. He wanted a contrite admission, not excuses or a play-by-play.

"It was an accident," I said. "I killed her. But I swear to you, I never meant to hurt your mom."

Sammy slipped the blade to the right. Though it was out of my blurred vision, the steel felt cool against my cheek, and its sharp edge threatened to slice me open.

"Bullshit. I asked to see her in the morgue because I didn't believe it was her. I barely recognized her after…"

He trailed off, unable to articulate the savagery. I'd convinced myself Sammy never saw what I did to her face in the name of covering up my own crime. He wasn't in court most of the trial, and I'd always hoped Sammy avoided reading and listening to any media coverage that detailed Summer's injuries.

I'd hoped Sammy's lasting image of his mother was the beautiful woman he'd seen earlier that day, not the corpse I'd left in his backyard.

"Do you know what it's like to stare at your dead mother, knowing it's her, but half of her face is caved in so bad you're not sure? I even asked one of the officers if they'd made a mistake. When the guy said no, that it was my mom on the table and Butch had done that to her, I got so wild it took two cops to restrain me. So don't sit here and tell me what you did was a fucking accident."

By the time he finished, Sammy's blade had dug into my cheek. And as the blood trickled down my face, I realized how wrong I'd been. He didn't want to hear how sorry I was. He wanted to know everything.

Perhaps most of all, he wanted to know why.

"You're right," I said. "I was angry, and I did go over there to confront her."

Sammy removed the blade and released my head. "Confront her about what? Are you saying she really was sleeping with you, too?"

"Not me. Ruth Ann. She was sleeping with Ruth Ann."

He leaned in from my right and was so close I could smell the Scotch on his breath. "Who?"

My sister was older than us and had been dead several

months before I killed his mother, but I'd still expected him to remember Ruth Ann. Her death had gripped Hinterbach. But then—as happens with heinous events—Summer's murder split the town's history into before and after, and much of what happened prior to the infamous act had been forgotten.

"My sister," I said. "Your mother and my sister—"

Sammy's punch landed flush on my left cheek. The tears that leaked out of my right eye burned as they hit the fresh cut.

"Try again," he screamed.

"It's the truth," I said. "Remember how your mom was training her? To run sprints in track?"

Rage fell from Sammy's face as memories flooded in. Nobody had suspected the affair, but their out-of-school relationship gave Sammy enough pause to consider what I'd told him.

"But she died six months before," he said. "So even if you're telling the truth, how would that justify what you did?"

"It doesn't. But I found out by reading Ruth Ann's diary earlier that day. Then I got drunk and decided it was your mom's fault my sister was going to college near home rather than here in Austin. I had it in my head that, if Ruth Ann had taken the scholarship at UT, she wouldn't have been driving on that road that night, and she wouldn't have been in that crash."

Sammy stood up and turned around, still holding the knife. "So you're telling me you killed my mother, the woman who helped you pass English because you couldn't read Shakespeare, who decorated our locker room and made us spaghetti lunches before every home game"—he spun around, streams of tears looking like scars on both sides of his face—"you beat her to death because you blamed her for a complete accident?"

Sammy charged at me, the tip of his knife leading the way. And as I waited for the blade to sink into my gut, I realized how stupid I'd been, craving my just deserts and hoping Sammy would kill me. Letting me bleed out on my office floor wouldn't relieve the anguish I'd caused by killing his mother.

My pain would last a few minutes. His would last a lifetime.

"You're not a murderer," I screamed.

Sammy pulled up short, though the knife made its way to my throat. "You sure about that?"

"Killing me won't give you any peace," I said. "I know you want the pain to stop. But taking another life will do the opposite."

Sammy's jaw muscles rippled as he withdrew the blade. "And your proof is what? Guilt over killing my mom out of revenge? You'll understand if I don't find that piece of ironic garbage very persuasive."

"Actually, I wasn't talking about your mother. I was telling the truth earlier. I never meant to kill her. I just wanted to tell her what an awful person I thought she was."

Sammy didn't like that, but he let one *hey, fuck you* suffice before allowing me to continue.

"After I realized she was dead, I panicked and wanted it to look like someone had attacked her on purpose. That's when Butch drove up and told your mom—"

"My mom's body, you mean."

I nodded. "Butch said he'd caused the wreck that killed Ruth Ann. He's the one who T-boned my sister and drove off, who left her to die in the middle of that highway, cold and alone. He didn't mean to do it any more than I meant to kill your mom, but I still blamed him. So I lied and said I'd seen Butch do it, and I kept lying until the day they put the needle in his arm.

"But you know what? After he died, I didn't feel any better about my sister's death or the way it depressed my parents and nearly broke up their marriage. Nothing changed, except now I also think about *him* late at night before the pills knock me out."

Sammy shook his head in disbelief. "I have to admit, you are one hell of a liar. But Butch was still living with us when your sister died. He wasn't the POS everyone thought. There's no way he could've hidden something like that from us."

"Call Veronica. She can back me up."

"Yeah, I'm sure she would lie for you. Her ass is on the line for that book just like yours."

I closed my eyes, wondering how much to tell Sammy about Veronica. Butch had been like a father to her, which made her akin to Sammy's stepsister. But my limbs had started going numb, and I was one wrong move from landing in the obits section of Sunday's paper, so I opted for the much shorter version.

"She was with Butch the night it happened."

Sammy looked at me like I'd started speaking in an alien language.

I nodded to my phone. "Call Veronica. It's her story to tell."

He stared at me for a few more moments before transferring the knife to his left hand and reaching for the device. I gave him the passcode, and he fidgeted with the screen before replacing it on the desk.

"It's on speaker." He pointed the knife, now back in his killing hand. "But don't say anything unless I ask you to."

The words had just left his mouth when Veronica answered.

"I told you we can't talk anymore," she said, the hum of I-35 in the background as she half-yelled into her car's Bluetooth. "I know it sucks, but—"

"Miss Stein, this is Sam Foster, the lawyer who's suing you." His voice had gone from menacing ex-Marine to attorney on a conference call. "Or, was suing you."

"Oh, hello. Why are you calling me from Beck's phone?"

"Because I just got done telling him the good news and we thought it'd be easier to call you from his phone."

Veronica paused, probably trying to sniff out the lie. "Well, I can't say I'm surprised, but I guess I appreciate the personal touch."

"No problem at all," Sammy said. "Say, we were reminiscing a little bit and got to talking about my mom and Butch Heller and that whole mess, and—"

"Beck, are you there?"

Sammy extended the knife but nodded at me to answer. "Yeah, I'm here."

"Are you okay?"

I locked eyes with Sammy. "Yeah, I'm fine. But before he goes, Sam here needs you to tell him about the night Butch killed our sisters."

It took a moment to register, but when it did, Sammy cocked his head.

"I'm calling 911."

Sammy and I shouted *no* in unison.

"Miss Stein, I promise everything will be fine if you talk to me. I'm just having a hard time believing the man who lived with my mom and me for years left the scene of a deadly crash. And now I know Beck's lying because he's saying more than one person died, when everyone in town knows Ruth Ann was driving back to college alone."

"Beck—"

"Veronica, please," I shouted. "Just tell him and everything will be fine."

Sammy's face went from angry to focused as Veronica told him about Butch and getting wasted at the kitchen table, then strapping Veronica's half-sister into their terrible-parents version of a car seat.

Sammy's eyes widened a bit when Veronica described the sound of shattering glass and the smell of gasoline.

Though he tried to hide it, Sammy's Adam's apple bobbed several times as Veronica soberly recounted Butch asking her to carry the baby from the floorboard of Butch's truck to her final resting place in a lonely field beside the highway.

"Satisfied?" Veronica asked after finishing the story.

Sammy ended the call without answering.

"I don't know if I can trust either one of you," he said. "But you have said at least one true thing tonight—I'm not a murderer. Not like everyone else I grew up with."

I closed my eyes and allowed myself to consider being alive

later. Assuming Sammy untied me, the only damage would be a small cut to my face. I pictured myself a week from now, rested, ready to think about a second career that would keep a roof over my head and provide adequate medical care for my father.

I was still visualizing the rest of my life when I heard the door to my apartment open.

57
___

BECK

PRESENT DAY

Sammy jerked his head toward the open office entrance and put a finger to his lips. Then he stepped toward me, carefully placing the soles of his shoes on my faux hardwood until I felt his slow breath on my earlobe.

"Who has a key to your place?"

"Just Veronica," I whispered back, still seated and tied to my office chair. "And you heard her on the phone. She was still driving on the highway."

Sammy nodded in agreement and stepped achingly slowly toward the door. After arriving, he crouched low and peered around the jamb, then carefully retraced his steps.

"Male. Armed. You have a gun in here?"

After I shook my head, Sammy turned and stepped toward the door, leaving me a helpless pig at the slaughterhouse.

I was looking forward to being alive, so I wasn't interested in watching while Sammy tried to save the day alone.

"Sammy," I stage whispered through clenched teeth.

He turned like he might throw the knife through my eye after all.

"Untie me. Then it's two against one."

He glanced back at the door, then moved behind me. When

he cut the rope, the tension broke and my toes fell to the floor—an innocent sound in any other circumstance, but potentially deadly in this one.

We froze. The steps were measured but getting closer. Sammy ripped off the rest of the rope.

"Stand behind the door," he whispered. "When you hear me yell, slam it as hard as you can into him."

Sammy moved quickly to the other side of the opening and put his back flat against the wall. As I took a few wobbly steps toward my post, he moved his feet away and slid down, his knees nearly at a ninety-degree angle.

I expected the seconds to tick by slowly, but I had barely positioned myself when he shouted.

I threw my shoulder into the door and pumped my unsteady legs. The crash and yelling were nothing compared to the gunshot that followed. I jumped and covered my ears, but Sammy and our attacker moved as one spinning mass to the back wall, a burnt orange ballcap flying off the shooter's head.

The man's shoulder hit first, then the side of his balding head cratered the sheetrock beside the bullet hole. Sammy was leaning against the man's chest, both hands driving the knife into his torso just below a ragged beard. The shooter's gloved hand was still gripping the pistol, so I rushed over and grabbed his wrist with both hands and slammed it against the wall. When the gun fell, Sammy took a step back and let the man slide down the wall, his chest heaving, gasping through blood.

But he wasn't dead yet.

Sammy leaned down and slapped the man's face. "Hey, look at me. Who sent you?"

His head lolled and eyes blinked open. Sammy yanked his beard, forcing him to look up at us. The man spat a mixture of phlegm and blood onto the floor. "Fuck you."

I wiped my neck and looked at my bloody fingers as Sammy continued his interrogation. Who wanted me dead? It couldn't be Franklin Jones or his lackeys anymore. Same with Grant Schuhmacher.

But if the suicide was staged, Sammy was asking the wrong questions. Who wanted Grant Schuhmacher dead? And why would they come after me, too?

I stopped Sammy from punching the hitman again and knelt beside him. "You work for Jim Flynn, right?"

His breathing was shallow and interrupted by bloody coughs, but he had enough life to smile at me.

"Who the hell is that?"

I shifted backward, stunned for a moment. Then I came to my senses. He was lying. He was probably trained to resist interrogation.

But I had to try.

"Quit covering for Flynn and Schuhmacher. You can't die twice, and we can make these last few minutes hurt worse than you could ever imagine."

The words escaped so effortlessly I believed them. But did he?

"I'm telling you. I don't know any Flynn."

Sammy picked up the gun and shoved the barrel against our attacker's temple, straightening his head. "Then who sent you?"

His breathing sounded like sucking blood through a broken straw. "Fuck... off."

"Who sent you to kill me?" I screamed.

The bearded man laughed, crimson spittle peppering my forearm. "Who said I was here to kill you?"

I looked at Sammy, who shrugged. "You think I told anyone where I was going tonight?"

If he wasn't in my home to kill me or Sammy... "Veronica? You followed her here and thought this was her condo, didn't you?"

The man smiled, and that's when I saw it.

I had to picture him without the beard, and with the clock

turned back more than twenty years. But it was him, the man in the photo I'd seen at the news conference.

"Lenny Floyd. You're the one who messaged Veronica, but instead of meeting her, you waited for her to leave and go home. Then you sent her an old photo, so she'd believe you and agree to drive out of town, giving you enough time to make sure she didn't double back before breaking in. Only she didn't go home. She came here."

Floyd was in the final moments of his life, but he still managed to nod. "I was going to kill her, then find a nice beach to retire on. Nobody I run with would talk to the feds. But they might talk to her for that much money."

The words had trickled out of him, his last breath spent uttering the word *money*.

Sammy shoved me out of the way and grabbed the corpse on my wall. He rummaged through Floyd's pockets and pulled out a black pouch, which he unzipped before quickly tossing it to my feet. I bent over and retrieved what must've been the toolset used to pick my locks.

I was still eyeing the pouch's contents when Sammy slapped my shoulder with something leather. I turned to find him holding up a black ID holder with a golden badge. Next to it was a photo of the late Agent Casey Kelley beside the letters *FBI*.

58

BECK

I was still staring dumbly at the badge when we heard a policeman announce himself. "Are you here, Mr. Beck? Someone called earlier and wanted us to do a welfare check, then a neighbor said she heard a gunshot. Call out if you're hurt."

One officer turned into three, turned into more police and EMTs, turned into a detective questioning us in my living room.

"Looks like you were right," the burly investigator said. "I just received confirmation that the man you killed is the fugitive Leonard Floyd. Now, tell me again what he said."

We repeated the story we'd already told at least three times. He nodded and seemed satisfied.

Then the detective looked at Sammy. "Now take me back to before he came in. What were you doing here this evening, Mr. Foster?"

The uniformed officers hadn't asked that. Sammy paused a bit too long before telling him the same lie he'd used on me.

"I noticed the open bottle of Scotch." The detective turned back to me. "I also noticed rope lying next to your office chair. It had a couple of slipknots and looked like it'd been cut with a knife. A good one, too, like the one you used to defend yourself. Or maybe the one that put that cut under your eye."

The truth could ruin Sammy. He'd drugged and kidnapped me, then threatened me with a deadly weapon. All I had to do was say the words.

But I'd driven him to it. And though I'd never make things right between us, doing this for him was a step in the right direction.

"It's going to sound stupid," I said. "But he was helping me with my next novel."

Sammy's eyes were saucers. The detective furrowed his brow.

I smiled.

"We were drinking, and I told him about a scene I was struggling with. A man has kidnapped my main character and has him tied to a chair. But I wasn't sure how my character would feel in that moment, physically. So, I asked him to do it. Then he cut me loose."

The detective blinked twice. Then he shook his head and flipped his notebook closed. "I've heard writers are strange, but that's the weirdest shit I've ever heard."

Sammy laughed and agreed. "I'm just glad he wasn't still tied up when Floyd broke in."

"Well, none of it's my problem for long anyway." The detective stood. "The feds will be taking over this case before breakfast. You better get comfortable, because you'll have to stay here and go through all of this again with them."

The detective left us on my couch as crime scene investigators hustled back and forth. The timing wasn't ideal with all the law enforcement surrounding us, but I had to know.

"You gonna turn me in?"

Sammy acted as though he didn't hear me, but I knew he was considering it. He had every right to run after that detective and amend his statement. I could see him telling the guy that, *well, actually, while I had him tied up, I made him confess to a rather infamous murder.*

Sammy turned to me, as serious as he must look in front of a jury. "You're an awful person. And you deserve to be punished for what you did."

I nodded. Killing me would've been counterproductive; I'd helped him see that. But watching me rot in prison must've seemed like a satisfying end.

I disagreed. For the first time in years, I no longer felt pinned down by the weight of my past.

"I won't confess to the police," I said. "I was ready to before, but not now. No amount of prison time will change what happened."

Sammy clenched his jaw. Released. Clenched again. "I spoke to Ranger Walker before coming over here. She explained why the evidence she has wouldn't be strong enough for a DA to prosecute. So, my initial thought was to convince you to turn yourself in. That's the only way you're going to jail for it. After all, with the attorneys you can afford, any confession I got here tonight would've been thrown out before trial."

Walker obviously hadn't given him any of my financial information, though Caitlin would step up for me again. Hopefully.

"But"—Sammy pulled a phone from his pants pocket—"I decided to record the confession anyway."

59

BECK

PRESENT DAY

"It started recording just before I woke you up," Sammy said. "I haven't had a chance to listen, but I'm sure it picked up what I need. It'll be compelling, especially after a little editing."

I was a bit confused. "You just said anything I told you tonight couldn't be used in court."

"True," he said. "But if your buddy Parker Mallory posts this, there'd be way too much pressure not to arrest and try you. And even if you don't go to jail, it'll ruin you."

I tried to appear calm as my mind raced with scenes of my mother hearing that audio, then taking phone calls from reporters asking about her homicidal son. She'd have to shield it from my frail father.

But those were the people who'd be most hurt. Not me. And if Sammy knew that, maybe he wouldn't follow through.

"I'm already ruined," I said. "Veronica called me earlier tonight to tell me I've been dropped by our agent and publisher. I'll never sell another book, unless someone wants to buy another *If I'd Done It* memoir. The books I've already published will sell like crazy for a few more weeks, then be boycotted by everyone. And that's assuming they aren't pulled from the shelves. Oh, and I'm just about bankrupt. In addition to pissing away a lot of my money"—I looked around my condo—"I've been paying for my father's live-in care after his stroke. And that came after I helped my parents retire on a ranch in Montana."

Sammy looked equal parts frustrated and confused at the ineffectiveness of his plan. "But you'll still be in jail while you wait for your trial."

"Been there, done that. What else you got?"

"Your parents," he said. "What'll they think when they hear you admit to killing my mom? Even if they already know you might've done it, hearing it is a whole other level of sickening."

And there it was. I had nothing to threaten him with that held the same stakes.

Except, just maybe, his new job. The one he served his country to get. The one he seemed so proud of earlier.

"And what'll your fancy-ass bosses think when they find out how you got that confession?" I pointed to the cut on my face. "Do it too soon, and this scar'll still be here."

Sammy's curse was so loud it drew the attention of the crime scene techs.

"He's fine," I said. "Isn't that right?"

Sammy's hands were shaking as he strangled his phone, which I'm sure he wished was my neck. He was never going to forgive me, but he also wouldn't kamikaze his career to get revenge.

"Rather than punish me," I said, "how about you find a way for me to make things right. I know a ton of people in media and publishing if you ever need to sway public opinion. And if you call, you know I'll answer."

He didn't respond, but I took Sammy's silence as a tacit agreement.

60

BECK
PRESENT DAY

The FBI agents showed up sooner than I'd expected. Agents Cooper and Graham said they were local and were just here to get our initial statements. The bags under their eyes suggested they'd been woken up for this task.

When we were done, the smaller of the two, Cooper, thanked us and asked if we had any questions for them. Sammy said no and stood to walk out. I, on the other hand, couldn't turn down the opportunity.

"Why do you think he had Kelley's badge on him?"

The agents looked at each other. Graham, who was built like a pro wrestler, answered. "In case he was stopped by someone. All people would see is the gold and the letters FBI, which explains why he's here after hours and why he had a gun. Makes you wonder how many times he's flashed it over the last twenty-odd years."

Before leaving, agents Cooper and Graham shook our hands. "Thanks for gutting that sonofabitch. The Bureau owes you boys."

I tucked that IOU into my back pocket and thanked them before walking them to the end of the hall. Sammy followed a few minutes later to avoid any awkward talk.

My condo was a crime scene, so I packed a bag. I'd already made late reservations at a downtown hotel for two nights and was looking forward to a soft bed and some room service. I just hoped my credit cards wouldn't max out before I could come back. In the meantime, I'd see if there was any chance of selling the place.

On the elevator, I thought about what else lay ahead. I didn't like the idea of Veronica working alone, but I gave her number to Sammy and said she might need help if Gavel Press used me as an excuse to break her contract. I also hoped they'd connect on a personal level. Veronica and Sammy had been mourning the loss of their father figure, and now they wouldn't have to do it alone.

And what about Shayla and Caitlin? They'd have each other's backs, as they always have. I counted them as allies, and I'd undoubtedly need to rely on them again.

My own future had never been so uncertain. I had no plan, which was equal parts scary and freeing. I'd finally broken free from the endless loop of awful that had been my life.

As the elevator door opened to the parking garage, I could hear the rumble of media and rubberneckers from just beyond the secured gates. The valet brought my Challenger around, and I'd just tossed the bag in its trunk when a voice called my name.

I turned to see Parker Mallory's face screwed into a smug grin. He quickly covered it with a cellphone. "Is it true that you've killed yet another person, Bart?"

The valet came running, but I put up my palm and said I could handle it.

"You know what Parker? I'll give you an interview. Right here, right now." I waved him forward. "Let's make sure you have good sound and light."

Parker was so eager for the opportunity, so willing to do whatever it took to become a social media sensation, that he did as I said, stepping forward and staring at the screen. When he started perfecting the focus, I closed the gap between us.

His cartilage caving on my fist was the most satisfying thing I'd felt in years.

313

ACKNOWLEDGMENTS

Though my name's on the cover, no book enters the marketplace without a phenomenal team, and this novel had one of the best. Fawkes Press continues to produce amazing work, and I consider it a privilege to have again contributed to their catalog. I will be forever grateful that Publisher Jodi Thompson believed in me and my characters. Her vision and patience were beyond measure as I wrote this novel (my first attempt at a sequel). She and Editor TwylaBeth Lambert were nothing short of miracle workers with this manuscript.

I must once again thank my best friend and brother, Jesús Ramirez, who allowed me a second round of pipeline research, this time deep in the heart of West Texas, where I befriended a host of other hardworking men and women to whom I owe an unpayable debt.

Additional thanks go out to the many novelists and fellow members of the Texas High Plains Writers who continue to provide camaraderie and friendship. Sharing the ride with those who can relate makes it so much more fun. I'd like to give special recognition to Taylor Moore, Jodi Thomas, Linda Broday, and Bruce Edwards. Your support over the last year has been extraordinary.

But this time around, family and friends played the most important role in getting this book into your hands. It's not hyperbolic to say *The Price of Silence* was written during one of the most difficult periods in the history of the world, and without such an amazing support system, writing a novel wouldn't have been remotely possible.

If you enjoyed this book and would like to support the creation of further pulse-pounding stories, please do one or more of the following:

- Leave a review on your favorite book review site
- Tell a friend about *The Price of Silence*
- Ask your local library to put Rick Treon's work on the shelf
- Recommend Fawkes Press books to your local bookstore

Readers make good books possible!

Visit us at

www.RickTreon.com

www.FawkesPress.com / newsletter